TORTUGA GOLD

WES DEMOTT

This 2012 paperback publication of TORTUGA GOLD is the first print release of this novel by Wes DeMott.

Cover photo courtesy of NORDHAVN

ISBN 978-0-9851741-0-1

The Pirate Song

To the mast nail our flag it is dark as the grave;
Or the death which it bears while it sweeps o'er the wave;
Let our deck clear for action, our guns be prepared;
Be the boarding axe sharpened, the scimitar bared;
Set the canisters ready, and then bring to me,
For the last of my duties, the powder-room key.

It shall never be lowered, the black flag we bear;
If the sea be denied us, we sweep through the air.
Unshared have we left our last victory's prey;
It is mine to divide, and yours to obey.
There are shawls that might suit a sultana's white neck,
And pearls that are fair as the arms they will deck.

There are flasks which, unseal them, the air will disclose
Diametta's fair summers, the home of the rose.
I claim not a portion; I ask but as mine
'Tis to drink to our victory - one cup of red wine.
Some fight 'tis for riches, some fight 'tis for fame;
The first I despise and the last is a name.

I fight, 'tis for vengeance! I love to see flow,
At the stroke of my saber, the life of my foe.
I strike for the memory of long-vanished years;
I only shed blood, where another sheds tears.
I come as the lightning comes red from above,
O'er the race that I loathe to the battle I love.

Chapter 1

Taz Keaton, muscular, tanned and shirtless, tried to get more speed out of the outboard, but it was already wide open and screaming like James Brown as it blasted his narrow fiberglass boat up the Central American river. He squinted for signs of the crashed jet in the muddy water or thick jungle canopy, but didn't see any clues as to where he would earn his three million dollars.

"Not looking good," he yelled to his partner, who was bouncing along in the bow.

Gordon Windsor looked back. "Yeah, but other than our lucky break last year in Cambodia, not looking good is about as good as it ever looks."

"That's a point. Keep an eye out for survivors, maybe a pilot or crew member who's been busted up but is still alive."

"Will do. Not likely though."

Taz glanced at the river's overgrown banks for anyone sitting in a clearing, maybe waiting in pain to be rescued, even though the speed and angle at which the corporate jet went down made it unlikely that anyone could have survived. Then he held his GPS in front of his face and took a quick check of his position as he steered around the stumps and debris of the Changuinola River that bled brown into the Bocas Del Toro archipelago off Panama's Caribbean Coast. The river was legendary for keeping her secrets, with her inaccessibility, the snakes and crocodiles, and the thick rain forest all contributing. If the jet wasn't visible now, it might never be, completely shrouded in a matter of days by strangler vines and banana leaves.

"Gordie," Taz shouted as he stood with a surfer's practiced balance. "We're approaching the crash site coordinates. Is that twisted thing sticking out of the mud over there a tail section?"

Gordie looked where Taz pointed and then glanced behind them. "I think so. I also think our competition's going to catch us. Couldn't you have gotten a faster boat?"

"It was slim pickings in *Empalme*."

"Next time let me get the boat."

"It's a deal. Do you think those guys back there have guns?"

"They look like soldiers, and they *always* have guns." Gordie looked again at the two *pangas* chasing them through the twists and turns of the ever-narrowing river. One of them was much closer than the other.

"I was kind of hoping–"

"The Panamanians are peaceful people, Taz, but every rule has an exception."

"And I usually manage to find them."

"Yes, you do."

Taz sat down and grabbed a railing. "Time for batting practice, Gordie. I'm turning to face 'em."

"Don't...you must think I love doing this."

Taz slammed the outboard to port, spinning the narrow twenty-foot boat like a top and nearly pitching Gordie out before Taz straightened again.

"Still with me?"

"To adventure, Taz."

"And to those who seek it. Get ready."

Gordie moved farther into the bow. "Next time how about I run the boat so you can face the bullets."

"I'd like to say there won't be a next time," Taz said as he aimed for the bow of the first boat, surprising the three soldiers onboard, "but it's a bad bet."

The soldier in the front of the other boat raised his rifle and started shooting.

"Don't worry, Gordie. They're bouncing like crazy in our wake. Who could aim while doing that?"

Just then a bullet tore into their panga right next to Gordie's hand and sent shards of fiberglass flying. "It appears that he can."

"Probably just a lucky shot. Are you ready?"

"Pass 'em starboard to starboard."

"I was thinking port to port."

"Don't screw around, Taz. I'm ready to tee off on the starboard side."

"And since when do we do things the easy way?"

Taz swerved back and forth over the centerline of the collision course as the two boats closed the distance at nearly sixty miles an hour.

"Damn it. Okay, port to port." Gordie shifted a little to his left.

"If you're going to get all pissy about it I suppose we can do it your way. Here we go to starboard. Ready...now!"

Taz shoved the outboard sideways as Gordie pushed away the rifle barrel just as the soldier got off a shot that whistled by his ear. The two boats banged together so hard it almost stopped them both and nearly sent Gordie flying over the bow.

The soldiers held on for the few seconds it took before the boats started to move again, scraping noisily along each other as Gordie raised the blue aluminum T-ball bat. He took a quick but powerful swing at the soldier in front, but the man ducked back so hard that he went over the rail and into the river.

"The driver's about to shoot, Taz. Looks like he's aiming at you."

"Noticed that. Anytime now, Gordo!"

Gordie yelled "*No fuego*" to the driver as he threw down his bat and grabbed the flare gun. The soldier hesitated, and while he did Gordie aimed at their fuel tank and fired, the phosphorous burning and hissing and melting everything, including the fiberglass boat and the plastic fuel tank.

"Glad they can swim," Gordie said as they raced away, while the other two men scrambled out of the blazing boat and swam like Olympians as the *panga* exploded.

"*No fuego*, Gordie? Really?"

"It was all I could come up with."

"Old Miss McAvoy would be so disappointed in your Spanish. Let's get over to the crash site."

"I wonder why the other boat's hanging back. And no, I don't want to go ask them."

"If that really is the wreckage, man, it's going to be a tough slog through the swamp to get to it."

Gordie looked back at his boss. "Say 'For a change,' Taz. I dare you, I even double-dog dare you to say 'For a change.'"

Taz flashed him that great grin of his. "Then I'm not going to say it. Just for a change," he said as he veered sharply off the river, sliding as fast and far as possible through the grassy flats toward the spot he thought was the crash site. A massive boa constrictor shot across the murky water to get out of their way.

"Man, did you see the size of that snake?"

"A fast one, too. We're about out of water, Taz. Are you planning to carry this boat back to town or drive it overland?"

"No idea yet."

Taz kept going until hard-grounding about sixty feet from shore and half that distance from the crash site. He killed the engine and leaped like a kid over the rail and into the knee-deep grassy edges of the jungle.

Gordie jumped too, but he caught his shirt on a cleat and tumbled in head first.

"Enjoy that, Gordie?"

"Funny guy. Let's just get what we came for and get out of here." He started running and Taz followed, their feet turning the water into frothy foam.

"You know what I think?"

"That we should be home watching a game?"

"What I think is that the guys on the other boat decided to wait for us to do the hard part of recovering the case."

"Smart of them. I guess that leaves us no option but to make our way out of here on foot." Gordie looked at the nearly impenetrable wall of jungle just beyond the wreckage. "Well, I must say that's typical news for a day out with you." Then, "Christ, I see a body over there."

"There were no reports or indications of survivors. If there are it will change things. We can't leave them out here to die, regardless of who they are."

"My God that plane's a wreck. Okay, you knew that. But it's totally torn to pieces. Where was the package? Was it cargo?"

"It's supposed to be in a shiny aluminum case that was with a passenger in the cabin."

Gordie sloshed ahead, but stopped short of a large clearing in the marshy river that looked like a small crater full of creamy coffee. "Do you see anything that even looks like it was once a cabin?"

"She sure hit hard. Let's find some sticks so we can set up a search grid."

"I think I see it floating over there."

"No kidding. Wow, that's one sturdy case. Go get it while I find a way out. I hear something."

"No, Taz, please don't hear something."

A black helicopter suddenly swooped over the edge of the jungle canopy and stopped quickly, hovering fifty feet over them with two men in uniform sitting in the open doors and aiming rifles.

"Sorry, Gordie. I knew I heard something."

"I hate helicopters. Now what's your plan?"

Taz raised his hands and looked up. "*Hola.*"

"That's your plan?"

"You want to try hollering *no fuego?*"

Gordie raised his hands. "*Hola*, Guys. Hey, how's it going up there?"

Taz looked around. "Think we can reach the cover of the jungle?"

"Depends."

"On?"

"On how much you're willing to get shot up in the process."

"I'll take that as a maybe. Let's split up so the pilot has to keep turning the chopper. Make it harder on his guys to get off a shot."

"You don't even want to consider giving them the case?"

"And change our name to Mayday Salvage and Rescue *and Give-away*? What would we do with all the old stationary?"

"Just a thought. Guess I'm ready. We'd better get going because I think I hear another chopper."

Taz turned to the noise. "That's a plane, not a chopper."

A soldier fired a burst from his automatic, the rounds exploding into the brown water at Taz's feet.

"Hey," Taz yelled. "I haven't moved. Why are you shooting at me?"

"I think they want us to walk toward that clearing over there so they can land."

"There's the plane. It's certainly not military."

An ancient tail-dragger, its doors missing and paint faded, banked over the trees with its engine sputtering from the clogging of old fuel. It dropped down to the river and skirted the water, buzzing so close to the remaining boat that the soldiers jumped out and started swimming. Then it climbed, coughing and wheezing like a sickly old asthmatic, and flew directly toward the tail of the helicopter, closing the distance until panic or good sense overcame the chopper's pilot and he dumped it to the left in an effort to get away.

The gunmen in the helicopter's doorway opened fire on the little plane, but their bullets scattered across the landscape as they hung on to keep from being tossed out of the open doors.

A couple of seconds before the plane collided midair with the chopper, a giant man with long hair and a beard jumped out and dropped to the swamp as the momentum of his plane carried it into the chopper and pushed the tangled wreckage of both aircraft a hundred feet through the sky before crashing into the water and exploding.

"Wow," Gordie said. "Now that's not something you see everyday."

"That was actually a couple of things I don't see everyday. Do you think he survived the fall?"

"Sure he did."

"You're sure?"

"I'm willing to bet my share on Sam if you want to bet against him."

"I'm not that foolish."

Just then the big man struggled free of the mud that must have broken his fall but then sucked him under. He rose up in waist deep brown water and used it to slosh the muddy slime off his chest. He was using his teeth to pull a big shard of metal from his massive left forearm as he slowly splashed over to Taz and Gordie.

"You two assholes should have waited for me at the dock."

"I left when the boss said to go, Sam. I didn't have a vote. Taz, back me up."

"And I, well shoot, Sam, I wasn't even sure you'd make it here from Nicaragua."

"I got here with time to spare, Taz. Hell, I could have taken the time to eat breakfast first." He looked around. "Great, so now I suppose we get to fight our way through the jungle? *Again*."

Gordie looked with him. "That's almost exactly what I said."

Sam pointed to the case Gordie was holding. "Is that what we came for?"

"This? No, this is a gift I picked up for my ex-wife but forgot to leave behind in my room."

Sam rolled his eyes as Taz said, "Let's see if those soldiers survived their crash, and if there's anything we can do to help them. Then we're good to go."

Gordie looked off at the wreckage of the two aircraft. "Let's be quick about rendering assistance. Panama doesn't have much in the way of a military, but it certainly has to be bigger than these few guys."

They hurried over to see what Taz hated most about the career he'd so anxiously chosen and vigorously pursued.

"The pilot's dead," Sam said.

"Co-pilot, too. And a door gunner. The other soldier must have been thrown clear. Let's take a look around."

"He beat feet," Gordie said, aiming out along a fresh path in the low marshland. "Headed off that way. You can see his tracks."

Taz took another look at the dead men and reminded himself that they'd tried to kill him and Gordie. Then he looked at the river and saw one overturned panga and another still ablaze and felt better that the men he and Gordie had fought were all still alive.

"We'll meet the client in Bocas Town," Taz said, shaking off the moment and moving on. "After that, whoever has the least number of leeches will buy the drinks. I'll pay you each your shares as soon as we get there so Gordie can't claim to have an empty wallet again."

"I still think you both are assholes," Sam said as he scanned the edge of the jungle for a way into it. "Come on, I'll walk point."

Taz laughed. "Hold onto the case, Gordie. We get to follow the big man."

Chapter 2

The three tired and muddy Americans worked their way along the muddy river and through the dense and humid jungle to a large clearing where there'd been a village or teak plantation not long ago. It hadn't yet become overgrown, but anything of value had been taken away, probably to be used again somewhere farther up or down the river.

"Hey Felipe," Taz said into channel twenty of his handheld VHF. "Do you copy?"

"Mister Keaton," came back a voice. "Yes sir, I'm standing by outside *Almirante*. I heard some very bad news earlier and am quite glad to hear from you."

"He's really close," Taz said to Sam and Gordie. Then, "We've found a spot for you to set down and pick us up, my friend, so get that old bird to take flight. We're at... are you ready for frequency changes?"

"Yes, sir. I've got my notes out."

"Good." Taz switched to channel seventy and said "Nine degrees, twenty-four minutes north."

"Copy."

He switched to channel ten. "With forty-eight point six seconds."

"Copy again."

Then to channel sixty-five. "Eighty-two degrees, thirty-one minutes west."

"Roger."

Finally he switched to channel seventy-nine-alpha. "With twenty-two point zero eight seconds. Did you get all that?"

"I'm on my way."

"We're looking forward to seeing you. Bring a hose and a big bar of soap."

"A hose?"

"Just kidding. See you in a few. Be careful, too. It seems like we've made some enemies around here."

"I'd say you're not just whistling...damn, what is it you Americans don't whistle?"

"Dixie. We're not just whistling Dixie."

"Yes, that's right," Felipe shouted over the slow winding-up of his rotor. "The airwaves are full of chatter about what happened. Mostly by the National Police."

"Well, come and get us. I can't wait to see what happens. I'll be standing by on the predetermined channels."

Taz switched the radio to channel twelve as Sam walked into the shade, sat down and leaned against a tree. Just as he closed his eyes Gordie kicked the bottoms of his boots. "Try to get a little more involved."

"Involved in what? There's nothing going on now but a wait. Leave me alone."

"I've got six leeches so far. How many for you?"

Sam grumbled out a low snarl as he lifted himself onto one elbow and pulled up a leg of his trousers. "Eleven. And one, two, three...hell, I've got almost a dozen more on that leg alone." He ignored the leeches and flopped back down.

"They've always loved Sam," Taz said. "That beats me. I've only found seven."

"Eight," Gordie said as he peeled a leech of Taz's neck. "That makes eight. Shit, it looks like I have to buy again."

"Gordie, they just don't seem to like you as much as Sam."

Sam laughed. "Who does?"

Taz was just about to sit down when he heard the thump-thump-thump of rotor blades. "I think I hear Felipe. Gordie, ease out there and make sure it's him."

Gordie stayed hidden by the shade until he recognized the old UH-1 that the young pilot had scrounged from the United States when it turned over the Panama Canal in 1999 and the American military went home. It was the only chopper of its kind and easy to spot, with bright graphics and colorful scenes painted all over it that made it look like one of the *Diablo Rojo* busses that rattled around the towns and countryside carrying locals, their wares, and the occasional backpacker.

The men dashed for the chopper, and the instant they'd piled through the doors Felipe took off, flying just above the tops of the shortest trees and weaving expertly through the taller ones.

"This is fun," Taz said into the microphone of his headset. "Hey Felipe, are you having fun?"

"Jeez, Taz," Gordie said, as a treetop flashed so close to his open door that he snatched in his legs. "How about letting the guy concentrate on flying?"

"Yes, I find this to be quite fun, Mister Keaton."

"That's why I like you so much. Here comes the water."

The old Huey pounded its way past the jungle, across the narrow beach, and out over the gin-clear water with mazes of reefs snaking wildly across the bone-white bottom.

"Look at that, Gordie," Taz said, as he leaned out of the helicopter and stared down at the beautiful Caribbean. "I never get tired of the tropics."

"Twenty-six," Sam said as he worked a leech free from the mat of black hair at the side of his face and then tossed it out the doorway. "My official count: twenty-six leeches."

"You're definitely not going to have to buy. Ready to get out?"

"Get me a little lower than you did at that freezing Canadian lake, okay?"

"When you start bitching, Sam, it means you're getting old. Besides, it's only your second time today to jump from a moving aircraft."

"Just a little lower. I'm not asking much."

"Felipe," Taz said. "How about dropping down to a hundred feet, close to shore but where there's some deep water."

"We're at just such a spot now, Mister Keaton. Hang on." He pushed down the collective and the chopper dove like an osprey.

"He must be anxious to get rid of you, Sam," Taz laughed. "Have you got a good grip on the case?"

"I'm out of here." Sam stepped to the door and, without hesitation, leaped out.

Felipe pulled off while Taz and Gordie watched Sam fall straight down, feet first with his arms straight up, his hands holding the case over his head. Just before he hit the water he let go of it, and his enormous body made an even more enormous splash.

"Bocas is just ahead," Felipe said as he banked the chopper so that Taz and Gordie could get a better view of the province's capital. The festively colored waterfront town was plopped onto the southern tip of Isla Colon, which placed it more or less smack dab in the middle of the Bocas Del Toro archipelago and a couple dozen miles from the Caribbean border that Panama shared with its neighbor nation, Costa Rica.

Dilapidated in a wonderfully charming way, Bocas, with its brightly painted buildings that lined the waterfront and all the streets – most of which had never seen a drop of asphalt – had much more in common with its closest island nations than it did with Panama. It was a laid back but exciting place where men and women of all stripes would go to hide from their pasts. A crazy wild spirit survived among the Bocas residents and visitors that melded the town's Jamaican charm with a pirate's attitude, probably like Key West back in the 50's. Bocas served proudly as a refuge for millionaires, misfits and miscreants, and a watering hole for them all.

Kids playing soccer on the grass runway of the town's only airport moved reluctantly as Felipe set his chopper down in front of the small block terminal that was about the size of a fast food restaurant. Then the kids went back to their game, getting in a few more minutes of play as the day's last scheduled flight from Panama City made its final approach.

"You think Sam will get here safely, Taz?"

"Safe for him? Sure. Probably not so safe for anyone who tries to jump him." Taz leaped to the ground, and then stuck his head back into the helicopter. "Thanks again, Felipe. Were you paid well enough?"

"I was paid much too well, Mister Keaton. Thank you. Thank you. Watch behind you."

Taz turned as three men in army uniforms ran up to him. Several more soldiers waited at the door to the terminal. The leader of the three men, whose pineapple face reminded Taz of Manuel Noriega, said, "Mister Keaton?"

"That's me." Taz grinned like a kid having fun. "Wow, where did you guys come from all of a sudden? Did you see them when we landed, Gordo?"

"I'm very impressed." Gordie pointed at one of the soldiers. "Did you see that guy? He ran like a deer."

"A deer? I don't know, maybe deer, but I think–"

"Mister Keaton," the officer said. "This is important business and we have been expecting you."

"Good. Hey, Skipper, do you happen to know a girl in this town – a lady really – named Isabelle?"

The officer looked confused. "Isabelle?"

"Yeah, Isabelle. Look, never mind. Gordie, step up here and introduce yourself, since he already knows who I am."

"I'd rather not."

"Gordie?"

"All right." Gordie smiled at the crowd of children gathering around them, then leaned toward the officer, smiled ridiculously, and reached out his hand. "Gordon Windsor. How ya doing?"

"I'm fine, thank you, but now for the reason–"

"Listen," interrupted Taz. "Since you know who we are, don't you think it would be polite to tell us who you are? That is how we do it back home."

"Mister Keaton is right," Gordie chimed in. "Just like back home. Hey, can we go inside to talk because I need to take a leak. A piss. *Comprende*?"

"Yes, I know to take a leak."

"You do? That's great. Then follow me because I'm sure not going to piss my pants in front of these kids."

13

Gordie moved. The soldiers quickly aimed their weapons at his chest. The officer snapped, "Stay where you are," and all the kids laughed

"Yeah, sure, funny, kids. Hey, let me see your ball for a sec." He held out his hands and a small boy tossed Gordie his ball. Gordie immediately kicked it at the soldiers by the door to the terminal. One of them caught it and smiled, then bounced it a few times on his knee and foot before kicking it back, just before the officer grew frustrated enough to pull out his pistol and fire it in the air, silencing everyone.

"Mister Keaton."

"And Mister Windsor," Gordie said. "I feel offended when I get left out."

"He really does."

The officer exhaled with frustration. "Gentlemen, I'm here about some very serious business. Several soldiers of the Panamanian Forces went missing today somewhere up the Changuinola River. They broadcast their pursuit of two gringos fitting your description."

"I get it," Taz said, "and you want me and Gordie to go find them for you. Gordie, what's our going rate for finding lost soldiers?"

"Depends on whether they're officers or enlisted?"

"Officers or enlisted?" Taz repeated to the officer.

The officer did not put his pistol away, but let it hang non-threateningly in his hand. "I am not here to *hire* you, Mister Keaton. I'm here to arrest you."

"For what?"

"For the murder of those men."

Taz smiled again, but this time there was the slightest touch of menace to it. "Look here, Admiral, I don't know what happened to your men, but I had nothing to do with murdering anyone."

"Me neither."

"Gordie neither."

"Just look at you two. You're filthy and soaking wet."

"We were looking at investment property on the mainland rain forest." He looked back at the helicopter. "Right, Felipe?"

"They were looking at investment property on the mainland rain forest. That's right."

The officer holstered his pistol and climbed into the helicopter. He searched it carefully for several minutes, and then came back to Taz.

"Where is the case?"

"You mean your case against us. If you ask me, I don't really think you have one."

"The metal case you found."

"Any idea what he's talking about, Gordie?"

14

"I *seriously* need to take a leak."

"General, my friend needs to take a leak."

"Seriously," Gordie repeated.

"He *seriously* needs to take a leak, so if you're going to arrest us, do it now and take us away to someplace with a pisser. If not, we're out of here."

He waited a few seconds before pushing passed the officer. "Come on, Gordie." Then to the officer he said, "Sarge, we'll be at Lula's Bed and Breakfast if you want to talk further."

As they walked away, Felipe took off in his wildly painted chopper.

"He looks like a piñata up there in that colorful thing."

"Just keep walking, Taz. I think I've got another leech, and it ain't in a happy place."

Taz laughed all the way through the terminal and out the door, where he waited for Gordie while drivers of a half dozen beat-up taxis and a kid with a scooter offered repeatedly to take them anywhere they wished on the island. When Gordie finally came out they walked the five blocks to the hotel.

They showered and changed, then waited four hours before walking up the small main street of Bocas, past the nice Italian restaurant, the internet café, the three ice cream stores, the five realtors, and countless bars. Two blocks from the ferry landing they went into a long, narrow bar built out over the aquarium-clear water. Fish circled the pilings and around the underwater lights that illuminated the entire aquatic scene.

A long pier extended even farther into the water, and it had a beautiful sixty-foot sailboat tied to the far end of it. The two men walked the long pier and then stopped as Taz stood beside the boat and whistled through his teeth. "Gorgeous."

"Hello, Taz," said an amazingly attractive woman wearing a very expensive looking dress, but barefooted. "And, of course, Mister Windsor."

"I always like it that Isabelle calls me Mister Windsor, Taz. Why don't you call me Mister Windsor?"

"I'll start right now, Gordie." Then, "Good evening, Belle."

"Please, gentlemen, come aboard. Care for a drink?"

"Beer, please."

"Scotch."

"Scotch and a beer. Light on the poison if that's part of your plan."

Isabelle tucked her legs up under her thin dress, posing like a cat in a royally comfortable position. "You're still silly, aren't you Taz. That's so cute."

"And I bet you're still untrustworthy, Belle. For the life of me I can't understand why I find that so attractive. Gordie? Any idea?"

"Because she's hot as Thai curry?"

"That's true enough."

"And you want to jump her like a battery?"

"That might be just a bit too much disclosure."

"There are people who pick at scabs and people who don't. Guess I'm a scab-picker. Anyway, I'm pretty sure she knows how you feel." Gordie looked at Isabelle and said "I meant all that as a compliment."

"And I certainly feel complimented." Then she leaned into the companionway and repeated the order of drinks in French to someone below. "And champagne for me," she added.

"Pretty nice boat you've got here, Belle."

"I suppose it's nice enough. My goodness, Taz, I wasn't prepared for how wonderful it would feel to see you again."

Gordie cleared his throat.

"And you, too, Mister Windsor. Of course."

"Nice to see you too, Isabelle."

"Is she chartered? Yours?"

"Did you retrieve the case?"

"Your case is as close as my payment."

She laughed. "You make the most interesting statements, Taz. Of course, saying that presupposes that you know where your payment is. Are you still as clever as you are silly?"

Taz rubbed a red spot on his nose. "Pardon me. Itching from earlier. Leeches."

"I think that one's a spider bite."

"Gordie thinks it was a spider."

"Of course," she said. "It must have been quite an ordeal in the jungle. I can imagine."

Taz looked at her dress, her fine jewelry, her thousand-dollar haircut and her carefully manicured nails. "Belle, I'd love to say that I doubt that you can imagine, but I don't. Not for a single second. And as to my money, well, you wouldn't have it on your boat for all kinds of good reasons. And you know I wouldn't accept it being too far away, either."

"Those are simple enough deductions."

"I'm a simple guy."

Gordie laughed.

"It wouldn't be in the bar we just walked through," Taz continued, "because that would be too obvious. So I'm going to take a wild guess that my money–"

"Our money."

"Right, Gordie. I'll bet that our money is under the seat of that shitty little boat you're pretending to use as a dinghy."

"Very good, Taz. Very good. Francois, would you please retrieve Mister Keaton's payment."

Francois, who'd been scowling the whole time as though he resented any other man being around Isabelle, served their drinks. Then he sat down his tray and climbed over the lifelines and into the dinghy. He returned almost immediately with a large bundle wrapped in plastic. He sat down in the cockpit, then looked up at a nearby balcony as he handed the bundle to Isabelle.

"Yeah, yeah," Taz said. "I saw your guy, too, Frankie. He doesn't need to worry about getting hurt unless you try to screw me."

"That, monsieur, is a ridiculously bold statement."

"Mister Keaton is a ridiculously bold man," Isabelle said.

"As is Mister Windsor," Gordie added.

"Of course. Sorry. And perhaps now would be a good time to make the exchange."

Taz sipped his scotch. "Belle, you know of course that the Panamanian government is onto us like candy on an apple. Soldiers will board your boat the instant Gordie and I leave. I expect we'll get arrested for whatever they can trump up, but they'll have nothing on us but suspicion. You, however, will have the case. Ever been in a Panamanian prison?"

"I have," Gordie offered. "I've certainly been in worse."

Isabelle moved a little under her sheer dress, as slow and practiced as a great stripper. "I have anticipated them coming aboard."

"And...okay, well, that's your problem to solve then. Our fee is all there?"

"It is. But first, aren't you curious about what's in the case?"

"I make it a point not to be, at least not with this kind of stuff. The search and recovery usually intrigues me more than the treasure. Besides, it's a Mayday Salvage and Rescue policy. We can't be held responsible for information we don't have."

"Long before I ever met you, Taz, I'd always noticed how respectfully they said that you were odd."

"By 'they' you mean the folks in Washington who first recommended us?"

"Not just recommended you. They endorsed you with such confidence that I've always been suspicious that you work directly for them. They said to never, ever, under any circumstances, dare to underestimate you."

"Did my name come up?"

Isabelle smiled. "Of course, Mister Windsor, they said not to underestimate you, either.

17

"We do work for the Feds on occasion," Taz said. "But we're pretty suspicious of them too, so they really have to talk us down off the ledge before we take their work."

"And there are still only three of you? Sorry I won't get to see Sam again."

"Business is getting more and more dangerous, Belle, so we use contract help a little more often than we used to. Like the sniper on that rooftop aiming at your man on the balcony."

Francois jerked around to look, but Isabelle didn't take her gorgeous green eyes off Taz. She was playing him hard, and he not only knew it, but he loved every second of it.

"But the original three of us," he continued, "have worked together a long time now and it seems to work out well. As we say in America, don't try to fix what's not busted."

"Interesting. Now, Taz, please, if you don't mind, the case."

Taz took another look at the man on the balcony, and at Francois, who had a hand on the pistol on his hip. But mostly he looked at Isabelle. She'd trained her eyes to conceal far more than her share of the world's secrets, but he knew those eyes extremely well and probably better than anyone. He would know at a glance if they broadcast even a hint of a trap. They did not, so he reached over the side of the sailboat and banged on the hull.

Sam surfaced next to the boat on the ocean side. He spit out the regulator of his re-breather and handed Taz a waterproof pouch with the case inside.

"Say hello to Sam."

Isabelle leaned over. "Very clever. Hello, Sam."

"Hey Belle."

She kissed her hand and then patted his head with it.

"And now, Belle, how about my fee?"

"Our fee," chimed in Gordie.

Isabelle sat back and smiled beautifully, then handed the package to Taz. He slid it into the pouch and then handed it back over the side to Sam, who disappeared under the boat in the night's watery darkness.

"Nice seeing you again, Belle."

"Hmm."

"See you next time, Isabelle," Gordie said. "Thanks for the drink, Frank."

Then Gordie and Taz stepped off the boat, walked down the pier, and took a seat at the bar.

"I'm leaving first thing tomorrow, Taz. I start a new job on Wednesday. Got to stay busy doing something between these adventures, but you know I'm always ready for anything, anywhere. Look, here comes the Gestapo."

Gordie nodded to the far end of the narrow bar as the soldiers from the airport rushed toward them. Most of them went right past and ran toward the boat.

"This should be fun to watch."

Three soldiers stayed to guard them, but Taz completely ignored them and said "I'm heading back to the States too. I'm about to get my boat out of the shipyard."

"Can't wait to see her."

"I had more leeches than you, Gordie, so you get to pick up the tab. You'll have to owe Sam a good night out. Hello, Sarge," Taz said to the officer-in-charge who walked up slowly and stopped in front of them.

"I found two more leeches in my underwear," Gordie said, "so are you sure?" Then, to the officer, "How ya doing, Commodore?"

Taz was just about to give Gordie his final leech tally when a tremendous explosion blew the sailboat in half, lifting the bow completely out of the water. The blast's concussion nearly blew Taz off his stool as it rolled through the bar, but he got to his feet and followed Gordie out on the pier just as smaller pieces of the sailboat rained down from the sky while flames from the burning fuel ate up the dock, keeping back the soldiers and the two bar patrons who dared venture out on the pier to help, risking their lives with no suspicion at all that the explosion was nothing but one component in Belle's elaborate plans for escape.

"Shit," Taz said.

"Say that twice, Buddy."

"Shit," Taz said again. "Poor Sam."

Chapter 3

Historic Ybor City
Tampa, Florida

Taz, dressed in old jeans, his favorite sneakers, and an expensive linen shirt, found an empty space in the middle of the employee parking lot. He despised, on some level, the large, covered space reserved for him alone that sat empty behind the big, five-story building that served as headquarters for twelve of his eighteen corporations, the other six being too far away or too firmly grounded in another culture to be effectively managed from Tampa.

He jogged across the lot and up to the entrance of the building designed to blend architecturally with the rest of Tampa's historic Cuban district.

"Mister Keaton," said the guard at the entrance as he rushed over, too late to open the door. "It's very nice to see you back after such a long time, sir."

Taz slowed down, and then stopped. "Hi. I'm so sorry, but I can't quite remember your name."

"I'm Lamont, Mister Keaton."

"That's right. Listen, Lamont, do you have a minute?"

Lamont smiled. "You sign my paycheck, sir, so I'm pretty sure I have all the time you want."

"It's actually an electronic signature."

"It works just fine for the bank." He laughed loud enough to echo around in the three-story atrium, which was disguised on the outside to look like a factory or warehouse.

Taz laughed too, and then led Lamont off to the side. He leaned against the wall as dozens of his employees walked slowly past, gawking as if amazed to actually see the handsome, mysterious entrepreneur who'd been canonized in *Forbes* two years earlier for his youthful success and his absentee management. Taz didn't know any of them.

"What's the feeling around here, Lamont?"

"Sir?"

"You must get a vibe of some kind as you see people coming and going, working early or late, leaving excited or bummed. What's your call on how my businesses are running?"

Lamont stammered a bit before saying "I'm nothing but a guard, Mister Keaton. How...I'm not sure how I would know."

"I understand. Do you have kids, Lamont?"

"I do," he said proudly. "Two big boys that play football and a little girl who'd melt your heart."

"That's nice. Tell me, Lamont, when they come in the door after school or a game, do you even have to ask them how things are going with them?"

"No sir, why I can tell the second I see them...okay, now I get what you're asking. It's a happy place, Mister Keaton. People like working here a lot. I never hear any grumbling."

"Good. Then would you do me a favor?"

"Yes sir. I'd be proud to."

"This is my personal card, Lamont. It has the phone number of the cell phone I carry as much as I have to. If you ever stop getting warm and fuzzy feelings around here, will you tell me directly?"

Lamont looked like he'd just been appointed to a Cabinet position, and the truth wasn't far off. He stared at the card, which he would probably frame, and then looked right into Taz's blue eyes. "You betcha."

Taz laughed. "I love it. Thank you."

By the time Taz got to his office, everyone knew he was in the building, and he hated the separating feeling of being special. People who worked for him never acted the same when he was around. It was not only one of the reasons he stayed away, it was also why he liked the adventures with Mayday so much. No one gave him any special attention there. He was just one player on an exciting team.

He flew past his secretary who, as always, had a table full of stuff for him to look at or sign or, more likely, ignore.

"How long will you be here this time, TK?"

"Hey Fran, I've missed you too."

"I never said I missed you."

"I could have sworn you did. My ears must still be ringing from last night."

"She was that good?"

He couldn't help but think of Belle. "Yes, but that's not why my ears are ringing. Anyway, I think I've already been here too long. How can you work in a place like this?"

"You let me design your entire floor, so it's kind of hard for me to complain."

21

He looked up from his big desk. "Pretty smart of me, huh? Anything for Mayday?"

"We're getting too many requests, but there aren't any you'll want. The easy ones I siphoned off to those looking for that kind of work. The foolish ones I declined altogether."

"Excellent."

"I have lots of stuff for your other businesses that you might want to–"

"Has any of my top management quit?"

"No."

"Gone insane, died, or lay comatose in a hospital somewhere?"

Fran sighed. "No, no, and no."

"Acted stupidly?"

"Stan Richards has started dating a twenty-year old, but other than that, no."

"Then let's allow them to do their jobs. Now please see if you can track down Sam." He rushed the words so as to hide his concern. "You might have to call heaven to do it. His regular number doesn't work, at least not for me."

"Sam?" She said the name with undisguised affection.

"There was an explosion last night in Panama."

"I'll get right on it."

Taz walked to the window as she left. He waited there, knowing that if Sam was still alive and anywhere he could possibly be contacted, Fran would figure out a way to reach him.

After ten minutes she stepped back into his large office. "Sam's on line two." She looked like she could cry at any minute.

"Thanks, Fran. Why not take the afternoon off?"

"Maybe a two-martini lunch. Will you be here when I get back?"

"No."

"Shocking. Okay, take care, TK. See you next time you slip through town."

"Sam? Oh...hang on." He hollered to Fran, "Give Lamont a decent raise for some additional work I've assigned him."

"Who? The downstairs guard?"

"That's him."

"I'll take care of it."

"Sam, are you there?"

"Hey."

"Jesus, man, are you alright?"

"I thought we were going out for drinks last night in Bocas, but by the time I got back and dry, and then got rid of the cash, you were both gone."

"Gordie and I figured you were obliterated in the blast so we left."

"Thanks for all your concern."

"We felt bad for a little while. About losing the money, that is."

"You're both assholes."

"Probably."

"I saw all the explosives under the hull while waiting for your signal. They had two underwater scooters hanging underneath there too. I figured I'd have plenty of time to get away, but with Belle you never know so I swam like Flipper once I had our cash."

"You never do know with Belle, that's for sure."

"Where are you?"

"Back in Tampa. Can you believe that Stan Richards is dating a twenty-year-old?"

"That's creepy. So you're spending a long day at the office? I love it."

"Try calling the odds on that."

"Somewhere in the range of not good to totally ridiculous. So, a few minutes there and then gone?"

"I'm heading out now to go to the shipyard."

"Have fun. I'm in Panama City. Landed two hours ago. No problem, either, and thanks for asking."

"How did Fran find you so fast?"

"Keep your nose out of my personal life."

"None of my business?"

"That's right. Anyway, I'm going to roll around Casco Viejo a couple of nights before I head home. We'll catch up soon. See you."

Sam hung up and Taz looked around his office. It was much too big and far too professional, but it served nicely as a great reminder of the trap in which he'd once ensnared himself. He would always be on guard about doing that again.

A half-hour later he hopped out of his car to look up at the boat he'd lusted after each and every time he crossed low over Charlotte Harbor while flying home to Naples in the corporate helicopter. She was a sixty-two-foot heavy-weather trawler riding at anchor in the warm and sheltered waters of Southwest Florida. The alluring geometry of such beautiful lines – her high, pointed bow, shapely beam, and low stern – had the same powerful effect on him as a short skirt on a narrow waist, and he loved it.

"Hi," he'd said to an old-timer splicing line behind the counter of a nearby marina when he finally took the time last year to see the boat. "Do you happen to know who owns that beauty out there?"

The man looked at Taz like a seasoned captain or experienced appraiser, deciding whether Taz deserved a short answer, a detailed one, or no answer at all.

"And by the way, what's your name? I'm T. Keaton. Do you sell Oreos here?"

"James. I keep 'em on the small shelf of groceries over there."

Taz opened a box and popped a cookie into his mouth. James looked at him like he wished he could eat Oreos and still be in as good of shape as Taz.

"Inspiration pills. They help me think."

"Roy Baker owns her. Fishes her up north in the summer and lives on her down here in the winter."

"That sounds like fun."

"Nice twin diesel. Big, solid boat. She's super heavy-duty fiberglass. Hull, decks, house - everything." He turned to look out the window. "That's Roy out on the fuel dock. He's pretty close to heading back north."

"Care for a cookie?"

"No thanks. Wife has me on a diet."

"Is that her I hear in the back?"

"No."

Taz leaned over the counter and smiled. "Cookie?"

"Hell, maybe just one." He smiled back and took three. "Come on, I'll introduce you to Roy."

"I appreciate it, James."

A week later, in yet another rejection of the carefully structured way he'd lived until seven years ago, the massive trawler belonged to him. Most of his friends were happy to tell him what a stupid decision it was, but the impulsiveness of it felt wonderful as he walked her wide decks alone that first night of ownership.

He moved her to a Tampa shipyard for a complete refit, and now, almost a year to the day later, with her new electronics, sparkling engine room, and a brand new interior from a fancy Miami decorator, he was about to make this eighty-ton love interest an important part in his future.

"Are you still planning to launch next week?" asked Pete, the young guy with a strong but lean body who expertly drove the shipyard's travel lift.

"Sure, as long as you don't pull the wrong lever on the lift and drop her on someone's toes."

"I've only dropped six boats this week," Pete laughed. "I'm getting better."

"Then let's launch while you're still on a lucky streak. The dinghy gets delivered today and the name goes on Friday. Are you coming to the party after the christening and launch?"

"You're inviting *me* to your party? I saw photos of one of your exclusive parties in *Esquire*, with lots of models and movie stars."

24

"I only sponsored that party for charity, and was there maybe ten minutes. This party is for my friends."

"Then sure, you bet. Thanks."

"It's been fun getting to know you, Pete. Did I tell you how much you remind me of a younger version of my good buddy Gordie?"

"Don't get all weepy on me just 'cause it's time to leave." Pete stepped back and looked way up above the fly bridge. "You've got state-of-the-art global communications, so you'll be able to call if you want or need anything from me."

"I will, although I hate being in touch. I've pretty much managed to escape that life and tend to see anything that can reach me as more of a tether than a tool. A leash, so to speak, and I don't like leashes."

"Have you ever run a boat this big? It's been most of a year since you brought her in here, but seems I remember you hiring a skipper."

"She's my first boat."

"Sorry?"

"She's the first boat I've ever owned."

Pete shook his head. "I can never tell if you're kidding, but I'm going to assume that you are because no one buys a world cruiser as a starter boat. Everyone here's going to miss your kidding around."

"Assuming I'm kidding."

"True enough. Where are you headed?"

"I suppose the best idea would be to go someplace where I could practice backing and turning this beast without hitting anything or running aground."

"I'd suggest the middle of the Gulf of Mexico?"

They stepped in front of the huge vessel, which was really a small ship, and leaned back to look up at her bow.

"Man, she is big, isn't she?'

"Good sized, Taz. I bet she's got good range, too. I'm guessing more than 1,000 miles between fueling."

"When I bought the new engines, the manufacturer said over 3,000 miles at an efficient cruise."

"Jeez, where I'd go if she were mine."

"Where?"

"What?"

"Where would you go?"

"Well...I don't really know. It's just something people say, you know, like 'What I'd do with a million dollars.'"

"What would you do with a million dollars?"

"I...damn, Taz, you may have noticed that not only don't I have a boat like this, I also don't happen to have a million bucks. Have you seen what I drive? So what does it matter?"

"Because I'm lucky enough to have both, but I'm not yet sure of the best way to combine them."

"So you don't work? I've been dying to ask how that's possible when you're not much older than me."

"I work, but I got lucky, I suppose, early on. Then I hired good CEOs who I pay very well to shoulder most of the responsibilities. That leaves me free to run the one small company I love. It's just a few of us and the work is intermittent, but always a blast. I just got back this morning from a small project in Panama."

"Is that where you meet women?"

"Panama?"

"Working different places? I've seen a couple of the beautiful ladies you've brought in here to show your boat."

"My sisters. Every one of them."

"I somehow missed the Asian lady's family resemblance."

"I meant they were *like* sisters. Wonderful young women helping me through a difficult time in my life."

"Does that line really work?"

"Never has for me, but you're welcome to take a shot with it."

"Do you want me to come along for a while after we splash her, just to make sure you don't knock off the mirrors or scratch the paint?"

"Are you a good skipper?"

"Compared to you I bet I'm awesome."

"I've supervised every bit of work that was done to her, and read all the manuals."

"Captaining something like this has to be as instinctive as it is intellectual."

"My instincts tell me to never take her out of a slip."

"And make a marina condo out of this beauty? Now that would be criminal. With her range and room you should head to the Keys and then to the islands."

"So that's what you'd do."

"Guess so. I'd head to Key West, and from there spend a year leap-frogging the islands of the Bahamas, Caribbean, and West Indies, hit South America and hang out for a while, then wander up Central America to Mexico and then, maybe, home. Or maybe stay on the merry-go-round and do it all over again."

"What about work?"

"I can work on boats anywhere. With luck I'd find a fantastic new place to call home while I'm out there exploring. Until then, I've got all the money I saved by being single for so long."

"Awkward around girls?"

"Not in the least."

"You really think you could leave everything behind and go away for that long a time? Up until seven years ago even I would have had trouble doing it. A few months, sure, but not a year that might turn into a lifetime if I liked it well enough."

"What happened seven years ago?"

"I rode a cruise ship around the Caribbean."

"That doesn't seem so life-changing."

"I got off for the afternoon in Belize and grabbed a cab for a tour. I was late getting back and the ship was almost to the horizon."

"They left you in Belize?"

"Yeah. It would have been funny except that I'd left my passport and credit cards on the ship, and only had a little cash left on me. So I found the harbor master and called the ship on his radio. They said they wouldn't come back, so I told them I'd find a fast boat to take me out to them."

"Did you?"

"At first the ship's captain said he couldn't risk trying to pick me up at sea, even if I could catch up to them."

"Liability, I suppose."

"But then I did the only smart thing of the day, which was to say that they couldn't risk leaving me behind and at-risk like that. So they agreed to let me board at sea if I could get out to them."

"What was it like, getting onboard a fast moving cruise ship in the open ocean?"

"I have no idea."

"But you just said–"

"Long after the sun went down, the Belizean guys I'd hired had me almost to the ship. The spray stung our eyes as we slammed through the waves and the salty water chewed our fingers where we held on, but all the while the guys running the boat were laughing like children and having a great time. I was too."

"I'm sorry to pee on your campfire, Taz, but don't you think they were laughing at you?"

"Most likely, but they really were having a blast doing it, and I thought to myself that it had been years since I'd laughed that hard or recklessly. Probably since I took over my first corporation."

"They had nothing to lose so it was easier for them."

"I think it was more along the lines of them knowing how to live each minute of every day in a way that made them happy. And if you're right that their way was easier, I needed to ask myself why I'd made happiness so elusive?"

"So what happened?"

"We pulled alongside the ship, which didn't even slow down. Every single passenger seemed to be manning the rails, watching our boat close the distance as the water sluiced between the ship's hull and ours. It must have looked dangerous to them but nothing short of terrific fun to my new friends.

"The ship opened a door in her side and lowered a ladder. Passengers looked worried and crew members seemed anxious, but my guys were still yucking it up. I sat there looking from the guys on my boat to the passengers on the ship and–" Taz snapped his fingers. "Just like that I chose another life."

He stopped and looked around. "Man, is this a beautiful day or what?"

Pete looked around too, as if something might have happened to change the day. "Wait, what do you mean, you chose another life?"

"I was thirty-five and addicted to buying companies. I'd been like that since my early twenties, when I caught a lucky break right out of college. It was plenty adventurous, at least it felt that way, and provided me with lots of money and recognition. But it wasn't really a life."

"And your guys on the boat were happier, or at least they seemed that way to you."

"They were happier, there's no question in my mind." He paused a few seconds. "Do you have faith in the company that trued my props?"

Pete followed Taz's eyes to the massive propellers, almost four feet in diameter and nearly a thousand pounds each. "They're the best. Never once heard a complaint."

"Know what I'm naming her?"

"Knotty Guy? Happy Ours? Aquaholic? I see plenty of boats with those names."

"*Wasafiri*. Bet you've never seen one of those. It's Swahili for–"

"It figures that you'd know Swahili."

"Just a few dozen words. Not a big deal since it's the primary language for much of Africa."

"Say something in Swahili."

"I just did."

"Right."

"What does *Wasafiri* sound like?"

Pete shrugged if off. Taz waited.

"I don't know. Safari, maybe."

"Exactly."

"Why would you name your boat after a hunting trip?"

"Because that's only what the word has come to mean in English-speaking countries. *Safari* really means to travel or journey. It could mean to wander."

"So you're the traveler."

"Nope. That would be *Musafiri*. *Wasafiri* is plural because I know of at least one adventurous woman out there who would enjoy this, and if she's ever onboard I want the name to include her. And instead of 'The Travelers' interpretation, I prefer 'The Wanderers' as a nod to Tolkein's 'All who wander are not lost,' because that's what I seem to be doing with my life."

"Wandering?"

"No. Appearing lost to everyone else as I enjoy what looks like wandering. So, I launch Wednesday morning, Pete, and I take you up on your offer to come along."

"Sure. What marina? Where will we be heading so I can reserve a slip?"

"Well, I was already planning to head to Key West, and from there I'm thinking I'll spend a year leap-frogging the islands of the Bahamas, Caribbean, and West Indies, hit South America and hang out for a while, then wander up Central America to Mexico and then, maybe, home. Or maybe stay on the merry-go-round and do it all over again"

Taz couldn't take Pete's stunned stare for very long without laughing, so he walked around his boat for the some-hundredth time, checking thru-hulls and cutlass bearings he already knew to be perfect. Over the last year he'd come to like Pete a lot, and would enjoy having him on-board for a few weeks or longer. But he knew how hard it was for someone to turn their back on an entire life. Taz's seven years of great adventures had taught him that family, finances, or freedom seldom changed the outcome. Most people couldn't wait to climb the boarding ladder and get back aboard the cruise ship.

Pete eventually joined him under the hull and leaned against one of the jacks supporting the massive boat. He looked unsure, as if fearing that the huge boat might fall over on him. "You mean it, don't you? I mean, I know you mean it. You'd take me along?"

"Yup."

Pete looked around the yard where he'd worked long enough to know every sling point of every type of hull, and how many quarts each type of diesel needed for an oil change. The cop who'd given him two speeding tickets driving to work had long ago taken a liking to him and started giving him warnings – three so far this year. Pete had a wonderfully familiar and safe life, which was both a blessing and a curse.

"Don't worry about it, Pete. I'm sure I can handle her."

"I'll bring my gear and load it tomorrow."

"Are you sure?"

"Absolutely not."

"Good. Certainty tends to take the surprise out of things anyway." Taz stuck out his hand, and when they shook he said "Really glad to have you aboard, Pete."

Chapter 4

10:02 A.M. on October 18th, 1718

Aboard *Queen Anne's Revenge*, Blackbeard's flagship, 219 nautical miles west of Havana, Cuba and bearing 279 degrees magnetic.

Waves crashed against the bow and threw spray high into the air as Queen Anne's Revenge ran off the wind under full sail, chasing the Spanish prey they'd seen at first light.

"Low she lies in the water, Captain," said Claw, the first mate, who, even though he was six feet tall still had to look up at Blackbeard.

Blackbeard lifted his spyglass to the dark eyes of his weathered face and studied the waterline of the large Spanish galleon a half-mile away. "Aye, much too low, I say. Why would a captain so load his vessel in such a season of fearful Caribbean weather?"

"Might there be extra cannons, sir? Or Marines? Surely they not be carrying slaves to home."

"'Tis either sinking, Claw, or gloriously overloaded with goods of the New World. Either way, it's a visit she's due from Queen Anne's Revenge."

"Her escort appears to be coming about, sir, and heading back to defend her. It's too yonder on the horizon to be sure, though."

"Then there's no use to the trickery of flying her flag, so let's be proud lads and hoist our colours, for we've already been guessed to be pyrates."

"Yet I see no sail for a vessel what should be trailing as a cover from her rear."

"Being a galleon, as it were, she herself might be the rear defence. If not, then by another pyrate or a storm the amaranth's been taken."

"Aye, sir."

Claw turned toward the decks and faced the crew that stood below him waiting for word of attack. They'd wanted to hear it all morning as they manned the rails and sharpened their axes, watching their ship close distance on the heavily laden vessel off their port bow.

"Lively now, lads, and hoist up the bones," Claw shouted.

The men cheered so suddenly it was like an explosion that the galleon's crew probably heard. At almost the exact same time their black flag unfurled, as big as a barn door, snapping in the wind off the stern of Blackbeard's 300-ton ship, its giant skeleton about to stab a lance through a bright red heart.

"Such a sight." Blackbeard said, drawling out the words as he squared his big, strong body with the ship's rigging and studied the flag he'd designed almost a year earlier. "Such a beautiful sight. Now watch ye and see how the galleon's escort sets all that's left of her canvas in her failing quest."

"Aye, Captain, its men are into the rigging now."

"But too late, ye see. The breeze this day favors our angle, so their fight with the trades and the Stream will keep them far away from their commission. And being as our prey is already fully rigged on a downwind run, they can do nothing more but prepare for battle."

"Battle," Claw repeated. "Then by your leave, sir, the keys to the armory and powder room."

"They have nearly double our cannons, Claw, yet we've over two hundred men what needs the bounty in her hold. Take her early shots if necessary, but I want her disabled with one salvo. And then in the smoke, we board."

"Aye sir." Then he turned to the crew. "A very close broadside with all port guns, lads. Then double-quick to the rigging and over the rails."

They cheered again. Claw turned back to Blackbeard and smiled. "It appears, sir, that the men stand eager for a fight."

Blackbeard handed him the keys. "Then by my leave, young Claw."

He left the deck for his quarters, returning just as Claw directed the helmsman to ease out from behind the other vessel's stern and blanket her with their sails, causing her to stall.

"Stand by to drop canvas," Blackbeard ordered as he stood behind Claw.

Claw didn't look back as he carefully guided the helmsman, "Aye, sir, we're at the ready. She's the *Espiritu del Mar*, Captain. The Spirit of the Sea."

"Aye, and soon to be more of a ghost than a spirit."

Claw laughed, and as he did he looked back, shocked as always at the sight of Blackbeard before battle. "Why you're the very devil himself, Captain."

Blackbeard smiled as he adjusted his cap over the wet rope he'd put under it and had already lit afire. The smoldering smoke rolled around his face and made him look demonic, even more so after he lit the slow-burning cannon fuses he'd tied into the long curls of his beard with red ribbons. "Aye, Claw, that I am."

His face now fully surrounded by smoke, Blackbeard moved his massive body to the foredeck in an exaggerated cadence, like a monster or ghoul, and ascended the steps with his back to the galleon as they drew even with her. The ships, each with their cannons loaded and ready, were separated by only a few dozen yards, and that distance was quickly closing as the ocean raced between the two large vessels with a rush that was building toward a roar.

Then with great theatrics Blackbeard turned around and faced the crew of *Espiritu del Mar*. He threw his smoking head back and gave a loud and maniacal laugh.

The Spanish soldiers, who had no doubt heard the legend of the devil that raided these very sea lanes, stood silently transfixed and staring at the phantasm who stood there, half afire from hell's own blaze and laughing at them with the fearlessness of a captain already certain of victory. They said nothing as Blackbeard's crews shouted and screamed and readied their guns.

"Fire the swivel guns, men," shouted the Spanish captain. "To guns, damn you. By God and your King, lads, to guns!"

But his men didn't move. They just stood in silence as Blackbeard stood close to his bowsprit, laughing at them with menace. Then the Spanish captain pulled out his smooth bore flintlock.

"Tis but a man, you fools. If not, let him wait for my shot and be damned."

The Spanish captain ran to the rail and took slow and careful aim with his pistol as the bow of Queen Anne's Revenge pulled even with his helm, the Spanish Captain and Blackbeard separated by only twenty feet or so. Then he pulled the trigger and sent a small ball of metal directly at Blackbeard's chest.

The slug travelled at an unnerving speed that was too fast to avoid but slow enough to watch. Blackbeard had expected a miss at that range, but stood grinning anyway as he watched the metal pellet come straight for him. He quietly reveled in the silent awe with which both crews watched as he waited in fearlessness, ready to win the psychological victory before even firing the first cannon.

The pellet struck hard and penetrated. Blackbeard wanted to rock back from the impact but did not allow himself to do it. Instead he forced out another laugh, even more psychotic than the first, and turned to his gun crews, smiling with obvious invincibility.

"Cannon crews!"

"Aye, sir," came back the shouted chorus.

"I shall meet you again in Hell, Captain Teach," shouted the Spanish captain.

"Cannon crews," Blackbeard repeated, watching as the ships finally drew even. "Kindly send the good captain to Hades to make ready my room. Now FIRE!"

With that command nearly 30 cannons blasted balls, nails, chain-shot, and explosives into the hull and onto the decks, instantly killing the captain, first mate, and many of the crew.

"To the rigging, now lads," shouted Blackbeard as he stepped up on the rail himself and tried to peer through the dull grey smoke of spent gunpowder. "And over the rails to take what's ours."

The Spaniards on deck directly across from Blackbeard must have decided to do battle with invaders who might be mere mortals, because they scattered from the spot where Blackbeard swung aboard with his pistols and knives and cutlass. So he walked the decks with impunity, ignoring the small, burning hole in his chest, hoping the distance would not have allowed the pellet to penetrate too deeply and trusting now fully in that same belief.

He strolled calmly through the battle as his men overwhelmed the leaderless Spanish. At one point he stopped to cut a man who was bettering one of his own, and then re-sheathed his cutlass as further proof that the devil needed no such protection.

Chapter 5

Gallants Point, just north of Beaufort, North Carolina and on the shore side of the flats where Russell Slough intersects the Intracoastal Waterway

A Marine F/A-18 tactical jet streaked low across the summer night sky, its roaring engines demanding attention from the men working on the Intracoastal dredging project recently funded by the United States Government and expanded off-the-books as residents paid privately to have small channels cut through the flats to their property.

Roger "Buzz" Cutts watched the plane with an angry kind of jealousy. Although he'd never even been in a plane, he could imagine flying something like that if only he'd stayed in school beyond the tenth grade and gone a totally different direction in life.

"While you're dreaming," he said to the darkness as he stood alone in the muck, watching slurry from the river pump onto the shore at his feet, "you might as well dream yourself a million dollars and a famous actress for a wife."

He looked back at the mud and was about to move the chute a few feet to a new spot when he caught a glimpse of it. He stared, transfixed, as it disappeared into the blackness.

"Shut down the dredger," he shouted into his walkie-talkie, trying but failing to control his excitement over what he believed he'd just seen.

"Are you sure you want to do that?"

"Just do it, damn it!"

"I'm winding her down," came a reluctant voice over the airwaves. "But I know how much you hate this side work on private channels, so if you're trying to screw it up you're going to take the heat. Boss man can hear this beast from his motel in Morehead City."

Had it been a trick of Buzz's eyes in the darkness of night? If so, he sure didn't want to lose the only real job he'd ever had by overstepping his tiny role in this yearlong project. "Okay, just let her idle while I check something."

He waded to the spot as soon as the flow stopped from the huge metal pipe. Muck immediately oozed over the tops of his rubber boots, the compost of water, slime, and sea grass colder than the night air. But that wasn't why he shivered as he groped around in the wet, black lava until his fingers actually touched it.

He lifted it up and wanted to scream, his brain going in a dozen exciting directions, none of which outpaced the instinct he'd learned in three decades of prison that it was always best, if equally impossible, to stuff down emotions.

He picked up his radio. "Forget it," he said. "Nothing."

"Yeah? Another nothing like that and you're going to get yourself fired."

Buzz's life had never given him any choice other than to answer each and every challenge he perceived from anyone, but he'd barely heard his supervisor's threat as he spit on the gold coin, which was about the size of a half-dollar, although thinner, and rubbed it shiny.

He slowed down his racing brain and made himself think in complete sentences, something he'd mastered as a way to control his temper enough to finally get parole.

"If the gold came out here," he said, using the simplest of logic, "then it went into the dredger where it's digging along the bank. That's where there might be more."

He waited a half-hour but no more gold came out. He wondered what the coin might be worth and considered that there might not be anymore. And he knew that losing this job would probably put him back in prison.

With those thoughts rushing through his mind he clipped his radio to the top of the pipe and walked away, struggling over a high wall and along the shore to the place where the dredger was finishing its excavation of a private channel and, hopefully, uncovering a new life for him.

THE WATERFRONT residents of Beaufort had grown used to the deep and powerful hum of the dredger's motor. Many slept better because of its melodic throbbing, now a sound so familiar as to be comforting, like coyotes howling on the desert or sirens screaming in a city.

The first people to have their sections dredged liked to tease those downriver that the low black form was creeping toward them as well, speaking with dread and submission as though it were the unbeatable phantom of one of the pirate ships that once plied their waters and called them home, long before an obscure U.S. Treasury Secretary first conceived of creating the Intracoastal Waterway in 1808.

Others took pleasure in the ease with which they could get their own private channel cut from the ICW, making their homes accessible to larger boats and increasing the value and usefulness of their property.

Few of the coastal residents, however, enjoyed the presence of the hardened men who drank in their bars and worked on the barges for the out-of-state dredging company. Locals resented that outsiders did the work when so many of them were unemployed watermen, so the strange men in town, and the inconvenience of their mile of floating pipe, mixed uncomfortably with their appreciation that the ICW was finally getting the maintenance it needed.

It had only taken a second for Derek Holmes, a very private man with extremely quiet ambitions, to wake up fully and realize that the dredger sound that woke him was not a sound at all, but rather silence, or close to it. As it worked its way toward his back door, getting closer to finishing the channel he'd hired them to dig, he'd forced himself to be tolerant of the noisy deckhands with their walkie-talkies and radios, the undecipherable sounds of both carried across the water and then lifted over the cattails of the muddy shoreline dotted with fiddler crabs, fish holes, and an occasional tire. But he heard almost nothing of those noises now.

The six-inch pine floors of their two-hundred-year-old home creaked when he got out of bed, waking his wife.

"What is it?" she asked, now sitting up in bed.

"Nothing, Theresa."

"It sounds like the dredger stopped. Why?"

"I don't know. A breakdown?"

The motor was running, but at idle, which meant the dredger's teeth weren't chewing into the muddy bottom. Oyster and clam shells weren't clanging against the sides of the oil-drum-sized pipeline as the massive pumps pushed the muddy mixture ashore, where it was dried out and used as fill dirt or topsoil somewhere up or down the coast.

"I still hear the engine."

"Could be lots of reasons they stopped dredging. Go back to sleep."

She dropped her head to the pillow as Derek went to the window and looked out. The dredger's lights were shining and cigarettes glowed in a congregation at one spot as though the crew was on a break, although dredger-stopping breaks normally only happened when they moved the barge a little. Then the dredger started up again

Derek kept staring for most of an hour since he wouldn't get back to sleep anyway. At one point he thought he saw a man in the darkest shadows of their yard, but it must have been a trick of his eyes, strained by his effort to better see the dredger. There was nothing in his yard but the small skiff that Theresa used to check the crab pots she'd placed here and there in the same river that ships once used to avoid the treacherous waters of the Atlantic. Especially those waters around Cape Hatteras that had claimed cargos and crews all the way back to when Europeans sailed the trade winds with goods from the New World, assuming they were lucky enough to avoid the storms and the pirates.

50,000 miles of interstate highways had ended the commercial era of the waterway at the edge of his yard, and his beloved ICW had, until very recently, slipped from importance in the national budget, its patchwork of man-made canals that connected streams with rivers and cuts and passes neglected to the point that it could no longer accommodate the vessels she was designed to carry. So the barges and tugs yielded to trawlers and sailboats – pleasure yachts heading south in the winter and north in the summer.

She was even too shallow for them in many places, and it was common to have yachts cued up at one end or the other of Mud Creek or Hell's Gate or a handful of other places with skinny water, waiting for a high enough tide to allow them to pass. Burned out navigation lights and missing day marks were seldom replaced, shoals shifted without being noted on charts, and silt filled in some areas to a depth of only a few feet. But that was finally changing following Congress's appropriation of new funding in 2009.

Finally, Derek went back to bed, assuming the silence to be of little significance, and completely unsuspecting that at the far end of the pipeline, in a massive puddle of ooze and slime and low-tide smells, a large man with bad teeth and calloused hands had found a golden coin that would rewrite history and destroy Derek's life.

Chapter 6

Taz stared up at the concrete underside of Tampa's Sunshine Skyway Bridge as he steered *Wasafiri* under it.

"This, Pete, is one way I love to add value to my life." He checked to make sure he was still lined up in the channel as he slid into the shadows of the twin-towered bridge that hung from hundreds of miles of cables stretched out in elegant simplicity. Then he stared up some more.

"You're right."

"I'm right? You really got my meaning?"

Pete glanced around the boat that he couldn't believe was now his home. "I actually have no idea what you're talking about, but since I've barely got my gear stowed I figure it's best to assume that you're right about everything for the time being."

Taz laughed. "Your berthing is comfortable?"

"As Mary-Ellen's arms."

"Is that your girlfriend?"

"A long and happy story that's over for now."

"I don't think I've ever heard those thoughts and words strung together. How long did you date?"

"Too long but not long enough. I'm afraid I totally missed your point, Taz."

"It doesn't matter. I was having a surreal moment as my life actually caught up with one of my best dreams. It doesn't happen often."

"You surely need to take a moment to appreciate that. But I'd think that you of all people would be used to seeing your dreams come true."

"Just because I'm rich?"

"No. Because you've got such white teeth." Pete laughed. "Yes, of course because you're rich."

"Success and wealth were challenges, Pete, not dreams."

"If you say so. Although I'm guessing it's a lot easier to make lofty statements like that when you're richer than cheesecake."

"Then maybe I can surprise you."

"That's not hard to do."

"Building a fortune from scratch requires a stupefying number of layers of pretense. Much of it is stuff that someone else might dream about but that has zip value to you."

"You mean having the right car, watch, and suit...that kind of stuff."

"And joining the right clubs, attending the necessary social events, donating to the proper candidates. It all sounds innocent enough, but if none of it is really who you are, at some point you find yourself deeply involved in a life that isn't yours."

"Yeah. A life of money, nice cars, and country clubs has to suck."

"You're kidding, I know, but it really can suck. I was lucky. Early on a good friend and mentor gave me a warning, and his heads-up almost allowed me to avoid it, but not quite. It's pretty much impossible."

"So come on and give it up. What's the meaning of life, oh wise one?"

"Tacos."

"Be serious."

"Naah. Seriousness is too much like cancer in that it loves to take over. And since serious stuff is often bad or hard stuff, pretty soon that's what you spend your time noticing. I'd rather notice the bridge."

"And so the bridge is what life's about? Let me see if I can understand the symbolism. It's about the connections we have, right? Represented by the opposite shores it ties together."

"No."

"The deep center channel that divides our–"

"You're not going to let this go, are you?"

"Probably not. Maybe it symbolizes the enormous heights to which we must go in order to cross over obstacles? The challenges–"

"Okay, here goes, but you're going to be disappointed."

"I doubt it."

"I absolutely love the architecture of that magnificent bridge. I drive over it all the time, sometimes just for fun. I park at both ends and study it while walking the old bridge beside it. But just now was the first time I've gone under it, and it was a totally different view from underneath. That was my point. By changing my viewing perspective I just got a completely new appreciation of something I thought I knew well, and a way to love it differently."

Pete laughed. "And to think we're only two hours out, Zen master."

"Then I'm going back to Tacos."

They motored smoothly into the Gulf of Mexico, turned almost due south, and then set the autopilot to take them to Key West. They sat back and relaxed, running at eight knots past the beautiful Southwest Florida coastline that eased slowly out of sight on their port side: Sarasota with her clear waters and art culture; Fort Myers, caught in the shallow curve between Sanibel and Bonita Beach that kept the water murky but the spring-breakers coming; Naples with its manicured opulence and Taz's old life; and Marco Island, known as The Rock, serving as the cultural bridge between the wealth of the coast and the fish camp mentality of Goodland, Chokoloskee, and Everglades City.

"Hope you managed to sleep," Pete said when Taz came up to take his shift. "I haven't seen anything since some lights of a condo at Caxambas Pass, but it's sure been a great night out here. Shark River's directly off to our left someplace. If we were closer to the coast we'd see Cape Sable at first light."

"Boat sounds good."

"Boat sounds great. You've really got a winner here." Pete tapped the autopilot to jog around a crab pot, its white float glowing nicely in the last bits of moonlight. "Ask you something?"

Taz hesitated, then said, "Sure."

"Out here alone in the dark for so many hours, passing a few of the places you've mentioned over the year that I've known you, I started to wonder where home is for you."

Taz raised his hands to his forehead and then gently ran his fingers through his blonde hair to push it back. "This is home." He stretched out on a couch on the fly bridge and closed his eyes again.

"*Wasafiri*? You mean she's your home until we get back."

"Nope. As the work on this boat came together, I realized the life of freedom she offered. So I called a realtor and told him to sell my Naples land anchor. The deal closed last week. I donated my car, the furnishings, and all the personal stuff I didn't bring onboard to charity. So this is my only home now. Wow, look at that sky."

"Wait, you gave away the Mercedes? Did you ever happen to notice the hunk of crap I drove to work?"

"I like your truck. It has character."

"And no backseat and holes in the floorboards. Jeez, how hard was it to get rid of everything you own?"

"Surprisingly easy once you decide to do it."

"Not the answer I expected."

"The decision was hard, though, because just like everyone, I had gifts I valued and stuff I'd collected, and it all meant something. But then I pretended that my house had burned down and I'd lost all that stuff anyway. Only this way I still had a choice of what to keep and to whom I should pass along some of it. That made it easier, along with my realization that what I owned kind of owned me."

"I still would have had a hard time."

41

"Americans tend to love their possessions so you've got lots of company. Which is why you'll probably go back to Tampa in a few weeks and consider your time onboard *Wasafiri* as nothing more than a vacation."

"Wow. Harsh."

"I'm sorry, Pete," Taz said as he sat up quickly. "That wasn't meant as an insult. It's just that everyone says they want to travel the world, or cruise for a year, or whatever, but when they finally get the chance most of them have a very familiar and comfortable life of lawns to mow and stuff to clean and an address where everyone knows where to find them, and that holds them back. I've got a friend who says that man is the only animal that builds a trap, sets it, baits it, and then willingly steps into it."

"When you put it like that, it should be easy to leave all that crap, to escape."

"But even when those people do get away for a week or a month of adventure, almost to a person they look forward to climbing the ladder back to the cruise ship – getting home to their conventional lives. It's almost impossible to break the gravitational pull of the familiar life that must be left behind in order to do something like this. Now go get some sleep. I'll take her for a while."

Pete left the bridge and Taz finished the shakedown cruise of 214 open-water miles. He couldn't have been happier with *Wasafiri*. She was dry and stable and reasonably fast, at least for a boat of her size and design. Her engines were smooth and her advanced electronics showed not only the charts and landfalls, but bottom topography as well as aerial views of ports and harbors.

They arrived off Key West and picked up the #1 marker at the entrance to Calda Channel, then carefully followed the well-marked but weaving course through the twists and elbows that had claimed hundreds of boats skippered by captains who'd steered the straight line-of-sight from Marker 9 to Marker 21, missing markers 12 through 20 altogether and getting a hard lesson in the time-honored tradition of not heading your boat to where birds were walking.

They turned to port at the Garrison Bight Channel and idled around Fleming Key, directly toward the old and unused seaplane ramps of the U.S. Naval Station, before looking over the cluttered mooring field for a spot big enough for them.

"Pete, get a boat hook and a line," Taz called from the upper helm. "I'm going to bring mooring ball forty-three amidships on our port side. You'll need to walk it back to the stern to get our line through its loop."

Pete ran along the deck with the boat hook and a heavy rope. "Got it, Taz, and don't think I still believe this is your first boat."

"I'm a quick learner."

"So was my dog, but it was weeks before she learned to bring back the Frisbee. I'm just going on record as seriously doubting you."

"All I said was that she's the first boat I ever owned."

"Mooring ball coming up. Easy. Easy. I've got it."

Pete walked the big floating ball to the much lower stern and passed a line through the eye-splice that dangled from the mooring.

"Think the mooring is anchored solidly enough into the bottom for this big of a boat?"

"Hope so. Standy-by." Taz picked up the microphone of his radio. "Garrison Bight City Marina, Garrison Bight City Marina, Trawler *Wasafiri*."

"Switch to Channel 69, *Wasafiri*."

"*Wasafiri* switching to 69," then "Garrison Bight, you there?"

"What can I help you with, Captain?"

"We just arrived and picked up one of your mooring balls. We're pretty big. Think she'll hold okay?"

"What number, and what's your length?"

"Mooring number forty-three. Our vessel was sixty-two feet and eight inches at launch and I think I managed to keep her that length on the way down."

The dock master laughed. "Hang on a tic." Then after a half a minute, "Yeah, that's really hard bottom there. It was blasted or drilled, and then poured. Not a mushroom rig, so you should be good. There's plenty of water, too."

"I'll come in by tender to do paperwork."

"I'm closing early so come by in the morning. To your adventure tonight in Key West."

Taz laughed. "Gordie? Is that you?"

"That depends on if you're a friend of mine."

"Give me a better option."

"Hey, Taz, welcome back. I heard you were on your way. So *Wasafiri*'s the name you picked for your boat. That's as weird as you are."

"And being dock master is the job you mentioned in Panama? Very nice. You've seen Sam?"

"I saw him yesterday. We have a story to tell you and were going to call tonight anyway. Let's get off the radio and meet for a drink at Irish Patrick's."

"What time?"

"Island time."

"Perfect."

Pete finished wrapping the line to keep it from chafing against the chock, then stood and looked up at Taz.

43

"I heard all that. I suppose this is your first time in Key West, too."

"First time. Come on, let's launch the tender and get cleaned up. We'll grab something to eat and celebrate *Wasafiri*'s first passage under our command. Then I've got someone you'll want to meet."

"Your friend Gordie?"

"Him, too."

Chapter 7

Key West, Florida

"Not many spots left for a tender," Pete said as they eased up to the marina's crowded dinghy dock. "Especially one as big as this."

"We'll put her in a slip if necessary. How about between those two inflatables?"

"Yeah, we can probably squeeze in there." Pete gently pushed the boats to make enough room for their whaler. They stepped ashore and Pete stopped to take in the sight of cars and motorcycles hurrying along the busy waterfront street or turning into the stores and restaurants that filled the other side.

Taz waited for him to move. Then, "Memorizing the scene for later?"

"Just trying to get a new perspective on it, like you yesterday."

"I thought you'd never been to Key West before."

"Maybe that's why I'm having trouble getting a new perspective."

"Smart ass."

Pete held out his arms like a revivalist preacher. "Thanks be to thee, O Lord, who hath permitted me to see something new."

"Wow," Taz said. "I never took you for being religious."

"It's what Ponce de Leon said after discovering Florida in 1513."

"I'm impressed."

"I've always liked it. You'll more than likely hear me say it again."

"It's a worthwhile line, and it's good to give thanks."

"Not in Ponce's case. Some Indian–"

"Native American."

"Some *Native American* didn't take kindly to his presence and shot a big ass arrow deep into his thigh."

"Ouch."

"Ponce later died in Havana from the infected wound."

"A lesson to be learned there, I guess. Hey, I know of a good locals-only restaurant a mile or so off-island. Want to walk it?"

"Sure."

The restaurant was a twenty minute walk in the direction of Miami, over the small bridge at Cow Creek and then down a side street until they got to a baseball field that needed some attention.

"Here we are."

"How does anyone ever find this place?"

"It's actually pretty legendary."

"So is the ancient city of Atlantis. Which, by the way, is probably easier to find."

They had a beer while they waited for their food, sharing the good feeling of a completed voyage, even a short one. The food came and they kept talking about how well *Wasafiri* performed and how comfortable she was.

They called a cab to take them downtown, and when they crossed back onto the island the driver tried to take them around by the airport so he could rack up the meter idling through the congestion of Duval Street. Taz asked him to turn right instead, past the anchorage where he caught a glimpse of *Wasafiri* and the marina full of charter fishing boats, transients, and the live-aboard boats that hadn't moved in years. Taz turned the driver onto Greene Street, where he and Pete jumped out at the side entrance to a noisy bar.

They walked around the corner and Taz smiled at the oddly typical evening crowd of people doing, or at least trying to do, the kinds of things they would never dare do at home. After a week or so it became a little tiresome, but each time he returned there was something about the free-spirited festiveness that made him instantly happy to be back in Key West.

Each bar they passed tried to lure them in with its loud music and laughter. Pete fell behind twice in half a block, and then caught up each time with the same question. "Where are we going?"

Taz stopped in front of a bar that was almost devoid of an entrance, just a big doorway and large window openings with no glass in them. A guitar player sat on the stage toward the back, working the crowd like a pro and always watching the people walking along the sidewalk.

"Here," Taz said.

Just then the guitar player stopped playing and waved at them. "Come on in, you guys!"

The crowd, obviously trained by the entertainer to join in the fun, all turned to face them and shouted, "Yeah, guys, come on in."

Pete was so anxious that he didn't wait for Taz. He stepped inside while the musician and the half-drunk audience kept watching him.

"Where are you from, stranger?" asked the guitar player, and everyone waited for Pete to answer.

"Tampa," Pete said, as if suddenly learning the thrill of being a celebrity.

Taz started laughing even before the whole room screamed "Who gives a shit?" at Pete.

"Welcome to Key West," Taz said as he passed Pete and headed to a table in the back, getting a nod and a laugh from the guitar player while a man and wife in matching shirts stopped Pete to buy him a drink for being such a good sport, and because they were celebrating something they couldn't quite remember at the moment.

"Hey, Gordie," Taz said as he sat down at one of the only two chairs available, his back to the door as he faced the back third of the room and the stairs to the balcony. "Thanks for the crappy seat. I guess you'll have to watch my back."

"Like all the other times."

"I don't know about all the other times, but the last time I was here you nearly let me get whacked by a jealous boyfriend."

"And I promise to do every bit as good tonight."

"Terrific."

"Hey, a guy anchored close to you said the boat you bought with a bag or two of your money is a real looker." Gordie turned to a big man sitting next to him who was cleaning his fingernails with the fid of a rigging knife. "Taz only looks like a bum. He tries hard not to show how wealthy he is."

"I'm only rich when compared to Gordie. But then again, who isn't?"

"You two are obviously old friends," the stranger said. "So where did you meet?"

"I'm betting it was somewhere that served us liquor."

Gordie lifted his glass. "And I'm not betting against you."

Just then Pete walked up to the table, proud of his free drink and the new friends he'd made at the bar.

"Pete, let me introduce you to the finest poker player you'll ever meet. Gordie, this is my friend, Pete."

"Good to meet you, Gordie. The finest card player, huh? Did you ever play in the World of Poker competition in Vegas?"

"Oh boy," Taz said, "here we go."

Gordie tried to kick Taz but missed. "Don't worry about me boring this nice fella man with stories of my past. I'll make it short and simple."

"I'll buy a ticket to see that."

"Pete," Gordie said, while ignoring Taz, "to understand what I'm going to tell you we need to pretend that Vegas is a totally different country, see, and that this totally different country, for reasons no one has yet been able to clearly explain to me, has declared me persona non grata, and that I–"

"Gordie's banned from Vegas. For life plus a day."

"That's not quite the truth, Taz."

"I'm improving the story."

"You're an ass. Still."

"I'm just fitting in around here."

"And you're still not telling the truth." He turned to Pete. "I assume you crewed down on this gorgeous boat of Taz's, right Pete?"

"Yeah."

"So I'm not talking out of school when I say that Taz is loaded."

"So?"

"So how does that boat match Taz's comment about trying to fit in?"

"What Gordie's trying to say in his ham-handed way," Taz added, almost reluctantly, "is that I've known far too many people who let wealth separate them from the normal world. I don't want that to happen to me and so I asked Gordie to pull my nose hairs when I might be losing my way."

"Wealth has never been my problem," Buzz laughed. "Afraid I can't relate."

"I think that's the only thing I've ever seen scare Taz," Gordie said with sincere amazement. "Even as he runs around the world on his crazy adventures."

Pete looked surprised. "What adventures, Gordie?"

"Nothing. Ask Taz when you get a chance. And now, Pete, it's your turn to tell us what your particular deal is with Taz? All of us have a role, you know, so are you a scientist? Diver? Pilot? Chemist?"

Pete started to answer but Taz stopped him, then looked around before leaning forward as if to tell a secret. Everyone leaned in with him. "You've got to keep this quiet, men, but Pete's a spy for Russia. During his time in America he's really taken a liking to our country, so I'm helping him feed his handlers some really good disinformation as we strategize a safe way for him to defect."

Pete picked up the game and looked around as though he, too, was concerned.

Gordie sat considering it, looking at Taz and then Pete. Finally he said, "Bullshit."

Taz took a drink from the waitress who leaned far over the table in order to kiss his cheek. "Thanks, Marcia. Yeah, Gordie, it is bullshit."

Gordie turned to the large man beside him, who laughed hard and showed a pretty rotten set of choppers. "Yeah, funny, sure, but the trouble is that Taz could have just as easily been telling the truth." He eyed Pete again as though still not sure he wasn't a spy.

"Well if Pete's not a spy," Taz said, "maybe this fellow is. Gordie, how about introducing us to your friend?"

"I'm Buzz," the guy said, and stuck out a calloused hand as he flashed what passed for a smile. "I'm a reconstructive dentist here in Key West."

There was silence again. Then Buzz laughed like crazy and so did Gordie.

"Very funny."

"I thought so."

"Pete," Taz said, "what would you guess Buzz does?"

Buzz sat back as though he both liked and hated the attention.

"No clue, Taz."

"Think about it. He's lucky enough to be able to work without fussing over how he looks. No offense, Buzz."

"None taken."

"He's got a working man's hands but he's drinking what is probably a single malt scotch. He's–"

"Are you some kind of a detective, Taz?"

"Just infected with curiosity. I want to guess that you're a fisherman, Buzz, but that's not quite right, at least not a fisherman from around here. You work hard but you don't work construction. And you're just visiting Key West, right? Been here a day? Maybe two? I'm guessing you're from...let's see, maybe Virginia. The lower Chesapeake Bay, perhaps."

"Not too far off."

"I can imagine that you run a crab boat up there and have just finished getting ready for the season. You're taking a vacation here to charge up your batteries for the several months of back-breaking work ahead."

"Not bad at all," Buzz said, "although I'm from a little farther south. Currently I'm in Beaufort, North Carolina, although home, I suppose, is Maryland. I work on a dredger, or at least I did. Lost my job last week."

"A dredger. Damn, I never thought of that. And Maryland's a state, not a home."

"It'll have to do because that's about as close as I can peg it."

"Did I get the vacation part right?"

"Not even close," Gordie said in a too loud voice before throwing back the shot of whatever the waitress had just set on fire in his glass. "He's here about treasure!"

Buzz jumped in quickly. "I came down to see the museum about the Atocha wreck. I've always heard that it's very interesting."

Gordie looked at something behind Taz. "Trouble coming, Taz."

"Guy or girl?"

Just then the guitar player pulled a chair over from a just-vacated table. "How's it, my brother?"

49

"Hey Rick, nice joke on my man here."

"Thanks." Rick turned to Pete. "Sorry about the 'who gives a shit' at the door. I do that to a lot of people."

"That's Pete," Taz said. "This big guy is Buzz. You know Gordie."

"Hey guys. Glad to see you. Taz, welcome back. Here for long?"

"Heading out in a couple of days. Pete and I are off to explore the Caribbean."

"Then we'll need to celebrate while you're here."

"Tell me, Rick, do you know that beautiful woman sitting against the wall, two tables from the stage toward the door?"

"I don't."

"You didn't even look."

"I don't have too. Every guy in this bar knows exactly what woman you mean."

"I feel like I'm wasting away."

"No you're not either."

"I am."

"You just got here. I haven't even talked to you yet. You're not wasting away."

"Let's go."

"No."

"I'll tell these gentlemen about the time you went out alone when staying with me in Kinshasa."

"Why do I call a man I hate my friend. I amaze myself."

"I'll join you in a minute," Taz said as he got up and motioned to their waitress, who caught up with him just before he got to the woman's table.

"Taz, one day it'll be me you're buying a drink. And it won't be in this place."

"I'm looking forward to that, Marcia." Then he stepped up to the woman's table while the waitress smiled and waited. "Hello. I'm TK."

"TK is not much of a name."

"Neither is my name, really, but TK still works. Who are you?"

"Professionally? Intellectually? Perhaps philosophically? I mean, honestly, who really knows who they are?"

Taz just smiled and waited.

"Okay, okay, I give up. Jesus, where did you buy that smile? I'm Tricia. This is my friend Wendy."

"Very nice to meet you both." He turned to the waitress, "Marcia, would you please do me the favor?"

"Of course I will, Taz. Ladies, what I can I get you from the bar or menu?"

"Taz? What happened to TK?"

50

But Taz had already walked off. He jumped onto the stage as Rick finished checking the tuning of a second guitar and was casually strumming Jimmy Buffett's *Margaritaville*.

Taz sat down on a stool beside Rick, and in Key West tradition they played the song pretty much like Buffett's version. But instead of "wasting away again in Margaritaville" they pointed the necks of their guitars at Tricia and substituted it with the line "wasting away again in Tricia's underwear," which initially caused an angry look from her that was quickly followed by a smile that crept to the edges of her eyes and corners of her mouth.

The crowd laughed harder each time they sang it while Tricia blushed and tried to look offended. Every man in Irish Patrick's and most of the women joined in the loud chorus until people on the sidewalk were crowding the entrance to get a look at the now-famous Tricia. All the while, Taz's eyes stayed with her.

"I hated that," she said when he went back over.

"You did not. Wendy, did she really hate that?"

Wendy looked around at the guys staring at them, every one of them probably thinking about Tricia and her underwear. Two other waitresses were bringing offers of more free drinks as Taz stood there waiting with absolute patience for her answer.

"Why don't you ask her, TK?"

"I wouldn't be able to hear her over the noise. Tricia, can we step outside to talk about whether or not you hated that?"

Tricia looked at Wendy, who'd just started talking to a guy at the next table. Tricia touched her hand and Wendy nodded that it was okay for her to leave.

As they headed to the door Pete caught up with him. "Do you want me to meet you at the tender later? Want me to go back to the boat? Wait here?"

"Have a great time, Pete. Whatever you do, just have a great time. We've got work to do tomorrow."

"Work? What work? I thought we were just going to wander."

But Taz and Tricia were already out the door.

Chapter 8

"Wow, that sure smells nice," Tricia said as she propped a pillow behind her and breathed in the smell of fresh coffee and pastry. "Did you wake up Wendy?"

"I'm not sure that would be possible," he laughed as he sat on the edge of the bed. "I'm sure you can hear her snoring."

"I've kind of gotten used to it."

"I didn't know which croissants you liked best so I got two of every kind they had."

"The chocolate ones look good."

She smiled while he gently spread a napkin across her lap. Then he carefully placed a chocolate croissant on a plate for the best visual presentation and handed it to her. "How do you like your coffee?"

"Just black, thanks."

"Interesting."

"Last night we talked about my years in Africa. You get used to black coffee."

"Was it a nice time?"

"Africa?"

"No, last night."

She smiled. "You shouldn't have to ask, Taz. I'm pretty sure I made it clear."

"I bet everyone on this floor knows."

"That's fine with me."

"It really was a nice evening."

"You never did tell me your name. Or why you first introduced yourself as TK but the waitress called you Taz."

"I'm Keaton. I use T. Keaton or TK or Mister Keaton when I'm unsure of myself. My friends call me Taz."

"So what should I call you?"

"Mister Keaton."

"How about I don't call you at all?"

"Then let's make it Taz."

She took a bite and he watched her eat. She somehow managed to look both sexy and fresh in the morning that followed a very long night.

"I know your name from work," Tricia said.

"I was afraid you might when you said you worked at State. You heard all good things, I hope."

"Weird stuff, mostly. And did you really talk the French ambassador's wife into table dancing?"

He laughed. "She was a great sport."

"The story's a good one. It gets retold a lot."

"Good." He stood up.

"Taz, while walking back here you warned that you'd leave in the morning, but do you really have to go so soon?"

"I do. I'd rather not, but Wendy's not really going to want a third wheel tagging along on the vacation you two have been planning for, let me guess, a year?"

"Almost a year. No, she probably won't. Can I see you once more, though? Where are you staying?"

"I'm on a boat."

"A nice boat?"

"Unfortunately it's not accessible to you because it's way out in the mooring field, so it has that going against it. But the next time I'm in D.C. you'll hear from me again. If you want, we'll see each other then. But now I have to run."

"That's not just an excuse?"

"A very good friend has an adventure story to tell me, and I'm dying to hear it."

"I love an adventure, so go. I really do understand." Tricia handed him her plate and then slid down into the bed. She smiled, and then pulled up the covers like she was heading back to sleep. "Bye, Taz. You are a very nice man."

"Good-bye Miss Vance. Thanks for a terrific night."

Taz stopped at the front desk and paid Wendy and Tricia's bill, then left the hotel and walked through Mallory Square. The street performers who set up every sundown were nowhere to be seen, and even the high-wire rigging on which the animals performed was gone without a trace. A tour boat idled slowly past, its captain repeating local history for probably the thousandth time to the handful of early-rising tourists who weren't nursing bad heads.

Duval Street was as heavily littered as always after the nightly onslaught of tourists and locals, many of whom competed to see who could act or look the craziest. But the trash crews were already busy cleaning up the tons of nightlife garbage, and in another hour or two the shops would open, the beer taps would start to flow, and the cruise ship *du jour* would pull into port and disembark a few thousand new tourists. Slowly but inevitably the native rhythm of Key West would build throughout the day until it swelled each night to its noisy finale.

Pete woke in a start on the hard fiberglass deck as something crawled across his face.

"Shit, what was that?" he asked no one as he bolted upright in *Wasafiri's* 19' tender, triggering a reaction from his stiff and cold muscles that had endured the cool night air without any covers at all. "Ow."

"How's your head?"

Pete jumped again and shifted around to see who was behind him. "Taz, did you put something on my face just now while I was asleep?"

"I can't believe you'd accuse me of that when I've brought you coffee. Here, and there are croissants in the bag."

"I didn't know what to do last night after Gordie and Buzz left. And my head hurts. Thanks for the coffee."

"How late was that?"

"Two. Maybe three in the morning. I think they went to a place that stayed open until five or five-thirty."

"Ouch, I know the place. I've thrown back too many in there."

"I'd already reached that point."

"You should have gone back to the boat," Taz laughed. "I really think you would have been much more comfortable sleeping there."

Pete rubbed his stiff neck while he took a sip of coffee. "Well thank you very much for the wonderful idea. I can't imagine why I didn't think of doing that instead of waiting here for you? Go back to the boat where I have a nice comfortable bed, wow, what a concept."

Taz pulled off his shoes and hung his legs over the dock so that they dangled in the perfectly clear water. "What did you think of Buzz?"

"Nice enough I suppose. I hope he's not dreaming of being a model someday."

"There's something a little strange about him, but he's probably a good enough guy. Maybe just blown a little off course like the rest of us."

"Maybe he's just wandering, like you?"

"Maybe. I don't think so, though."

"So what's the story with you and Gordie?"

"There are far too many to tell."

"That's obvious."

"But the good news is that if Gordie has attracted Buzz's attention, or Buzz has attracted his, there's a brand new story about to unwind and you, with luck, are going to be smack in the middle of it."

54

"Does it involve more bugs crawling across my face?" He stomped on the rock-roach as it shot across the deck.

"You never know. Did you notice the look Buzz gave when Gordie mentioned treasure?"

"He certainly reacted."

"So either he was embarrassed about being a tourist at Mel's museum, which he had no reason to be, or he was pissed off that Gordie hadn't kept quiet about what he'd told him."

"Gordie doesn't seem like the kind of guy who talks out of school if he was trusted with a secret, although he did kind of dime you out over your fear of money."

"Because I asked for his help in keeping me centered. But you're right that he's not one to spill secrets. And he can drink like a Russian farmer without slipping his tongue, so it sure wasn't the alcohol. He was knocking back those shots so he could blame it on the alcohol."

"What are you going to do?"

"It's time to go to work, my man. I think we should hang out here a few days, talk to Gordie and Sam, see why Buzz came to Key West, and figure out what's going on. Buzz is a little rough looking but that doesn't mean he's not smart enough to present a challenge."

"He was quick witted with the dentist line. Are you always looking for challenges?"

"You should go back to the boat and get a nap. I'll register our stay with Gordie at the dock master's office and then get together with Gordie and Sam over lunch."

"How will you get back?"

Taz looked across the small marina to the narrow pass that went out to the acres of mooring field where *Wasafiri* was tethered at the far side. "I'll swim."

"That's quite a swim," Pete said as he fired up the whaler and Taz threw off the lines. "But suit yourself. It'll give me a couple of hours in the rack. Have fun."

Taz pulled some walking-around money out of his wallet before throwing it into the boat as Pete idled away, then he walked along Wahoo Dock toward the road. A couple was making noisy love inside the cuddy cabin of their 23' boat and a guy in the next slip was chuckling about it as he rigged rods for a day of fishing.

"How long have they been at it?"

The fisherman looked at his wrist where his watch would be if he wore one. "Let me see...just about all night."

It reminded Taz of his own great night, and that's what he was thinking as he walked around the corner of the converted construction trailer that housed Garrison Bight City Marina Operations. The parking lot was, as usual in the mornings and afternoons, full of cars pulling boat trailers. Drivers jockeyed to launch their boats while ramp monkeys – old men who no longer took to the sea in ships but instead stood around in good-natured judgment of those who did it badly – manned the piers beside the ramp. At this particular moment they were laughing at a guy trying to launch an 18' center console.

"Pull that stern line harder," the driver of the car shouted to a teenage girl who was probably his daughter. "I'm backed into the water up to my bumper and the boat should have slid off the trailer long before now."

The young girl pulled harder. Slowly the trailer's upright guide posts moved sideways toward her.

"You forgot to take off the straps," hollered Taz to the driver. "Right now your boat *is* floating. It just happens to have your trailer hanging underneath."

"Spoil sport," shouted one of the ramp monkeys.

"Hey, Gene, I saw you fall in the drink once while straddling between the dock and a boat, so give the guy a break."

"If you don't have a photo of my splashdown, TK, I'm going to swear it never happened."

"Mister Keaton?"

Taz turned around to the sound of his last name, which, outside of the office, was unfamiliar and uncomfortable.

"Yes, officer, that's me. Good morning." And then, while making it clear that he didn't need to read the name tag on the man's uniform, he added, "Your name is Bill, isn't it? I've seen you around town."

"It is, but I'm afraid it's not a good morning, Mister Keaton."

"T.K."

"We found Mister Gordon Windsor dead this morning. I know he was a good friend of yours?"

Taz's legs weakened and he felt like he was going to puke or fall down or both. He looked for a lie in the policeman's eyes, even though he was sure he wouldn't find one. Not even a cruel person said things like that unless they were true.

He fought hard to find some way to hold onto his insides and maintain some control. "Gordie will always be my friend" was all he managed to say.

"I understand. I'm very sorry. We're not sure of the exact circumstances, Mister Keaton, but a zone car found him behind a stone wall on Caroline Street."

"Was it an accident? I think he'd gone to the Parrot and was probably pretty toasted."

"Not unless he accidentally fell on a rigging knife."

A gory spectacle of his best friend's bloody body battled for dominance in Taz's brain, but yielding to it would have taken too much attention from what he might learn about what happened, and what he'd definitely have to do about it.

"He had this in his pocket," said the officer. "I can't let you keep it, but we're wondering if it might mean something to you." He handed Taz a card that said ATLANTIC COMMERCIAL DREDGING.

"Someone wrote something on the back. I assume it was Mister Windsor."

Taz turned over the card and immediately recognized Gordie's lousy handwriting.

Taz, a guy working for this company told Sam and me a story you're never going to believe. To adventure, right?

"Any idea what he meant? What he knew?"

Taz had nothing positive to gain by showing his feelings, and he risked lots of negatives, such as having Key West's finest keep a vigilant eye on him as they searched for clues about Gordie's death. Murder – particularly non-domestic homicide – was terrible for tourism, which meant that solving it was essential before some level of fear set in among the tourists. The cops would press hard in all directions to make an arrest, but they could go back to Irish Kevin's and learn almost everything Taz could tell them, so he really had nothing to offer anyway.

"I wish I'd gotten to hear the story he mentions. I love a good adventure."

"You have no idea what he meant?"

"No. You might ask Sam, though, or Marcia, our waitress at–"

"I already talked with Marcia. And you probably know that Sam tends to throw rocks at cops. We'd have to torture him to talk to us."

"It wouldn't help much."

"I know. Marcia sent me to find you so you'd hear it before the news broke publicly."

"That was nice of her. Nice of you too, Bill. I bet you've had a long night."

"You could say that."

"I haven't had a decent breakfast yet. You've got to be hungry, Bill. Care to join me?"

The cop looked surprised, probably too used to people avoiding rather than inviting him.

"I'd sure enjoy some coffee and a pancake or two. But I have to pay my way. Rules."

"I know just the place." Then, trying to lift the mood and open up their dialogue, Taz pushed his love for Gordie far enough away to make a lame joke by opening the driver's door of the patrol car and acting like he was getting in. "I'll drive."

The cop was clearly glad to shed some emotional weight. "I don't think so."

"Okay," Taz said. "But maybe next time."

Chapter 9

As soon as Pete got back aboard he went to sleep and didn't wake up until two in the afternoon. He took a hot shower that felt great and then paced *Wasafiri*'s decks with his eyes constantly checking the wide expanse of water for the splashes Taz might make swimming out to the boat or, perhaps, drowning while making the effort.

Pete had attended two years of college on a swimming scholarship, but the only use he got out of it was a lifeguard's job during the summers. The funny thing about being a lifeguard, though, was that Pete would probably never stop feeling responsible for others in the water. He seriously doubted that Taz might need his help, but it was more than a mile swim from the marina and he wanted to be watching, just in case.

He walked back to the stern and was surprised to find a fresh trail of water from the transom boarding ladder all the way through the main salon.

"How did you get back without me seeing you?" He asked as Taz came back into the salon, toweling off but still dripping onto the beautiful rug that covered the highly polished floors.

"I saw you watching for me. Thanks, by the way, for standing by."

"No problem. But how did I miss you?"

"I needed the challenge of getting back without being seen."

"Nicely done, although I still can't figure out how you did it."

"How about firing up the engines and taking us to the main channel and then out through Fleming Key Cut."

"Roger that," he said without hesitating, even though he had no idea why their plans had suddenly changed, or where they were headed next.

"Gordie's dead."

Pete stopped suddenly. He stared and wanted to ask the obvious questions, but he'd learned a long time ago to hold back on questions when he'd been asked for action, so he rushed over to the lower helm and turned the keys for both diesels. The buzzers hissed as he ran the throttles to full and then back to half, pushed the start buttons, and then heard the big engines growl to life like a couple of caged but dangerous animals.

"Firing up the chartplotter. Radios are on. Radar on. GPS is locking in."

"After you head around to the Atlantic you can pick up Hawk's Channel. Plot a course to Miami. I'll slip the mooring ball. Then I've got a call to make."

When Taz sprung to the bow Pete stood ready to engage the props and take the enormous strain of the vessel off the line that attached it to the mooring, but as Taz grabbed the rope Pete was amazed to see him pull the massive boat forward and take enough strain off the line to un-cleat the bitter end and throw it overboard. Then he hauled the rope through the mooring ball's loop and back aboard *Wasafiri*.

"You're free, Pete. Make way."

"Wow. Underway."

As Taz ran back through the main salon Pete said, "I'm sorry about Gordie."

Taz stopped his dash for the chartroom and looked carefully at Pete. "I can't yet comprehend my loss."

"He was a real likeable guy."

"Yeah."

Taz started off, but then stopped and came back. "Listen, Pete, you've got to be careful around me, okay? Sometimes people near me get hurt, even strong, capable people like Gordie. If you want to get off in Miami I'll pay to fly you and your stuff home. We'll still be friends. Think about it."

Taz shot below as Pete resisted the urge to answer quickly, and instead ask himself what he really knew about Taz, which was, actually, almost nothing. He was rich, sure, but had he come by it honestly? Or could he be dealing drugs or running a Ponzi or cheating old women out of pensions?

But none of that seemed likely. Although wealth tended to draw people to anyone who had it, and being charming was a necessary character trait of a scam artist, Taz seemed to have real friends who liked him a lot and wanted to protect him. That added a great deal to the equation.

Beyond that, Pete had heard positive rumors around the boatyard since the first day Taz arrived and signed in. Someone in the office thought that they'd recognized his name and did an internet search that produced thousands of hits about the unconventional businessman who worked unnoticed on the production lines, ships, and loading docks of companies before he bought them, getting a feel for how everything worked and deciding if he really knew how to add value to the business.

And finally, although Pete's job had introduced him to lots of other people with fabulous wealth who owned nice yachts, he'd learned that the people who owned expedition yachts like *Wasafiri* were an odd lot and not easily understood. For all of their power and traditional beauty, yachts like

Wasafiri weren't show boats designed to impress gawking dock-walkers. They were big, strong and dependable sea-going vessels built for heavy weather and the toughest of times.

And so, figured Pete, was Taz.

So the only question Pete still needed to answer was whether or not he was tough enough to keep up.

"I'm ordering some gear, Pete. You're about six feet and 180 pounds? Certified diver?"

"I'm about that size. And yes I'm certified."

"What did you decide, my friend. Are you in or out? Take a second."

"I guess I could say that you might as well haul up the boarding ladder, Taz. I'm not climbing to safety."

Taz looked him over and smiled. "You'll probably regret it in some ways."

"I regret the calories in pizza, but eat it anyway."

"Exactly." Then Taz went back to his call. "And buy us a truck, Fran. Nice but not flashy, something like the Hilux you got Gordie and I to use chasing surf along the Azuero Peninsula. Title it to Peter Riley. Fax whatever he needs to sign to the boat. Thanks."

He winked at Pete. "The truck's for not giving you my Mercedes."

Taz went to his cabin. When he came back he was dressed in white jeans and moving slowly, as if settling into the slow, trawler pace of *Wasafiri*. After they rounded Whitehead Spit and entered the Atlantic, they turned east.

Taz pointed toward an array of huge antennas just over the beach at Truman Annex. "Spy stuff, Pete."

"All of it?"

"Most of it."

"I can't take the truck, Taz, but thanks all the same."

"I don't like owning personal things other than this boat and whatever's on it, so you're actually doing me a favor."

"Couldn't you have just rented something?"

"Not part of the plan."

"What plan?"

"The one I still need to plan. Besides, the way things go with me, the truck will probably end up pretty close to worthless anyway."

"Feel up to telling me what happened to Gordie?"

"I don't, but you deserve to know. The police say he was murdered. They wanted to question Buzz but he's nowhere to be found. I spent the morning looking too. He's gone."

"Any idea where?"

"Pretty sure I know exactly where he's gone, which means that *Wasafiri* is going to cruise to the Caribbean by way of North Carolina. Are you still in?"

"I've never been to North Carolina."

"God the water is beautiful out here in the Atlantic. Let's move to the fly bridge and watch the bottom go by. You'll swear you're going to hit the rocks and coral heads on the bottom, but they're much too deep."

"Again, I'm sorry about Gordie."

"I'll see you topside, Pete."

Chapter 10

1:18 P.M. on October 18th, 1718

Temporarily adrift aboard the Spanish galleon *Espiritu del Mar*, with *Queen Anne's Revenge* alongside, 225 nautical miles west of Havana, Cuba.

The panicked Spanish crew had spread sand over the decks while watching the black-flagged vessel approach, but too much blood had already been shed and the footing was treacherously slippery. Falling meant vulnerability, and probably an instant death by an enemy's axe or saber.

Blackbeard walked the decks unchallenged, the smoke from his hat and beard trailing behind him. "With me now, Claw!" He almost laughed out the order as men fought and died around him on his newly captured ship. "Our eyes we're now to throw upon our prize."

"Her escort ship has turned off and headed north again, Captain."

"Aye, she has nothing more to protect, and wisely sees no point in losing the lives required to sink this fine vessel from beneath us."

Both men climbed slowly down two levels of decks, with Blackbeard leading the way. Twice he stopped to stare down Spaniards they encountered below decks, who wanted to run when they saw the smoking specter of Blackbeard, but couldn't quite seem to move their feet until he pushed them aside and walked through their ranks, leaving them unharmed for his crew to murder, if that be the course of their lives.

When Blackbeard got to the ship's hold he needed all three of his pistols to shoot through the big brass lock.

"She's too dark inside, Claw. Fetch us a lantern."

Claw hurried off and returned in minutes, but by that time Blackbeard was already inside the hold, his eyes slowly growing accustomed to the darkness.

"There be no light in here," Blackbeard said in a voice of disbelief, "because she's full clear up to the crossbeams. She's much too full. Must be three hundred chests stacked amongst us in this vessel."

"'Tis why she carries herself so low in the water."

"Aye. The light."

Claw held it high.

"As I reasoned," Blackbeard said, "all the chests carry the king's mark."

"Yet not before have I seen this particular stamp."

"Nor I, but it's surely the king's mark. A new mint they must have commissioned, and that be their stamp. Break ye open a chest."

Claw pried open a chest and flung back the lid.

In the darkness of the hold and the shimmering of the light, Blackbeard stepped back and gasped, which, even with the treasure Claw saw surrounding them, surprised him so much that he gasped too.

"'Tis too much," Blackbeard said softly, almost fearfully, as light sparkled and danced off thousands of shiny gold coins.

"Aye."

Neither men seemed able to speak as they forced their eyes away from the chest and looked as best they could around the hold. Every available space was loaded full with crates, or chests like the one they'd just opened.

"What might this ship be rated for cargo, Claw?"

"Fifty tons, me thinks, Captain. Maybe half that again."

"Aye, and she's overloaded."

"Probably transporting close to a hundred tons, then, sir."

Blackbeard sat down on the open chest and shoveled up a handful of gold escudos, the most popular and valuable coins for his men to steal.

"Open ye a yonder case," said Blackbeard, pointing at several stacks of longer crates that were half the height of the chests. "For I bet on your soul there be ingots in them."

Claw dashed over to the stack of sixty or more crates, but they were stacked so high that Blackbeard had to help him build enough steps to bring one of the crates down from the top, both of the men struggling with the weight of it.

"To the lock, now, Claw. With some haste, if ye please, as my eyes be waiting on ye."

Claw pried off the lock and threw back the lid. The lantern's light reflected brightly off rows and rows of neatly stacked bars of gold.

"More than too much, Claw. My mind...I cannot fathom."

"With the same mark, sir. 'Tis a lifetime's worth of plunder, Captain. Well done to you."

"And to you, Mister Blackwood. Me thinks we'll not pay the good Governor of North Carolina his due on this bounty."

"But know he will, sir. As he'll hear back of the money what flows from our purses."

"Then we'll pay the crew's shares out of my own purse of past plunder. And yours if so ye wish, as I readied a fortune last trip out and plan this booty to hide. For to spend it now could well be our doom."

"Aye, sir. As you wish."

"And Claw."

"Sir?"

"Any man what speaks of my plan shall die by a tickle of my sword. If they be drunk when they talk, then their family be mine to slay as well."

"Aye, sir."

"Then take ye command of *Queen Anne's Revenge* and leave me half the crew, along with the ship's carpenter and his helper. Cast the survivors of the *Espiritu del Mar* into longboats with my compliments. If there be a brave man about what desires to join our ranks, bring him to me."

"Aye, sir."

"Then to home, Claw."

Claw took another look around the room. He couldn't help but smile. "With the greatest of pleasures, Captain Teach. A course I'll set to Beaufort, sir."

Chapter 11

"That's American Shoal over there," Taz said to Pete without really looking. "It's claimed dozens of ships over the centuries that captains have ridden the Gulf Stream through the Straits of Florida. Looe Key is just ahead."

"Did you used to live here in the Keys? You sure know it."

"I've retreated here, Pete, ever since I did some interviews that made me foolishly famous for my fifteen minutes."

"Retreated from what?"

"Questions, mostly."

"I didn't mean to pry."

"I have no intention of letting you."

Taz started to leave the bridge, but then stopped and came back.

"I'm sorry, Pete, that was unbelievably rude of me. I'm just not in a very good mood today. You understand?"

"Of course I do. It was obvious that you and Gordie were close."

"Go ahead with your question," Taz said, forcing a smile that lacked its usual brilliance. "I long ago prepared answers for the interviews I no longer give about my past, future, girlfriends, parents, and most of all, how I managed to make so much money."

He watched Pete scroll through the predictable choices, impressed and appreciative when he used his one chance to ask, "Did you ever learn how to cook? Because I'm starving."

Taz almost managed to laugh. "We have two full freezers of lobsters, steaks, and just about anything else. What would you like me to make for you?"

"If that grill over there works some dogs would be good. Or hamburgers."

"Then it's dogs and burgers coming up. Let me know when we're within a few nautical miles of Fowey Rock."

"Will do."

"And Pete?"

"Yeah?"

"I am glad to have you along. And I still owe you an answer."

The next day they rounded Fowey Rock and entered Biscayne Bay, then idled slowly into Dinner Key Marina where two employees waited at the end of a slip, staring out at *Wasafiri* as she glided toward them.

"I'm going to back her in, Pete. Prepare some lines. Port side is primary. We have a pretty strong cross-current running through here so let's stick it the first time."

"Port side primary. Roger that."

The wide channel shrunk dramatically as Taz motored *Wasafiri's* enormous hull a little up-current of an empty slip. He shoved the transmissions in opposition of each other to spin his boat around, then put both engines in reverse and gunned them to get out of the cross-current before it swept him away.

"Stern line coming," Pete yelled to one of the men on the dock as he heaved the heavy line.

Taz shifted into forward and hit the throttles. The big boat stopped suddenly with the transom almost at the seawall.

"Bow line on."

"Engines now in neutral."

They finished making *Wasafiri* secure and Taz tipped the dock workers, who walked off smiling.

"Do you see that, Pete?"

"What?"

"That great sunset. Man, what a stunner. Gordie would be pissed if I let something that beautiful pass me by without celebrating it, so I guess it's time for a cocktail."

"I'll buy."

"You're on."

They went into the restaurant and sat at a high-top table in the bar, looking out at the marina and the lights of Coconut Grove.

"What can I get you gentlemen?"

"Beer, please."

"Four Flaming Lemon Drops," Taz said. "But don't light them yet. Thank you."

The waitress looked confused, but then shrugged. "I'll be right back."

"For Gordie?"

"We have to say good-bye."

After a few minutes of silence, Pete asked, "Feel free not to answer, but how long were you two friends?"

This time Taz did not hesitate. "We played basketball together in high school. He was a senior and I was a full-of-shit freshman who somehow managed to make the varsity squad. He came down with a rebound in practice one day, and when he spun around he busted my jaw with his elbow."

"Sounds painful."

"It wasn't that bad. I wasn't even sure it was broken until I woke up in the morning with it lying on my pillow." He laughed. "But since neither of us could afford cars he helped me carry my stuff home after practice while I held my mouth in place. We've been friends ever since."

The waitress brought the drinks, which Taz distributed around the table, a drink at every chair. "Can you leave the lighter?"

"Sure."

Pete picked up his beer but sat it back down. "I guess we're waiting for something."

"I saw him as we idled in."

"Saw who?"

Just then a giant of a darkly-tanned man with long hair and a beard approached the table. He was muttering something and looked extremely rough, although his clothes and everything else about him were spotless.

"Never figured it'd be Gordie to go first," the man said as he picked up the lighter and lit the shots. "Bastard who killed him."

"Did you get Gordie squared away?"

"The cops were pricks. His family was really cooperative. They'll bring his ashes when they come our way. To Gordie," he said as he raised a glass.

"To Gordie."

They each threw back their shot, leaving Gordie's glass where it sat burning on the table. No one spoke as the big man walked around the table and hugged Taz like he loved him dearly and was proud to show it.

Then, with a tear on his cheek, the big man reached for Gordie's glass and held it up high before repeating "the bastard who killed him" and throwing back the burning liquid. There was reverence to the words, almost like it was a prayer that, because of the venom with which it was said, had been poisoned into a threat, or worse.

"Pete," Taz said. "Meet Sam."

Sam didn't say anything to Pete. He just stared and asked, "What's with the kid?"

"We're a man short, Sam. I think Pete is worth trying on for size."

"This kid?" Sam looked at Pete's lean frame and his smooth, youthful face that was such a sharp contrast to Sam's weathered skin. "The last time I looked I remember us being a team that never quits. Never, not ever. Can you even imagine committing to that, kid?"

"Easy, Sam. Why don't we let him eat dinner before you run him off?"

Sam scratched at his beard and then he walked away, muttering.

"Quitter," Pete shouted.

Sam stormed back and got right in Pete's face. "What did you say?"

Pete sipped his beer and glanced at Taz while watching Sam. "Did you meet this big ape on the basketball court too, Taz?" Then, to Sam, "You asked me a question, Mister Muscles, and then backed off as soon as you got a touch of heat from Taz. So you'll understand why it's hard for me to be impressed with your big talk after seeing you cower like that."

Taz stood and backed away from the table. "I'd be careful, Pete."

Sam was smoldering, and a little confused by Pete's courage. "I did that because Taz–" He suddenly turned back to Taz with the same look of menace. "And shit, Taz, while we're on the subject I can't even believe you let this punk call you Taz."

"He's a friend."

"I backed off of you, kid, because Taz–"

"Listen, Double-M, I don't even pretend to know what it is you fellows do, but–"

Sam looked at Taz. "Double-M?"

"I'm guessing Mister Muscles."

"Terrific."

"But I'm willing to bet your favorite umbrella drink," Pete continued, "that I can clear the bar you just tripped over without much of a run-up."

"Shit, I bet you've never even been in a fight."

"I came pretty darn close to holding my own when my little sister and I got into it once as kids. And what's your record, tough guy?"

"I'm alive."

Taz eased back to the table but kept his drink in his hand. "That you are, Sam." Now let's cool down or we're going to get thrown out of this place again."

"I'll go order a round, Taz. I could use the space." Sam stormed off and Pete watched him go.

"He's a little theatrical, Pete, and very pissed off about Gordie. Don't let him run you off just yet."

"Man, I really wasn't expecting that kind of confrontation. He sure made a big point about staying alive."

"And it's valid. But our world isn't really that scary. Or at least not all the time."

"Is it worth a trip to take a look?"

"Were you scared standing up to Sam? I've never seen anyone do that before."

"What's the worst that could happen? A beating if he won? Maybe loose a few teeth."

Taz laughed. "*If* he won? I don't mean to insult you, Pete, but that's rich."

"If he won, that's right."

"I think, then Pete, that you might find the trip worthwhile. Get yourself a taste of it and then let me know what you think."

"I will."

When Sam walked back with another round, Pete said "Taz...that's *Taz* to me, Double-M, just convinced me to stay."

"Glad to have you," Taz said, smiling but still holding his drink so it wouldn't get knocked over if a brawl broke out.

"Swell," grumbled Sam. "That's just swell."

Chapter 12

Sam managed to calm down a little during dinner, but he sat with his back to Pete and completely ignored him as he said, "So you two met Buzz in Key West?"

"He was with Gordie when we caught up with him at Irish Patrick's."

"You think that ugly bastard killed Gordie? I think he did."

"I do," Taz said. "And the police do too. They've got some kind of a witness they're keeping under wraps."

"I met Buzz when he came into Mel's Museum. I was changing a display and heard him ask the cashier about a gold coin he had."

Pete leaned in far enough to be in Sam's vision. "I'm having fun picturing you working retail?"

"Sam was actually part of the team–"

"Forget it, Taz. I'm just going to ignore him."

Pete moved to the seat beside Taz so that Sam couldn't avoid him. "Let's see how long you can manage."

Taz watched to see if Sam would stay in his seat or remove Pete's head from his shoulders, relieved when Sam relaxed a little and said "You've got stainless steel balls, kid. I'll give you that. Do you have any brains, or are you just courageously stupid?"

"I'd like to know about the coin you saw."

"Yeah," Taz said, "me too. Was it of historic value? Or maybe just a replica he bought online?"

"The kid won't understand the significance," Sam said as he cut his steak. "And you're going to think I'm lying, wrong, or crazy."

He took a bite and chewed while they waited. He swallowed. They continued to wait. Sam smiled. "Ready? I hope you are, because what I'm going to tell you almost made me crap my pants."

"Jeez, enough with the theatrics. Just tell us already."

Sam smiled even bigger, and then took a sip of beer. Finally he said "*Espiritu del Mar*."

Taz choked and started coughing. It took more than a minute before he could get out the words, "No way."

"Yup, as impossible as it sounds, Buzz had himself a coin from the fabled lost treasure of Tortuga Gold."

"I don't believe you."

"I don't believe me either."

Pete looked back and forth between them. "Tortuga Gold?"

"That's just the name treasure hunters and, well, pretty much everyone calls it."

"Why?"

Sam was getting more excited as they talked. "Because the wreck of one of the two ships carrying the gold was found in the Dry Tortugas, not that far from the *Atocha*."

"So it *was* found. And Buzz had some of it. What am I missing?"

"No, it was never found."

"But you just said–"

"That one of the ships was found."

"Here's the deal. In October of 1718," Taz said, "right in the thick of the hurricane season and just three years after the end of Spain's wars with her neighbors, the *Espiritu del Mar* and the *Conquistador de las Americas* had already waited an extra month in Cartagena for their gold cargo to arrive and be loaded. The rest of the fleet had gone on to Havana without them, and then home to Spain."

"They waited because..?"

"There was a fire at a new mint Spain had established in Colombia. It delayed the processing of gold."

"The mint," Sam added, "burned to ashes a month later due to a terrible explosion, and it never reopened."

"Only one ship stayed behind with the other two, but it didn't carry any gold when they left. Its role was to act as the amaranth when they sailed, bringing up the rear and defending the other two against pirates. So altogether there were only three ships."

"How many ships would there have been normally?"

"The size of fleets varied, of course, over the three hundred years of sailing from Europe to the New World and back before and after each hurricane season. But it could be as many as thirty. The *Nuestra Señora de Atocha* and the *Santa Margarita*, which Mel Fisher discovered–"

"And which still hold more than half a billion dollars of treasure," Sam added.

"Sailed in a fleet of twenty-seven, I think. Maybe twenty-eight."

"So three ships made them pretty vulnerable to pirates," Sam said, now much too enthralled in the story to care about his fight with Pete.

"Why didn't they just wait for more ships? Or join the next fleet passing through?"

"Because Spain was broke from years of wars and desperately needed the gold."

72

"So pirates attacked the ships and stole the gold?"

"No one knows, Pete."

"But Sam just said—"

"That they were *vulnerable* to pirates. Actually, the records show that the *Conquistador de las Americas* got pretty busted up in a storm and moved all of its precious cargo onto the *Espiritu del Mar* while anchored twenty miles west-southwest of Key West. Then they headed to shore to make repairs but ran aground and broke up at the Dry Tortugas."

"What about the *Espiritu del Mar* and the other ship?"

Taz grinned. "For years no one had a clue to what happened to her. Then she was found by accident twenty years ago off the North Carolina coast in one hundred and fourteen feet of water. But – and now this is where it gets exciting – all the gold and everything else of value was missing. Even her cannons were gone."

"Which means," Sam said, with almost no trace of dislike toward Pete, "that not a single piece of the one and only shipment of gold from that short-lived mint has ever been found. That makes it almost mythical."

"So either the gold never really existed and the ship was a decoy for some reason we'll never know, which is what Sam has always suspected, or the gold disappeared like a magician's trick. Or someone took it but never had a chance to spend it."

They all sat quietly. Sam and Taz couldn't stop smiling.

"Buzz said he worked in North Carolina," Pete said after a while. "I'm sure they have internet and probably even a museum or two up there, so why would he go all the way to way to Key West to ask people about his coin?"

"Good question. Sam, do you think he had any idea of its significance?"

"I seriously doubt it, but he was a hard man to read. I walked over to him and said 'I know your coin, friend. It bears the stamp of a mint that burned down after processing only one shipment of what's come to be called Tortuga Gold.' I figured that would rock his world."

"What was his reaction?"

"Nothing but a stare as empty as Pete's head. I would have gotten more of a reaction if I'd told him he had a booger dangling."

Pete laughed and started to say something, but Sam kept going. "What I didn't tell him was that not a single escudo has ever been seen until his."

Pete looked doubtful. "How could you possibly know that for sure? I mean, aren't there thousands of gold treasure coins out there in collectors' hands, and isn't it possible that some of them are Tortuga Gold?"

"Nope."

"And so I ask again; how can you be so sure?"

"Because" Taz explained, "the coins you mention were hand-stamped, not screw-pressed, until 1732, and that inherent irregularity is the first clue. Back then the mints would beat a strip of silver or gold flat, use snippers to cut the coins in planchets, or blanks, and then place them in the bottom half of a die. They covered that with the top half of the die and then struck it with a hammer."

"The stamp," Sam added, "typically included the king's name, or symbol of his royalty, the last two digits of the year, the denomination, the assayer's initials, and a mark that identified the mint."

"The Colombian mint used XA as their mark. And so, because that mint never processed a second shipment, you'll never see XA on a coin unless it's Tortuga Gold."

"Like Buzz's coin."

"You're really sure, Sam. And it wasn't a fake?"

"I'm absolutely positive."

"Then," Taz said, "I suppose Buzz would have gone to Key West for several reasons. Mainly because the *Atocha* is a famous discovery that's on permanent display, easy to find, and surrounded by experts who know treasure. When you think about it, where else could he go for access like that?"

"And he probably wouldn't want to wander around the Carolinas asking questions about a gold coin he'd found in the area."

"Good thinking, Pete. Just imagine it, years ago a treasure ship is found with no treasure onboard. And none of it has ever turned up until now."

"Maybe the rest was melted down."

Taz got up and started to pace the floor, avoiding the tables by the windows that were full of diners. "That's reasonable thinking, and it's certainly one theory that was heavily investigated. But even back then gold was well regulated and a record would have been found somewhere. Damn, I wish I had an Oreo."

"Is it a lot of gold?"

Sam turned back to answer him. "Just the gold itself, without allowing for historic value, was estimated at four hundred and fifty million dollars a few years back."

"I've got to find some Oreos. Be right back." Taz left Pete and Sam staring at each other.

"Oreos, Double-M?"

"Yeah."

"Care to enlighten me?"

"Care to drop that Double-M bullshit?"

Pete made a big show of pondering it, and then said "Okay."

"Deal, kid. Taz and I backpacked through the jungle once and Oreos were the only food he carried. He'd eat snake or bugs or whatever else he could find along the way, but he wanted his Oreos when it came time to think."

"What jungle? Were you looking for gold there?"

"No. And to be honest it was actually more of a rain forest. We walked from Belize to Portobello, which is all the way at the bottom of Panama. Sir Francis Drake died there in a bay called *Nombre de Dios* and Taz got a wild hair one day to see it. He's been intrigued with pirates ever since."

"Drake was never a pirate."

"Depends on who you ask, because along with being a famous circumnavigator he was certainly a privateer, and there's no question that the Spanish thought he was a pirate for raiding their ships, even if he did have a Letter of Marque, the blessings of the crown."

"Taz told me that a cruise ship left him behind in Belize. Was your journey around the same time?"

"We lost him for a year down there and had no idea where he was. His Board of Directors assumed he'd died and took over his businesses. I eventually found him teaching English in a little school that he built with his own hands. They named the road in front of it after him, which was nice."

"That is nice. And while we're being all chit-chatty, Sam, what's your story?"

"What do you care?"

"Let's pretend we're speed-dating and you've got three minutes to make yourself sound human."

Sam almost laughed, but caught it.

"I worked as a fireman for a few years but never got the chance to test myself. An occasional car or kitchen fire, sure, but I took the job with images of me cradling small kids or beautiful women as I emerged heroically from a flaming disaster. I saved a small dog once and actually went back into a burning building to get a crying little girl's pet iguana, but that's as heroic as it got."

"No fireman calendar photos of you?"

"Sorry to disappoint you. I left the job to search for Taz, who, by the time I tracked him down, had this crazy idea to find out what it must have been like for the early explorers hacking their way through the jungle. He was determined to make it all the way to Portobello. I thought he might have gone crazy down there during the year he was lost to us."

"He seems so powerfully grounded."

"He is. Now more than ever, except that he doesn't care a bit about dying. I've never seen anyone so free of the fear of death. I'm not sure where it comes from, and it's certainly not a death wish, but you need to keep it in mind."

"So that I don't get killed too?"

"So you can help me keep him safe. Hold him back sometimes. That's how I saw my role during our hike down the coast and through the jungle. I had more interest in learning to sew than I had in doing that, but I went along to protect him. We each carried a pack, machete, and compass."

"And Oreos."

"But no money. We learned who we were down there with only those few things and our determination. What Taz learned was merely a reinforcement of what he'd already come to suspect in Belize, which is that he was a slave to his corporations, that they owned him and not the other way around. When he walked away from all that and formed Mayday Salvage and Rescue, I signed on."

"So you're still protecting him. Do you own a stake?"

"Either you're stupid or you're blind to what Taz is about. All team members are equal partners, except Taz. He deducts expenses and splits whatever is left in equal shares among the rest of us, but never takes a cut himself. Mayday is all just adrenaline for him, or maybe a long series of tests he chooses to give himself. I'm not sure I know."

Pete slowly rubbed the rim of his glass.

"I know, kid. Now you're wondering if you'll get the same deal if you can keep up with us. The answer is yes, although I'm going to try my best to get rid of you."

"Because you learned how to be an ass down there in the jungle?"

"Because if you can't handle me then you're completely unprepared for the challenges we face, the stuff only a few specialized companies in the world will touch. *Mayday* Salvage and Rescue, get it? People only call us when they're really desperate, when no one else has the guts to help."

"Is Taz self-destructive?"

"No."

"He certainly sounds like he is, so how can you be so sure?"

"Because he's totally and absolutely in love with life. He engages everyone and everything as if it's going to be the next great experience of his life, seldom missing a chance to connect or taste or appreciate. He loves people and gets a real kick out of making them happy."

Pete smiled and finished his drink. "He sounds just like you."

"Don't start having wet dreams about me, kid."

Chapter 13

Pete was up at six the next morning, surprised that Sam and Taz were already dressed and looking like they'd been up for a while.

"Morning, guys. You two don't sleep, I guess. Too excited about Tortuga Gold?"

"Sam and I have to go, Pete. Watch the television a minute." Taz went down to his cabin as Pete turned to hear a newscaster talking about a ship being hijacked off the coast of Venezuela.

"We're prepared to report" the newsman said, "that the ship is a U.S. flagged vessel. That's a bit unusual, isn't it Commander Greer?"

The camera shifted to a man in a U.S. Navy uniform. "It is more common for corporations to register ships in Panama or Liberia or a handful of other countries where liabilities and costs can be mitigated. A super-tanker of this size flying under the American flag, yes, I suppose it's unusual."

"And the owners? Do we know that yet?"

Taz ran back up the stairs. "Yeah, I own it," he said to the television. "Are you ready to move, Sam?"

"I am. Listen Pete, a delivery captain and his crew will be here any minute to take *Wasafiri* up to Beaufort, North Carolina. You can ride along or go home and meet us later or do whatever else you want. Let's go, Taz."

They took quick steps to the door.

"Wait a minute," Pete said as he ran around in front of them. "I thought we were after Gordie's killer. I only just met him the one time, but even I'm anxious for a little vengeance."

Taz stopped abruptly. He looked troubled, but not angry.

"Listen Pete, our trip to find Buzz has nothing to do with vengeance. It's about adventure and, if we're lucky, perhaps a little justice. But no vengeance." Then, "That's all I can allow it to be."

"I'm not sure I understand, but I think I do."

"It might help to appreciate how few chances there are in life to really have a guts-in-your-throat adventure, a chance to win or lose, maybe even survive or die, without the handrails and safety nets that society is always building around us."

"You think Buzz will still be there after you get your ship back?"

"Of course."

"What makes you so sure?"

"The age-old reason that pirates never venture far from their treasure for long."

They stepped out of the door of the main salon and tossed their gear onto the dock.

"Wait, I'll come with you."

Sam turned around and pushed Pete back into the cabin. "No."

Taz checked his watch as he stepped in front of Pete. "Listen, Pete, those men on that hijacked ship work for me, and that makes it my responsibility to do whatever I can to secure their release. If I fail in negotiating that, things will, by the pirates' choice, get pretty nasty. You shouldn't want any part of that."

He turned, and then turned back. "For the record, though, I thought it was cool that you decided to join me on *Wasafiri* and not climb to the cruise ship we talked about once. But going with us now would be like swan diving from its bridge deck. This is a little too much to expect from you, or at least too much too soon."

"And you'd be nothing more than another life I had to protect."

"I'm a damned good diver," Pete said as he got back on his feet.

Taz looked at Sam. When they both looked at Pete, he said, "How else will you two know if I can take Gordie's place or not?"

"You can't," Sam said abruptly. "And don't ever dare believe that you can."

Pete stepped close to Taz. He spoke quietly. "You loved Gordie and I get that, and I also get that it took years to get to that point. But right now you're penalizing me for that friendship. You have no idea whether or not I can take his place, at least in my contribution to the team."

Now it was Sam who checked his watch. "Aw shit, Taz, we've got to get moving. Let him come and get killed if that's what he wants. Kid, if you belly-flop doing that dive of yours, make sure I get to see it."

"Give me one minute to grab my shoes."

"Shoes," Sam said, looking out at the huge pile of his gear on the deck while Pete ran below. "The kid needs to get himself a pair of shoes."

Chapter 14

A corporate jet screamed down its final approach into Miami Executive Airport just as an employee opened the chain link gate and allowed Taz, Sam and Pete to drive their rental car onto the tarmac. They got their gear out and piled it up neatly, ready to toss it into the plane and then jump aboard.

The pilot lurched to a quick stop and then rushed back to open the door. "Good morning, Mister Keaton. Nice to see you again, sir."

"Thanks, Don. Were you told where we're going? Do you still have enough fuel?"

"Corporate is filing a flight plan from here to Cartagena. If that's correct, I'm pretty tight on fuel."

"Let me ask you something. If your wife was in trouble down there, would you take the time to refuel?"

"No, sir. I'd risk ditching at sea or crashing while trying to get to her."

"Then that's good enough for me. Let's go."

They loaded in less than a minute and the plane went right back into the air.

Taz's cell phone rang and he listened without talking, then hung up. "The Venezuelan government is throwing up resistance."

"Shocking," Sam said as he pushed his huge frame deep into the leather seat and closed his eyes.

"Are they crazy enough to back the pirates?"

"No, Pete. Taz isn't saying that because *they* would never have the balls to say that. At least not to us, regardless of how much anti-American sentiment Chavez has managed to stir up over the years."

"Sam's right. What they're doing is demanding payment for my ship's unauthorized entry into their territorial waters. They're calling it a criminal violation. They also say it's anchored in a protected underwater sanctuary."

"Is it in their waters?"

"It is. But the captain was made to go there by the pirates. Still, it's my ship in their waters, so the point has merit."

"That's insane."

"They also say we did some illegal dumping."

"Probably bodies," Sam said, his eyes still closed.

"Not funny. They say we polluted by failing to comply with Annex V of the MARPOL treaty."

"The international agreement intended to prevent dumping from ships."

Sam opened his eyes. He and Taz looked at Pete with surprise.

"What? I have to put those stickers on the insides of boats in order to comply with the law."

"I'm glad to know you read it," Taz said. "I have no idea whether that allegation is true or not."

"It's bullshit and you know it. They're just making it hard on you because of the colors your ships fly."

"What I know, Sam, is that I have to accept their position and factor it into our actions. We can't start a war down there."

"A war might be fun." Sam laughed.

"Maybe a little war," Pete added. "But I'd have to get a note from my parents for a big war."

Sam was still laughing when he asked, "Where are your parents, Pete?"

"Dallas. Why?"

"So we know where to send your body."

"Funny."

"We'll send a nice note too. I'll write it myself."

"Funnier still. Why are we going to Cartagena if your ship is off the coast of Venezuela?"

"There's an old airbase there we'll use as a staging area. Sam, you've got some help on the way to join us?"

"The closest I could find on such short notice were teaching at the training camp in Nicaragua."

"They're on their way?"

"Yeah, in their own transport plane." He grinned. "Branson saw the news on BBC and offered one of his airliners if we needed one. But he asked us not to shoot it up as badly as last time"

Taz laughed. "Did I ever say I was sorry for that?"

"I think so."

"I'm pretty sure I did."

Pete had sat wide-eyed and listening. "You've got to be kidding me. You don't just pick up the phone and call...what are these guys anyway, mercenaries?"

"They prefer to be called commandos, Pete. But if you'd like to call them mercenaries I'll be happy to pick up your teeth after they get their hands on you. Here." He punched a speed dial number and handed his phone to Pete, who laughed nervously as he ended the call.

"They're the just-in-case team, Pete. I can probably negotiate something with the pirates, but we need to be prepared if I can't."

Taz's phone rang again and he put it on speaker.

"Mister Keaton, this is Byron Philippi at State."

"Yes, Byron, how's that little girl of yours?"

"She's...wow, thanks for remembering. She's doing well. The surgery went perfectly and she's fine."

"Very glad to hear it.

"Look, Mister Keaton–"

"TK, remember?"

"Right, TK. On behalf of the Under Secretary for Political Affairs and, of course, the United States Government, I've been asked to relay our sense of discomfort at your being so personally involved in an international incident over which we haven't yet gotten much of a handle ourselves."

"I understand, Byron, but let me ask what you would normally do, assuming it wasn't my ship?"

"Well, other than negotiate, and without that country's request for military assistance, there really wouldn't be much of a role at this time for–"

"Come on, Byron. You can tell me with the truth. You'd call Mayday Salvage and Rescue, wouldn't you? By the way, thanks for referring that job in Bocas del Toro to us."

"Oh sure, you're welcome."

"So if we're being honest here, you know and I know and I'm pretty sure Sam knows that right about now our phone would be ringing anyway. Sam?"

"I can almost hear it ringing."

"Sam can almost hear it ringing, Byron. And well, you're in luck, because we're already on our way."

"It's odd that I don't feel all that lucky."

"You have to learn to relax and stop worrying that we're going to start a war down there. Sam?"

"We're not going to start a war down there."

"Did you hear that?"

"No."

"Just as well. Sam tends to lie."

"Oh, great. With each passing second I'm feeling so much better."

"I've got to run, Byron. It was wonderful talking to you. I'm sending your beautiful little girl a puppy."

"She's allergic."

"Hermit crab, then. And Byron, I need your help with the Venezuelan government. Do your diplomatic magic about some charges of maritime violations they're throwing at me. And get us some kind of emergency visas."

"Please, no hermit crab. I'll see what I can do."

"Then I already feel better."

"As you should, Mister Keaton."

"TK."

Chapter 15

Sam stepped out of the dilapidated hangar and was glad for the warmth of the sun. He tuned the long antenna of the single-side band radio he'd rigged up in a hurry and then ran back inside to rebroadcast his transmission.

"There they are. I've got the ship now, Taz."

Taz took the microphone. "*Quiero hablar con el jefe pirata*," he said.

He waited a minute and then said it again. He waited some more.

"I am the boss here," came the response in English. "And how dare you call us pirates. You feel it's wise to begin our talks with an insult?"

Sam rolled his eyes. "Great, not only do we have to deal with pirates, but ours happen to be morally outraged at being called pirates."

"Just another name for a thief on the water," Taz said off-mike. "It's actually kind of amazing how we glorify them." Then, "By every definition, you are pirates. But what would you prefer me to call you?"

"I go by El Leon."

"No fooling? The lion? Do your parents call you that? I mean, it is sort of a dramatic name, don't you think?"

"And now you're making fun of my name."

"No I'm not. Well, maybe I am, but it's just because I'm trying to get a grip on what kind of guy calls himself a lion. You should appreciate my effort to understand you because it's up to you and me to work out a solution to this problem."

"You sound like a fool. Are you a fool?"

"I probably am, Leo, but look, I'm not here to bullshit with you, all right. Fool or no fool, lion or no lion, I want my ship and you want...what? Let's talk about what you want."

"This is your ship?"

"Yes. It's a beauty, don't you think?"

"You actually own it."

"Is there static on your radio or are you hard of hearing? Yes, I own it."

"One man owns this ship," Leo laughed, and someone else laughed in the background. "You must be very rich."

"Chances are pretty good that I'm rich enough to solve this problem without anyone getting hurt. Does that sound good to you?"

Taz waited.

Then, "We want twenty million dollars. We are all prepared to die here if our demands aren't met."

"Yeah, yeah, I'm sure you are, but let's be honest about that for a minute, okay? I mean, you kind of have to say you're willing to die, right? You wouldn't be very good pirates if you let me think you'd quit easily."

"Now I am sure you are making fun of me."

"I am absolutely not making fun of you, and I'm very worried about what you might do to the crew. But since we're both sitting here wasting time running up our battle flags you should know that we – that's me and all of my expertly trained warriors – are just as prepared to die in the process of killing you. But it doesn't have to go down that way if you'll just keep whatever promises you eventually make to me."

"We are reasonable men."

"Good, that's a good start. And please keep in mind that if you hurt a single member of my crew, we go to shooting, no ifs ands or buts."

"Understood."

"Good again. Now that we're talking, you said you're prepared die and I believe you. But do you really want to end your life on that ship? I know I don't want to end mine there. And my men don't."

Silence again. Then, "None of us *wants* to die."

"Good, so let's keep this honorable between us and we'll both be home soon. Where is home for you, Leo. I'm from Florida."

"Florida. Miami. Disney. It's beautiful there. I've seen pictures. It looks much the same in Valencia, where I'm from."

"I'll tell you what, Leo, I'm going to get off the air and let you think about your demands. See if you can be a little more reasonable than twenty million, which in Venezuela is probably enough to buy the presidency, I suppose."

Leo laughed. "Yes, perhaps it might be."

"Why don't I radio you again at six o'clock? But I need to talk to Captain Frazier first. Just for a minute. You can listen."

"I decide what people do. Not you."

"I get that. But let's look at ourselves as a committee of two, Leo, because we need to work together to get this done. Now I vote to let me talk to the Captain. How do you vote?"

Sam walked to the door of the old hangar and looked up in the sky.

Taz waited. Five minutes passed. He would not ask Leo again. He turned toward Sam and shouted, "Is that our guys I hear flying in?"

"Yeah. The transport from Nicaragua."

"Great. Have them unload the chopper and spool it up."

"This is Captain Frazier."

"Good afternoon, Captain. T. Keaton here."

"Yes sir, Mister Keaton. How are you, sir?"

"Better than you, I suppose. Is your crew safe?"

"As of a minute ago, yes sir. The pirates are keeping us all together. I'm not allowed to mention where."

"That's fine. Glad you're all okay. We're going to resolve this quickly. Cooperate with The Lion and have your men do the same. Do you understand and agree?"

"Yes, sir."

"Good. Oh, just one easy question while I've got you. Make sure it's okay with Leo before you answer, but I'm concerned about the ship grounding on the tide swing. Can you tell me how many fathoms of water you have under your keel? Two fathoms? Five fathoms? Ten?"

The captain hesitated, then, "The Lion says I can answer. It looks like seven fathoms, Mister Keaton."

"Seven fathoms. That's good. Thank you. Be safe, skipper."

Taz put down the mike and turned to Sam. "I'm taking that chopper to Valencia. Stay here and do a run-through just in case I fail."

Sam slid the trigger into a shoulder-fired missile and didn't look up when he said, "Will do. Have fun."

Chapter 16

If Taz got killed or did not come back, Sam was ready for war. He and his multi-national commandos had agreed on a plan and then ran through the drill five times, which was probably four times more than necessary for the veteran soldiers. Fields of fire were assigned, along with compartments to search and who had responsibility for prisoners, triage, and the dead.

He sat down on the floor and leaned against the hangar wall.

"Do you get butterflies before something like this?"

Sam looked at Pete almost sympathetically. He wanted to give him a short answer, but instead he said, "I did when Taz, Gordie, and me first started doing this kind of stuff, probably because, like you, it was all new to me and seemed so dangerous. And I was afraid to die."

"Not now?"

"It's no longer new and now I don't even think about dying. In fact it never crosses my mind. That probably helps keep me alive."

"How can you be so relaxed when you're so obviously ready for some serious battle?" He looked around at the tough-looking misfits in the hangar, playing hacky-sack or organizing their gear or working the coils from their fast ropes. "Jeez, I feel like I'm in a remake of *The Dirty Dozen.*"

Just then a black man in an even blacker uniform stepped over. "I want to know, Sam," he said in English, although he would obviously have been more comfortable speaking French, "who is the twerp? You say twerp?"

"Yup, we say twerp. I brought him along to see if I can get him killed, Jean-Louis."

"Sounds fun. I am very happy to help out if I can."

"I'm happy to accept your help."

"Okay, okay, I get it," Pete said. "I don't belong here."

"Are you afraid, my young friend?"

"No Jean-Louis, I'm not afraid. I'm just not trained like you."

"Oh, well you're in luck because that is the easy part. Your name is Pete? That is the easy part, Pete. None of us were trained at the start. I can train you quickly if you have the main thing that we share."

"A death wish?"

"Exactly."

"Really?"

Jean-Louis laughed, big and friendly, and the men listening to their conversation did too. "Of course not. We have families, Pete, most of us. And lives we love very much. We do not have death wishes."

"So you share...what?"

"A very simple acceptance that one day we *will* die doing this. Tonight? Maybe tomorrow? Who knows? None of us expects to live through this attack, if it actually happens, but we all know that some of us probably will. It is a good odds."

"A good bet, you mean," Sam said. "And I'm pretty sure it's going to happen tonight."

Pete looked between the two of them. "Then I guess I'm a little envious of you guys."

"Then come with us. Sam, bring the twerp along with you. Twerp, you have my personal invitation." He walked away laughing.

"What do you say, Twerp?"

"Is that nickname going to stick?"

"I can only hope." Sam looked down, as though embarrassed to actually be part of a meaningful conversation with Pete. "Look, the thing is...well, I guess it's that Taz has rubbed off on me to where I feel that being afraid to do this kind of stuff isn't really living. Until I got to that point I was like a dog on a leash, you know? I didn't realize it at the time, but I'd limited myself to doing only what I was sure I could handle. I wouldn't allow myself to go farther, to strain at the leash to get somewhere unknown. You're probably not to that point yet and may never get there."

"What kind of gun is that?"

"It's an H&K MP5, the weapon of choice for most special ops teams that can afford it. Ever shoot a gun?

"I won a prize at a carnival."

"Well that certainly counts. You know you're not coming with us, right. Assuming we engage, which, as I said, I'm pretty sure we will. I'll let you ride in the chopper and watch from above, but disregard Jean-Louis' invitation because I'm in charge of this mission."

"I thought Taz was."

"Damn it, Pete, it absolutely grinds my stones to dust that he lets you call him Taz. But no, if we go to war it will be impossible for anyone to get ahead of Taz. I'll be in command, though, because he could never give orders to hurt people. It conflicts with some kind of karma vegan Mother Theresa horseshit he's got banging around in his brain."

"I would probably just be in the way."

"You would definitely be in the way. I hear Taz's chopper."

All eleven men left the hangar and went outside as it landed and Taz jumped out.

"You're late, my man. You were supposed to call the pirates at six."

"I'm ready, Sam. Fire up the box."

Sam walked slowly to the table and tuned in the frequency, then handed the microphone to Taz. "We should probably talk first, Taz."

"El Leon," Taz said. "El Leon, El Leon, this is the owner of *Patriot*."

"Hello owner from Florida."

"I'm sorry, Leo, but there's been a change. Here's what I've done."

"I have never liked changes."

"Listen to me. I've set up a fund of five million dollars for schools and teachers and small business loans that will get disbursed throughout Valencia over the next two years under your name as long as no more ships are hijacked. It's as close as I can come to making you rich for doing something wrong."

"And nothing for us?"

"El Leon, you'll have to appreciate the larger benefits here. Girls will love you and families will respect you. The money will make all of you heroes at home."

"With no money."

"But alive. Real live heroes to your families and friends"

Silence. Then, "I will talk it over with my men, but we'll want something just for us. Call back in one hour."

The radio went silent.

"Maybe they won't be rich," Pete said, as they all stared at the radio on the table, "but they will be getting away with it."

"Did I fail to mention that none of the money gets distributed until their community turns them over to the police? Turns out they've been trying to catch El Leon for some time for running cocaine. I almost feel like I won."

Sam put his hand on Taz's shoulder and held it there as if to keep him in place when he said "You didn't win, Taz. You didn't even come close."

Taz looked in his eyes, knowing the voice was too compassionate for anything but bad news. "What?"

"While you were gone a very pissed-off pirate called to say they killed Captain Frazier and threw his body overboard. Someone looked at the depth under the ship and realized they were in sixty fathoms, and that there were seven pirates. They killed him for telling you how many of them there were."

Taz stood silently. He looked around the hangar at the men. He looked at the microphone on the table. He looked toward a heaven in which he had no faith and calmly said, "We attack the instant it's totally dark."

Chapter 17

Pete sat on the aluminum deck of the chopper, looking ridiculous in his white t-shirt, baggy plaid shorts and sneakers while everyone else wore dark grey or black uniforms that were much better suited to a nighttime raid.

"Sixty seconds," said the pilot through Taz's headphones.

"We're one minute from go," Taz repeated to the team. Then to Pete, "Miss the boatyard yet?"

"No."

"Good. You're going to have one heck of a view from up here."

"It's dark."

Taz smiled and moved his feet off the ropes as Jean-Louis and another man snapped shackles onto the metal frame by both doors. "Yeah, but it won't be for long."

"Good luck, Taz. Guys."

Jean-Louis held the rope, coiled and ready. "Luck is for amateurs, twerp. I truly hope to see you again."

"Be safe."

"But that would mean missing all the fun." Jean-Louis laughed like a happy kid.

Just then the chopper banked hard and stopped abruptly. In an instant the ropes were tossed and dangling down to the deck, with Taz going first and leading the men as they fast-roped down. The sky suddenly switched to hurt-your-eyes bright as the chopper's massive floodlights shone down onto the enormous ship and into its wheelhouse.

A man stood on one of the helo's skids, scanning the decks with a smaller spotlight while a guy on the other skid held a big machine gun, searching for targets. He fired one burst, and then another, the noise deafening Pete while the spent cartridges ricocheted around in the metal cabin.

"Good shooting, that's two down!"

"The wheelhouse," hollered the pilot as he stayed hovering directly in front of it. "I've got two men running out of there."

89

Pete crept to the door, hanging on as the pilot rocked and jerked around to avoid being an easy target. The massive tanker was right underneath them, and Pete saw that the team had split up and gone down separate sides of her, while Sam chased after Taz as he ran to the wheelhouse.

Another burst, the muzzle flash lighting up the other side of the chopper. Then another.

"I got one of the men, but the second guy's too close to Keaton," the gunner said. "He'll catch shards of metal or fragments off the steel if I shoot."

Pete watched Taz run up and tackle the pirate, taking him down and surprising the pirate enough to drop his gun. They fought old school for a few seconds while Sam stood back, aiming and ready but not shooting. The pirate broke free at one point and ran to the rail, then leaped over and made the seven-story drop to the ocean. He disappeared under the surface.

As stupid and unnecessary as it was, Pete couldn't resist the temptation. Maybe it was Sam, maybe Taz, or maybe what Jean-Louis had said. It didn't matter because something had suddenly changed in him.

He backed across the chopper, hoping to get a lottery winner's amount of luck and enough momentum to carry him out past the deck of the ship and to the ocean. Then he ran like a sprinter, passing the machine gunner as he hurled himself into a long-jump that carried him out the door and into the flood-lit sky.

"TAZ, CHECK it out."

Taz followed Sam's eyes and saw Pete falling from the sky, his arms flailing for the control he was gradually getting. "Did you tell him to do that?"

"I sure wish I had."

"I wouldn't jump from that high. Would you make that jump?"

"I guess I would if I had to, but I'd never choose to do it."

"Not sure I'd ever do it. Think he'll clear the ship?"

"It's going to be close. We'll know soon. If we hear a splat it will be bad news."

The gunfire had stopped and the night was quiet again, as if all the world's attention was focused on Pete, who managed to gain control and jackknife into a dive that almost pile-drove him head first into the deck that he missed by only a foot or two.

"Pretty good dive if he survives impact with the water."

"I'm going to give the dive an eight. Nine if he lives through it. Where in God's name did you find this guy, Taz?"

They ran down the bridge steps and got to the rail just as Pete stopped hitting the pirate who'd jumped overboard, and began dragging him back to the ship by his hair, keeping the pirate's face out of the water so he could breathe. He got to the accommodation ladder and rested until some other men came to help.

"I'm really starting to think that you have grit, kid," Sam said when they met on the main deck.

"Don't even think of trying to kiss me."

"How do you feel? How'd you like that?"

Pete was sucking air like a bellows, but smiled and said, "Taz, I'd say it was probably life-changing."

Jean-Louis ran up and picked Pete off his feet. "Twerp! You did very well. I am quite proud of you."

"Thanks."

"What are our losses?"

"Taz, we had none. Only a few wounds. One through and through bullet. Nothing to speak of."

"That's good. Look, I'm insured for this but it will be cheaper for my company to pay the bill than absorb the increased premium. So let's get back and settle up."

"I'm good," Sam said.

Pete shrugged. "Me, too. Heck, I'm living on your boat and eating your food. That's good enough for me. Damn, I think I broke a rib when I hit."

Jean-Louis looked solemn, then said, "Taz, my team normally splits a full share, but since this was so much fun let's just go to Cartagena where you can buy us dinner and drinks for payment."

"This is where I really need to be careful," Taz said to Pete. "Last time I went out with these guys the tab was over sixty grand."

"But to be fair, that also included the bribes to get us all out of jail."

"And was still cheaper than paying them a share, although far more dangerous."

"That amount, my friend," Jean-Louis said, "is less than even the fee for the chopper and the cost of ammunition. So we'll have to spend more this time. We agree?"

"What the hell, it sounds like fun. Painful fun, but fun all the same. Now I'm going to talk to the crew and get them moving my ship. Byron's taken care of the legal issues and our Navy is standing by to escort her to sea. Sam, you're out of here?"

"Yeah."

"Then I'll see you in Beaufort. Try to find Buzz before I get there." Taz walked away and disappeared down a stairwell.

"Cool that you passed up payment," Sam said to Pete after the others had left. "Our fee for recovering a merchant ship, depending on location, is two to five million dollars, plus expenses. Your share for tonight would be close to a million."

"A mill...shit, Sam!"

Pete walked away and then spun back around. "No kidding? Really? A million dollars?"

"You'll have a lot more chances." Sam smiled and stuck out his hand. "You're sure not Gordie, but as of right now you are part of the team."

Chapter 18

Derek Holmes walked slowly, methodically, from the barn in which he spent most of his time to the house where he ate, slept, and did little else. He was dirty, as usual. Not greasy, either. Dirty.

"Hey, Theresa."

"Please let me throw those clothes into the wash before you sit down anywhere," she said, staring, as always, at his filthy clothes with amazement, completely unable to comprehend how he could get so covered in dust while working inside a climate controlled barn. She had no problem, however, comprehending that her husband would never let her see whatever it was he did in there to get so dirty.

"Thanks. I'm going to grab a shower."

"After that I want to show you something."

He stopped on the stairs. "What?"

"Nothing that won't wait. Go ahead and get a shower."

He silently waited and made no effort to look patient. It was the only way he knew to be, or, perhaps the only way he needed to be. If the latter, the fault was probably hers. Or so said her mother.

"It's nothing." She spoke the words quietly, having learned over the years that although Derek was a decent enough husband, he would always quietly dominate her. "It really could have waited. Now please don't overreact the way you did last time, but someone's been on our property."

"Another homeless man, I'm sure. Where?" His slow, carefully pronounced question of one simple word conveyed powerful implications of how she knew he would protect what was his.

"Digging."

He exhaled and looked at his feet. Then he looked at her again. "Digging *where*? Taking vegetables from the garden?"

"No, *digging*."

He walked back and spoke to her like a parent to a child. "What, just digging around in the yard? It doesn't make sense."

"If it made sense to me I probably wouldn't have told you."

93

He flashed a look of contempt for her compassion for the homeless souls who wandered through town and often took refuge on their land for as long as they could, protected from the law by their perimeter wall that was designed, but somehow failed, to make a fortress out of the property. They did not deserve her concern, he felt, and certainly not after they'd trespassed on his land.

"And when I eventually did find out we would have fought about it."

"Over the last four days someone's been digging along the shoreline on the other side of our seawall, in the mud."

"Four days?"

"Nights, actually. I check during my morning walk around the property, and then again in the evening. All the digging seems to take place at night, especially during the hours of low tide."

"Then it's probably just kids digging fiddler crabs for bait."

"You need to see the holes. Come on."

She walked out to the wrap-around porch of their historic home and he followed her down the steps. On the way to the water she pointed toward some oaks near the water's edge, two hundred feet inside of the seawall. "Someone dug around those trees last night, and then filled it back in."

"Weird."

"Behind there, too." She pointed to a short hedge they'd planted five years ago. "I think they dug there when high tide kept them out of the river."

"It's probably nothing, but I'll call the sheriff. We have to do something or the next thing you know they'll be digging up our roses to give to their dates." He smiled, trying to break the intensity he'd shown earlier.

"You need to see the holes."

They walked the last hundred feet to the seawall and looked over at the deep craters at the edge of their newly dredged channel.

"Those are really big holes."

"You're not angry with me?"

"Do I seem angry?"

"I never know, Derek. God, I wish I did, but I never do until it's too late."

They stared down at the mud for five minutes. During the long walk back to the house Derek called Sheriff Mathias. "Bob, it's Holmes."

"Yes, Mister Holmes, what can I do for you this fine evening?"

"I've got someone, or maybe more than one person, digging up my property."

"That's a little surprising, Mister Holmes, seeing as how, well, private, I guess is the word I'm looking for, the missus and you are. I don't really know anyone who'd want to go on your property. I mean that in the best of ways, you understand."

"I'm certain I understand your meaning, Sheriff. I hope my meaning is just as clear when I tell you to have your men patrol the water's edge of my property by boat, at night."

"My boys don't much like being out there at night, Mister Holmes, especially with nothing going on but maybe some fisherman getting their bait in the mud flats of your property. I'd be happy to have a patrol car drive through there easy enough, though. He'd get out and walk to the seawall and run those fellows off for you."

"I don't want your men on my land."

"I know very well that you don't. I suspect everybody in town knows how you feel about your privacy."

"To which I'm entitled."

"That you are, sir. Although you can see how it makes my job kind of hard to do."

"Nevertheless, I expect you to do it."

"And to be honest, Holmes, I expect you'll be disappointed in whatever it is I do or don't do about your visitors, so get a good grip on that piece of logic and try not to go where you're heading next because I don't deal very well with threats. I never have. A childhood thing, I suppose, that I can't seem to outgrow." He hung up.

"Is he pissed off at you again?"

"Our sheriff is an idiot."

"I sort of like him."

"He'd never survive in a real city."

"We didn't either."

They walked back into the house and Derek got a small pistol out of a table drawer.

"Really, Derek? You're going to shoot someone for digging in the ground? For trespassing?"

"No. I'm going to be prepared to shoot someone if they decide to do more than that." He walked quickly toward the door.

"Where are you going?"

"To check the locks on the barn."

"The barn. Of course, I should have known. God help us if anyone gets into your precious barn."

He let the screen door slam behind him.

Chapter 19

The Morehead City Municipal Docks were only a few years old, built in the small sliver of Bogue Sound that raced around Sugar Loaf Island before re-joining the main body of water from which the island had separated it.

The docks were nice but far from full, probably because the water sluiced along in front of them with so much speed that sticking a boat into a slip was as hard as sipping martinis on a galloping horse.

"Must have been tricky," Taz said as he looked over the bow at the fast-moving water while checking Wasafiri's lines, making sure the hired captain had her secured the way he wanted. "Look at that water swirl."

"Running like a river."

"It is a river, Pete."

"Right"

Taz pointed to a nice silver Toyota sitting in the parking lot with the invoice still on the window. "There should be some keys hanging off the wheel at the lower helm for that truck over there."

"I saw the keys. I already told you I can't take it."

"Then I'll have no choice but to pay you the share you earned in Venezuela."

Pete looked down and stared at the deck for a half a minute.

"Thanks," he said, "but I didn't earn that money down there, and I did nothing to earn the truck. It's real hard for me to take stuff I don't earn." He laughed. "That's my dad talking in my head, I guess. Anyway, I'm having a great time going along with you, and some fun adventures, so I think that's plenty. I'll call us square, Taz, if you think we are, although I'm certainly getting the better deal."

"That's interesting. Well, let me ask you this, do you mind if the rest of us use your truck?"

"Be my guest." Then he smiled. "No smoking in it though. And don't drive it too hard. Drinking and driving don't mix, always wear your seatbelt, and never bring it home out of gas."

"Your dad again?"

"My mom, actually. This is a cute town. At least what I can see."

"Cute? Really?"

"What?"

"Nothing. It just sounds funny to hear a guy with the guts to leap twenty stories from a helicopter in order to duke it out with a pirate in the waters off South America call something cute."

"I think that restaurant's cute. That general store's really cute. That girl walking along the seawall is–"

"Cute. Okay, I'm with you. What about that big guy walking the gangway to our boat?"

"Our boat?"

"Figure of speech."

Pete laughed. "You mean that really ugly guy?"

Sam climbed aboard and looked at the two of them smiling. "Are you two ladies having fun? And who called me ugly? I heard ugly. Who said it?"

"I've missed you, Sam. And I was using the word 'cute'"

"He was," Taz said.

"Shit, that's even worse. How was your trip up?"

"Fine, except for the airport security hassles. What have you found out?"

"I located Buzz. He's hanging around this big, wooded estate on the water, hiding out in the woods during the day and turning dirt throughout the night. The gold, if there even is any, is most likely on or near that property."

"But he hasn't found it yet?"

"Doesn't look like it. If he has, he must not think he got all of it."

"If he's digging by hand he has no concept of how much gold there is."

"True enough. I walked the perimeter of the land, which is about twenty-five acres."

"Did anyone see you?"

"What kind of stupid question is that?"

Pete stood in front of him, grinning about the enormous difference in their sizes. "It is," he said, "just a little difficult to imagine you sneaking around anywhere unnoticed."

"The Rocky Mountains, perhaps," Taz said.

"At night, maybe."

"Almost the entire estate is walled in," Sam continued, ignoring them. "What isn't protected by walls is low and marshy. The only easy access is by water."

"Have you had a chance to catch up with Jake?"

"He was waiting for me at the airport."

"And the gear I ordered?"

"He and I already moved it onboard. I sent the bill to Fran, who says to tell you hi."

"Thanks."

"Jake also said to tell you there should be pretty good waves later this week, just in case you get a chance to paddle out and surf. Maybe run the boat to Hatteras and anchor in the sound and surf the lighthouse."

"I'd love that, but we'll probably be too busy."

"That's what I told him."

"How big?"

"Damn."

"What?"

"I just lost the bet. He was sure you'd ask how big the surf might be, but I said you'd have your head in your work. The surf websites are estimating eight to ten feet."

"Maybe we'll get lucky and still catch the swell. Did you test the gear already?"

"Yeah."

"Then let's break it out and launch the tender. We've got work to do after dinner."

"It'll be good and dark in three hours," Sam said. "So let's get started."

"Hey Sam?"

Sam turned to Taz, surprised at the sound in his voice.

"Yeah?"

"How did you feel when you saw Buzz?"

"I'd just as soon not talk about it."

"I understand." They both walked to the rail and stared out in silence. Pete hung back.

"Sad, Taz. It felt real sad that a man like that could just take away a friend like Gordie."

"I'm sure it was emotional."

"I found out this morning that he did decades of hard time for murdering a little girl. I mean, Jesus, a little girl! Killing Gordie probably meant nothing to him. What a son of a bitch."

"Thanks for holding back on your desire to kill him. I know how much you want to."

"Yeah. Want to know why?"

"Why what?"

"Why I held back."

"Okay."

"It was because I was too angry to think straight. Heck, I could feel that I was blood-blinded for vengeance, and I'm smart enough to know that makes a man powerful, sure, but careless and stupid as well. I probably would have gotten hurt or killed in a reckless, ill-planned attack. Buzz is a big-time loser, but I'm betting he's a damned dangerous one and not to be trifled with.

"I'm onboard with that."

Sam gripped the rail hard. Taz watched without speaking, waiting for the thick stainless steel to crumble or collapse in Sam's massive hands. "I want–"

He stopped when his voice cracked.

"It's okay, Sam. You don't have to talk."

"I want so badly to kill him, Taz."

"I know."

"It's the least I can do for Gordie. Did you know I was only two blocks away from where he died at the time the police said he was murdered?"

"I did not know that."

"I could have saved him."

"Yeah, and I know you would have. It didn't work out that way, though."

"I am going to kill him."

Taz took his time before saying "We fight, Sam, and sometimes people get hurt. Occasionally people die. But we're not murderers."

Sam looked down at the swirling water. After a minute he said, "Not today, anyway. We'll see what tomorrow brings." Then he turned toward Pete and wiped his eyes. "Come on, kid, we've got work to do."

Chapter 20

November 5th, 1718, aboard Blackbeard's secondary vessel, *Adventure*
034° 28. 476' North / 076° 13. 136' West
(23.5 nautical miles east of Beaufort Inlet, North Carolina)

Blackbeard stood at the rail of *Adventure* and watched his men scurry around on the decks of *Espiritu del Mar*, stripping her of everything of use or value.

"The blocks and the tackle," he said to his trusted lieutenant who stood beside him. "And all her line and rigging what's fit to re-use, Claw."

"Aye, sir." He looked out over the horizon and smiled. "No vessel approaches, sir, so none will know 'twas us what took her."

"Spain will surely search for her, but without reward for their labor."

Claw laughed, but just as he did Blackbeard grabbed his shoulder, turned him, and pulled him to his face. "Claw, listen well to what I say. A task I'll soon give that troubles my soul."

"If the task should be mine to own, then please sir, in me your trust is well placed."

"Would be the blood of yer life on my sword if 'tis not."

Claw studied the gruesome face that showed uncharacteristic concern.

"Aye, sir. It is the great Captain Teach himself that I serve, and 'tis through him that I prosper. I have no insubordination in my soul, sir, and never comes a day that I might."

"Good, Claw. 'Tis good. Upon our return to port ye must pick some of the crew to bury that treasure well. If there be a raiding party what makes attack, give no quarter at all, make good use of the swivel guns, lead the men well and follow they will."

"Aye, aye."

"Luck be to ye, Claw, and life to you alone among those poor men what served me so well."

"With my gratitude, sir. And now it looks like the men have accomplished their tasks aboard our prize."

"Then bring them back aboard."

"Well done, lads," Claw shouted from the rail. "Primary boarding party return. Secondary squad to stand by on her decks."

All but a few of the men leapt back aboard *Adventure* with all the quickness of their brutal training.

"Set fire to the galleon, Captain?"

Blackbeard looked over the graceful lines of the beautiful big galleon, her ornate carvings, the high aft cabin, and her bright paintwork. She was the grand prize of his career, even from his days as a privateer, and he hated to lose her. But to keep her would attract more attention from Spain than he could survive, and he knew it.

"No, Claw, no flames for the end of such a glorious vessel. Let her die as a noble ship dies and send her to the bottom."

Claw looked at Blackbeard. His smile bent the long scar on his face. Then he shouted, "Scuttle her, lads. Hole her bottom and send her down."

Blackbeard and Claw stood together and listened to axes splintering the bottom. They fell fast and hard for most of an hour before the ship started to lower herself gracefully into the sea as the men finished their jobs, clambered back aboard *Adventure*, and cut the heavy lines that held their prize close.

Every man took a spot on the rail and watched as seawater gushed into *Espiritu del Mar*, dragging her lower and lower into the water until finally she groaned one last protest and disappeared.

Chapter 21

Wasafiri's nineteen-foot whaler tugged at its painter as if anxious to get underway and start looking for treasure. Sam and Pete had already loaded it with wetsuits, tanks, re-breathers, flippers, masks, low-noise underwater fluxgate magnetometers, pinpoint probes, and stainless steel tools for scraping and digging at the bottom if they actually managed to find something. But it wasn't yet time to go.

Pete and Sam stood in the galley leaning against the cabinets as Taz finished washing the dishes from a light snack.

"That should hold us for another couple of hours," he said. "Most folks will be in bed by then and the night will be as dark as an ex-wife's heart. We'll eat a real dinner after we get back."

Pete looked surprised. "You sound like a man who took a bad ride on the marriage train. I had no idea."

Taz laughed. "What? No, not me. I was merely speculating, based on what I've seen. Heck, what we've all seen, I suppose. Move, this pan goes in the cabinet behind you."

Pete stepped aside and unlatched the cabinet. "It was my sister's ex-husband who had the black heart."

"I'm sure it cuts both ways."

"Did you ever come close to getting married, Taz? I almost did."

"To Mary-Ellen? The woman you mentioned before?"

"Yeah," Pete said in a sad tone.

"What held you back?"

Taz suddenly looked worried. "God, please don't tell me she died and that I'm twisting a knife around in a deep wound."

Pete laughed. "She didn't die so don't worry. She joined the Peace Corps and went away, promising to come back in a couple of years. I went to see her once in Darfur and we've continued to stay in touch through the internet, but you know how things go."

"Long distance relationships are tough."

"We both still hope for someday. And you, Taz?"

"I really like the idea of marriage and think it would be great. I guess I've just been too busy."

Sam said "Bullshit" under his breath.

Taz laughed as he punched Sam hard in the arm. "Shut up."

"Ow. I didn't really say anything."

"And said a lot by doing it." He hit him again.

"Stop hitting me."

"What are you talking about, Sam?"

"Nothing, Pete."

"It certainly sounded like a challenge. Come on, what are you trying to say?"

"Nope. I wasn't trying to say anything."

"Good," Taz said.

Sam moved to get out of Taz's range, and as soon as he was he said, "Isabelle."

Taz made a quick lunge at him, just to make him jump. "Big surprise that you would bring her up."

"Who's Isabelle?"

"Sam's got a big mouth," Taz said. "Isabelle is a really cool lady."

"Is that all there is to it, Sam? She's just a really cool lady, like Taz says?"

"No, Pete. She's amazing, and much more than that. In fact she's–"

"Harder than one-armed hang-gliding to love," Taz said. "I think it's dark enough outside so let's get moving."

"It's still a little early."

"Not any longer, it isn't. Let's go."

They climbed into the tender, left the docks, and motored into the turning basin used by the seaport's ocean-going ships. They passed the massive storage tanks of the port terminal and then turned left as the Intracoastal headed north, passing under the sixty-five-foot high bridge that connected Morehead City with Radio Island and Beaufort.

Taz cracked open the throttle after they cleared the bridge and the whaler jumped up on plane without a problem, even with all the gear onboard.

"I'm surprised she runs so well with all this weight," Taz said. "You must have dropped a few pounds, Sam."

"I'm all muscle and you damn well know it. Slow down at green marker thirty-five and make a turn to starboard. Watch out for the shoal I showed you on the chart."

"I see the marker."

"The property where Buzz has been digging is way off to the right on that point of land. You can barely make it out from here. We have to go up a county-maintained channel and then into the owner's private one. You'll want to slow to a quiet idle pretty soon."

Taz turned right at channel marker thirty-five and then backed off the gas. The boat quickly settled down in the water.

"From here north," Sam said, pointing, "it's just one big shoal. Other than the private channel that goes right to his doorstep, the water's only a couple feet deep."

"I've done night dives on sunken hulls and in the blackness of underwater caves," Pete said, still trying to find his place in the rankings. "But I don't think any of those were as dark as this."

"There's not even a trace of moon tonight," Taz said as he guided the tender slowly up-river, following Sam's directions. "Or lights from houses. It's dark, for sure. How do I look, Sam?"

"Your hair's a mess but you're good on course."

"I'll take your word for it."

"Tide is coming in fast, so let's anchor way up-current of this man's property and let it carry us past. It'd be too hard to fight it the other way and still check the bottom."

"Should someone stay with the boat and then pick us up later? I'm an excellent swimmer, but I'm pretty sure it would be impossible to swim back against that current."

"I plan to leave my gear wherever we land and walk back along the shore. We'll go get it with the tender later."

"Oh."

"I see a good spot to anchor."

"Sam sees a good spot to anchor. Feeling the adrenaline yet, Pete?"

"To adventure."

"And those who seek it. I'm going to neutral, Sam. Be ready with the anchor, and make sure she's set."

"Well thank you so much. I would never have thought of that on my own."

"Just mentioning it in passing."

Taz killed the engine. Almost instantly the swift current caught the boat and started to sweep it away. "Now," Taz said quietly, and Sam eased the anchor over the bow. The boat suddenly lurched to a stop as the anchor caught and dug in hard, spinning the boat around quickly to face the powerful flow of water.

"Happy, Taz?"

"Like a kid with an ant farm. Let's get wet."

They slung on their dive tanks and strapped them tight, tested their regulators, found enough hands and clips for all the tools and electronics they carried, and then slipped into the water and hung onto the dive ladder.

"Pete, you take the deep channel that goes to his house and try for thirty-foot sweeps. They're going to be fast sweeps because of the current, so pay close attention to your metal detector. Sam and I will try for sixty-foot sweeps in the flats on either side. When you're done make your way to rendezvous about a half-mile downriver."

"So you're going to slide like salamanders along the flats while I struggle with the current and depth," Pete said, grinning. "I'll remember that for next time."

"Okay." Taz smiled and pulled down his mask. "Flip the order. I'll take the channel. See you both down river."

And then he was gone.

"Is he always like this, Sam?"

"Pretty much. Be careful in the shallow water so close to shore. It'd be easy for someone to spotlight you there, which is why Taz thought it would be best for you to stay deep and invisible."

"Will do. See you in later."

They let go and were quickly swept away.

TAZ SLITHERED toward Sam and Pete, who were sitting on the muddy bottom in waist deep water, tormenting a blue crab.

"Did everyone have fun?"

"I didn't find anything, Taz, except beer cans and a length of chain that wasn't even old."

"Pete?"

"No treasure, Taz. But there were some weird holes very close to shore."

"The dredger we saw on our way out must have recently dug that channel to the property," Taz slipped off his tank and sat in the mud beside them, "because it was uniformly deep. So nada, huh?"

"I didn't say that."

"Then what, Pete?"

"I did manage to find a very nice large stump with roots like tentacles at the edge of the intersecting channel. It swallowed me whole as the current plowed me into it. I lost my mask for a while and struggled to get away from it."

Taz looked at Sam for a second or two before they both laughed.

"Yeah, friggin' hilarious. It scared the crap out of me."

"I'm sure it was terrifying. Let's get to the other shore and walk back to the boat."

"Wait a minute." Sam's voice was as low and measured as a sniper. "I see a light moving along the edge of the property."

They flattened out in the mud and watched as a light threaded along the water, just on the other side of the seawall. Then it stopped. The light went to the ground, and from its dull glow they could see someone digging.

"What in the world is that guy thinking? Just so you know, Pete, in spite of the legends and movies about buried treasure, pirates rarely did it. Right Taz?"

"That's right. In fact most of them spent their money as soon as they got it on drinking, gambling and whores. Those few who did keep some treasure wanted it accessible and ready to move if they were attacked, not buried deep in the ground someplace."

"Well," Pete said as he strained his eyes against the darkness, "if that's Buzz–"

"I'm pretty sure it is. The guy's got a big build like his, anyway."

"Then he's got a piece of Tortuga Gold and we don't, so he must know something."

"Good point. Who's ready to make our way back to the tender?"

"Why don't I go get it? Wait here and I'll be back soon."

"No running lights, Pete. Use the paddle and the current."

"I hope I'll remember where I'm leaving you guys. If not, good luck getting back." He laughed lightly as he slid away in two feet of water and disappeared into the darkness.

"He's kidding, right? Do you think he's kidding, Sam?"

"I'm still trying to figure the kid out."

"You like him?"

"He's okay I guess."

Taz waited.

"Yeah, I guess I do."

"Good. Try to keep him from getting killed, okay?"

"Spoil sport."

Chapter 22

Sam was wet, naked, and still drying off from his shower as he walked into the main salon of *Wasafiri*. He'd been the last one to clean up, having rinsed and stowed all the gear they'd used on the dive while Pete started their late night dinner and Taz handled a problem in Tampa.

"Whatever you're cooking smells really good, Pete."

"Thanks. It's my mom's recipe that," he turned toward Sam. "Whoa! Hey man, go get some clothes on."

"I'm still drying off. My clothes are right here so what's the big deal? And I'm starving."

"No food for naked men. Naked gorillas either. New rule."

"Good rule," Taz said. "Get dressed, Sam."

"Just a bite, please. Some bread or something before I fall over."

"For god's sake, here." Pete cut off a slice of sourdough bread and then walked away from the counter.

"Good." Sam tore into it. "That's a lot better for all of us."

"Do company benefits cover counseling, Taz?"

"I think I should check. How long before dinner?"

"You too?"

"It smells so good."

"I *know*."

Sam pulled on some jeans and then dragged a size too-small black shirt onto his big arms and shoulders. "I know that look on your face, Taz."

"You must be thinking of my other look. This is a new one I've been practicing."

"Nope, you're thinking about going to the property where Buzz is digging."

"Oh, that look."

"And trying to talk to the owner."

"What could it hurt?"

"It's just a little obvious course of action for us, don't you think?"

"I suppose, but then again, this is a weird deal. We're not being paid to recover something. We don't have a client asking us to rescue anyone. And we're certainly not out to steal the treasure from the guy, even if one actually exists and does happen to be on his property."

"You know what I think?" Pete stirred the rice noodles. "I'll tell you what I think, and it's that Buzz just got lucky finding that coin. Couldn't it have just fallen off a ship or out of someone's pocket?"

"That's certainly possible, but even if you are right it's still interesting – intriguing, actually – that even one piece of Tortuga Gold was actually here in Beaufort where it *could* fall off of a ship or out of a pocket. Up until now there's never been a clue as to where it went. No salvage record, captain's log, or historical notes of any kind."

"And since it was such a huge shipment of gold, you can imagine that the best scientists, historians, and treasure hunters have spent lots of time searching for it. Not to mention Spain itself. They searched the New World for two years before giving up."

"Sam's right. Buzz's coin is the first clue ever, the first time anyone seems to have seen the gold since it was loaded from the mint. So now where's the rest? It's not on the ocean floor with the ship, we know that for sure."

"It didn't disappear into thin air. And Ballard doesn't have it."

"Are you sure, Sam?" Taz laughed suspiciously. "Did you call Woods Hole?"

"I didn't, but since Bob didn't raid the Titanic when he found that ship, I doubt he would have raided *Espiritu del Mar* when he found her. Besides, if he did, and he had the Tortuga Gold, he'd be busy showing it to the world. It would be in museums everywhere and there'd be a traveling display. Ballard funds his expeditions by being a damn smart promoter. I'm starving."

"Soon."

"Pete will feed us, and then what do you say we pay the owner a visit? What's the man's name again?"

"Holmes. Derek Holmes. Locals call him anti-social, so splash on some charm before we leave. You're just going to walk up at midnight and tell him he might have treasure on his property? Dinner ready yet?"

"Two minutes."

"Sure, why not. Heck, he'll probably laugh in our faces. And the lateness of the hour will add a sense of mystery."

"And probably get us shot, so you go first, Sam."

"You just shut up and keep cooking, Pete. And just so you know, Taz, from what I hear this guy doesn't sound like the 'laugh in your face' type. There's a big unfunny wall around the property and a solid metal gate to help prove the point. Pete, soon?"

"Oh for crying out loud just sit down and eat. I'm never volunteering to cook again."

"Change into that pink shirt you own, Sam."

"Why?"

"It makes you look nicer."

"So what?"

"Just look at yourself. Would you let someone like you come into your house in the middle of the night?"

Sam looked down at the tight black shirt stretched across his massive chest. Okay."

THEY DROVE the Toyota truck over the high bridge under which they'd passed earlier, and then followed the GPS toward the Beaufort-Morehead City Airport. They turned onto a road that went close to the shore heading out toward Gallant's Point, passing lots of nice new homes and even more small shacks along the way.

They turned down an unadorned driveway with a simple black mailbox on which the house numbers where neatly painted.

"Wow," Pete said as he climbed out of the truck. "Impressive gate."

"If you're impressed by concentration camps. I told you this guy was anti-social."

"You said that the locals call him anti-social, but it looks to me like he's pole-vaulted way beyond anti-social and landed somewhere near insanity."

"Let's not rush to judgment, Pete. Sam, maybe he has his reasons."

"By reason of insanity?" Pete laughed at his own joke. "There's a buzzer on that post."

Taz walked over and pushed the button. The response was almost instantaneous. "How can I help you?"

"Mister Holmes?" Then Taz whispered to Sam, "That was sure quick. Do you see a camera?"

"No."

"There has to be a camera for him to be so ready to answer at this time of night."

Sam looked around them. "Or an alarm of some kind."

"How can I help you?"

"Mister Holmes my name is T. Keaton. I'm here with two colleagues named Sam and Pete."

"How can I help you?"

"Well...hey, this is a live person, right? It sounds like a recording? And please don't ask again how you can help me."

"I'm a live person."

"Good. That's good."

Taz hated to reuse any words from the question but couldn't find an easier way, so he said, "How you can help us is tricky because I'm not sure that you can. But we might be able to help you. I'm not positive, but maybe."

"Oh, so you're selling something. Good-night."

"No, no, wait a minute! We're not selling anything. Heck, we don't even have anything to sell. Sam?"

Sam leaned toward the speaker. "Nope, nothing to sell."

"See?"

"That proves nothing. Good-night."

"Wait a second, Mister Holmes, you've got a dangerous man digging on your property, a murderer with a long prison history." Taz turned to Pete. "Did I say that too fast for him to understand me?"

"It was pretty fast."

"I thought so, too."

Silence.

"I think he'd already hung up by the time you talked. I'll push the buzzer again."

"Hold up, Pete. I bet he's still there. He has to be curious, and therefore he's thinking and still listening. Aren't you listening, Mister Holmes?"

"Mister Keaton, even if we make the ridiculous assumption that you're right and that I do have a dangerous man on my property, what could or would you do about it?"

"Nothing, probably."

"An interesting answer. Then why are we talking."

"Because I know the reason he's there."

"And that reason might be?"

"Are you ready for this? I doubt you are, Derek, but here goes anyway. He's on your property looking for gold."

"Gold. Really, Mister Keaton, that's boringly predictable."

"I know it must be, given this area's long relationship with pirates and all that, right?"

"Correct."

"Foolish, right?"

"Absolutely."

"Except that in this particular instance, this particular killer has already found some."

Sam leaned close to the speaker. "I saw it."

"Sam saw it. Thank you, Sam."

"I find that highly unlikely."

"Yeah, me too, but it's the truth all the same. And this particular gold coin is part of an enormous fortune that's well documented but has never

110

been found. Until maybe now. I doubt this guy knows that it's worth several fortunes, actually, but I also doubt he'll leave until either he finds more of it or digs up your property like a gopher while looking."

After more than a minute Taz turned to Pete. "Did I say all that clearly enough? I didn't rush the words?"

"No. It was plenty clear. He's ignoring you because he thinks you're crazy."

"He wouldn't be the first."

Just then a heavy bolt clicked, a large motor whirred, and the solid metal gate swung slowly open.

Chapter 23

Derek Holmes' gravel driveway twisted forever around old growth trees and neatly trimmed hedges. Although it was totally dark when the Mayday team set out earlier in the tender, the shroud of trees forced the night impossibly darker once inside the gate, creating a creepy feeling that closed in on their truck like a crowd of zombies.

Pete looked out the passenger window while Sam rode in the bed. "Jeez, this feels like the setting for a slasher movie."

Taz reached over quickly and squeezed his leg. "Boo!"

Pete jumped and hit his head on the ceiling. "Oh, that's really funny. What are you, ten years old?"

"I only wish I was. Take as many pictures as you can. You know infra-red?"

"I'm figuring it out. Who could live as isolated as this? I've seen more inviting places in old Hitchcock movies."

"I could live like this."

"No way, Taz. You like people too much."

"I do like people, but I like being alone too. I could live out here like this for six months or so. Then I'd need a social fix. There's the house."

"That's not a house. It's a barn of some kind. Maybe. I'm not sure, can't tell."

"I'm not sure what that is, either, but get a picture. There's the house way over there."

"I'm a little surprised by how nice it is."

"It's old and kind of classic. I like it. That must be Derek Holmes on the porch."

"I was expecting Tony Perkins," Pete said. "In a dress. With the big-ass knife in his hand that he used on the poor woman in the shower."

"You watch too many movies, and you're creeping me out."

Pete squeezed Taz's leg just above the knee and said "Boo" in retaliation for earlier. Taz's right foot stomped the gas and the truck shot briefly ahead.

"Hey, I'm driving. Not fair."

"No rules for me." Pete laughed. "You should keep that in mind."

"I'm going to park over there."

"By those graves?"

Taz looked all around. "What graves?"

Pete laughed. "My mistake."

They parked and stepped out, took a slow look around, and then walked toward the house. The man on the wrap-around porch had a handgun of some kind in his waistband.

"There's someone on the right side of the house, Taz."

"It's a woman, Pete. Thanks. Sam?"

"I'll keep an eye on her. You go do your dialogue thing."

"Good evening, Mister Holmes. I'm T. Keaton."

"So I assumed. And I'll also assume the big man is Sam and the skinny kid is Pete."

"Skinny?"

"Roll with it, Pete." Then, "You're right, sir. Very good. Mind if I ask you a question?"

"Shoot."

"See, that right there is the question. I see that popgun in your belt and, well, if you have any plans on using it we'll just turn back around and leave. I can't honestly be sure that we're here to help you, I guess, but I'm positive we're not here to hurt you. Just being honest."

"You mentioned gold. What do you know? I mean, for crying out loud what are you talking about?"

"I don't really know too much, and certainly nothing I'm going to discuss out here in the dark. If you want to invite us onto that porch of yours, we'll discuss it over a beer." He turned to Pete.

"You did bring the beer, right?"

"Sorry."

"We forgot the beer, Derek. Do you have any?"

No answer.

"I hear they serve really cold beer at...what's the name of that place, Pete?"

"The woman's gone to the back of the house and disappeared," Sam whispered.

"The Net House."

"Right you are, Pete. The Net House has cold beer."

"And good oysters."

A few seconds later a pretty woman stepped through the front screen door. "Honey, who are your friends?"

"Hello Missus Holmes. You are Missus Holmes, right?"

"I am."

"I'm T. Keaton. This is Pete. The big fella over there tells us to call him Sam, and to be honest with you I'm not about to argue with him. Would you argue with him, Pete?"

"I wouldn't argue with him."

"Please call me Theresa. Join us on the porch, won't you? I'll get some cold beer."

Taz watched for whatever look she might give her husband before she went back inside, but never saw one. It was as if they'd rehearsed this until their performance was letter perfect, maybe for the few occasions they actually invited over company.

"Sit down in any of these chairs out here," Holmes said.

"These are nice Adirondack rockers."

"I suppose. They're made out of recycled bottles so that they won't rot. Theresa bought them. She's into that ecology sort of thing."

"You're not into it?"

"I think the chairs should be the real thing and made out of wood. What's this all about, anyway?"

"Well, Derek, my colleagues and I are in the salvage and recovery business and we–"

"You mean old cars? Repossessions?"

Taz smiled. "I suppose we would do that if the price was right, maybe go after a priceless exotic or fire-breathing classic, but so far we haven't been called on to do that." He took the bottle of beer that Theresa offered. "Thank you very much. It's warm out here tonight."

"You're welcome. Not buggy, though, so that's nice. Where are you from?"

"The west coast of Florida.

"I love Florida."

"You mentioned gold, Mister Keaton, so I'm going to make the assumption that you mean some kind of a silly pirate treasure. After all, North Carolina isn't particularly famous for gold mines."

"You're right, Derek. I did mention gold."

"Well let me tell you something before you get all wound up. This whole area has always endured crazy people looking for buried treasure. They walk the beaches with metal detectors and dive the waters with probes and right now it seems that one of those assholes is digging in my yard. But just because pirates once used this inlet as a raiding point for passing ships doesn't mean they left gold stuffed into every knothole and burrow."

Taz turned to Pete. "Hear that? Don't waste any time searching knotholes or burrows."

"Got it."

"Because Mister Holmes is probably right." He turned back to Derek. "Actually I'm sure he's right if he chooses to go to that extreme."

"I just don't believe in chests of gold. It's childish."

"You don't believe there's treasure left anywhere? Not from all the European ships that looted the Americas, many of which sunk or were raided?"

"Not really, at least not the way people think. Back then lots of stuff was considered treasure, things like medicine, silk, weapons, the ships themselves."

"Tobacco," Sam added. "Tools, cotton, rum."

Taz gave him a dirty look.

"Good," Holmes said, "So you gentlemen do have an idea of what I mean. Now, do I believe that some of that is still around? I do, and I believe it's worth digging up and preserving. But gold? That borders on the ridiculous."

"You do know that treasure from that era of our history is frequently found, right? Being a Floridian, I happen to know that more than 2000 ships sunk of the coast of my state alone, and most of them are still being discovered. On a per mile of beachfront basis I bet North Carolina has more sunken ships than Florida because of the rough sea conditions along the coast."

"And because of the pirates in whom you seem so intrigued, I assume."

"That's right, Mister Holmes."

"Not too long ago," Sam said with the confidence of someone very familiar with the topic, "a guy named Kip Wagner discovered the 1715 Plate Fleet off of Vero Beach. He paddled out in an inner tube, an *inner tube*, and found the treasure in a couple of feet of water a few feet offshore. It'll probably turn out to be the richest find ever, eclipsing even the *Atocha*."

"That find was an exception."

"Not true, Derek, and I'm starting to suspect that you're enlightened to facts you're slow to acknowledge, such as the twenty million dollars of treasure that gets recovered from our coastal waters every year, and the three million shipwrecks still holding an estimated ten billion dollars. Those ships went down for whatever reason and the treasure, in most cases, is still there to be found. That's why we're here. Want to hear a story?"

"A short story?"

"Derek, be polite." Theresa turned to Taz. "I bet you're talking about a pirate story?"

"Yes, ma'am, it's a pirate story. At least I expect it to turn out as one."

She poured her beer into a glass and drank. "I think a pirate story would be fun. Please, go ahead."

"Derek?"

"You might as well, seeing as how we're all sitting around like foolish kids at a middle of the night campfire."

Taz took another sip of beer, then, "In 1718 a ship named *Conquistador de las Americas* was busted up in a storm and, well, to keep the story short, it sunk near the Dry Tortugas. Before it sank, though, it transferred its half of a golden fortune – which long ago got dubbed Tortuga Gold – to another ship, the *Espiritu del Mar*, which was found off your coast without a trace of the gold aboard."

"I read about that find."

"Oh, so you do have some interest in pirates, and perhaps even some belief in treasure."

"It was news. I read newspapers. I am aware of what I read in those newspapers."

"You, Derek, are a very hard man to entertain." Then Taz smiled and leaned closer, whispering as though telling a ghost story. "Here's why I'm both confused and excited. The man who's digging on your property, the man I called a killer..." he paused. "That man has a piece of Tortuga Gold, and as far as I or anyone else knows it's the only known piece of it ever found."

Derek didn't even react. "And you're telling me he found it on my property."

"Absolutely not."

"But you just said–"

"I'm telling you that he's here looking for more. That fact would lead any reasonable man to deduce that he found it here, but it's only an assumption. Let's be honest, though, and acknowledge that he's not searching here because your welcome mat is bigger than where he actually did find it."

Pete laughed and so did Theresa.

Derek stood up and walked to the end of his deck. He stared out over his property for a long time. Then he walked back, his beer empty.

"Mister Keaton–"

"Why not call me TK?"

"Mister Keaton, I love our home and I love our land. I assume you to be smart enough to figure out that we also love our privacy. If there's a golden treasure buried here, well, I guess that's where it's going to stay, because I'm not going to sacrifice the tranquility we've sought for so long just in the interest of gold."

116

Taz sat silently and watched Holmes walk back across the porch and touch Theresa's shoulder before sitting back down.

"I guess I can understand that, Derek. You really do have something nice here and I like it a lot now that I'm over the creeps. Can I ask how old this home is?"

Derek smiled a little. "She's well over two hundred years. Not sure exactly, but the records indicate it was built around 1780 by a shipwright. There weren't any roads to this area here until the 20th century, so everything from materials to tradesmen had to come here by sea."

"Care to see inside?"

"Absolutely, Theresa. Why, thanks so much. We'd love to."

Derek scowled and then said, "Theresa likes company a bit more than I do. But I guess it wouldn't hurt to show you around."

"Thank you."

They got up and stepped inside and Sam said "Wow."

"You know antiques, Mister...?"

"I'm just Sam. I know this old tin was used to carry musket flints, and that box carried small bags of gunpowder. This is a French officer's sword, probably from our Civil War, and that's a navy enlisted man's cutlass, favored for close-in battle around a ship's rigging. Those on the wall are non-military, probably forged and hammered in some village to outfit privateers or–"

"Pirates. Very good, I'm greatly impressed with your knowledge of antiques."

"Would you please consider selling me this cutlass? I collect them, and as you and I both know this is an incredible item that's worth a lot of money that I'll gladly pay."

Theresa laughed. "That will be the day, Sam. Derek never sells anything and absolutely just hoards this stuff. They'll do a television show about him someday."

Derek turned away from her. "Anyone have thoughts on this chest?"

"Well," Taz said, his amazement over Derek's collection luring him into the conversation, "almost anyone, maybe even me, would call it a treasure chest if they found it in a cave or a hole, but it was actually a navigator's locker, the place he stored and locked his astrolabe, spyglass, nocturnal, cross-staff, charts, rulers and calipers."

Taz turned to Pete. "The navigator was probably the most important person on any voyage. Although the captain ruled the ship and the men and made the big decisions, there were others onboard who could do that job. The navigator's trade seemed like a dark art to the men onboard, and he protected his secrets like a sorcerer."

"And a ship's crew protected the navigators during battle," Sam said. "They kept them safe at all times."

"Very good again." Derek opened the chest and revealed all the items Taz had just described, each one in excellent condition and looking ready to be put into use.

"That, Derek, is truly impressive. I've never seen anything like it before."

"I think it's the only one in the world that's so complete and perfect. I'm very proud to have it."

"Of course you are. God, it's amazing."

"I know. It belonged to Anne Bonny's navigator."

"Pete, did you know there were a few great female pirate captains?"

Pete was gawking around the house in fascination. "Uh-uh, I didn't."

"So Derek, why were you so difficult outside about pirates. I mean, you've got a houseful of evidence that proves your interest, and almost every one of these items is museum quality and worth a lot of money, yet you value your ownership of them enough to keep them here."

Derek picked up a flintlock pistol and carefully took a soft cloth to its brass. "My primary interests, Mister Keaton, are the ocean, the men who sailed her, and the artifacts they left behind. Some of those men sailed under a nation's flag and some, I suppose, sailed under a skull and crossed bones. But I search for things that might actually exist, such as you see here. I don't look for the kind of treasure we're wasting time discussing tonight."

"Did you know the area history when you bought this place? Did you know that Blackbeard was only one of the famous pirates who sailed out of here and called these waters home? If I remember correctly, he even married and moved ashore in Bath, a few miles north?"

"Yes, yes, and I know that the call of the sea rang more loudly in his ears than the siren song she sang, and so he returned to pirating, which, by the way, he only did for two years."

"Blackbeard was only a pirate for two years?" Pete sounded astonished. "I've heard so much about him."

"He was a colorful guy, Pete. The stuff of legends and ghost stories."

"During those two years," Holmes continued, "he raided merchant ships for the goods that he later sold to locals, undercutting the price of goods imported from England. He was the big-box discounter of his time."

"Yet, Derek, you don't believe his treasure, or that of some other pirate, might be on your property."

"I read everything there was about pirates when I was a kid. My father and I actually used to camp on this property and he'd help me look for old swords or things."

"Find any?"

"No," he said flatly. "At least not back then. But what I did find were lots of old arrowheads and fascinating pottery and...well, I display part of that collection over there. So, as a young boy I decided that those items would be what I would choose to seek and collect, artifacts that actually exist, and not imaginary chests full of a dreamer's gold."

"I guess I understand. It's nice that so much of your collection came from right here."

"When I had a chance to buy all this acreage from the state I figured it would be a great place to practice my hobby, right in my own yard. So I do."

"You know, it's possible that the Tortuga Gold that Buzz – that's the man's name – found came up from the bottom when you had your channel dredged."

"It was criminal that the federal government allowed this wonderful commercial waterway that I love to get in such bad shape."

"But it was nice that we could pay to get our channel dredged when they fixed it," Theresa added. "I could barely get out in our skiff before."

"And it really doesn't interest you that a fortune in gold might be on your property or perhaps just on the other side of your seawall?"

"Of course it does. I admit to being intrigued and tempted. But I've already said that I have no intention of turning our lives upside down over gold."

Taz pulled out a picture of Buzz that Sam had taken. He handed it to Derek. "You may not have a choice," he said, suddenly solemn. "This man is probably on your property right now. This man killed my best friend with a rigging knife. This man wants the rest of Tortuga Gold."

"This man," Sam added, "will stop at nothing to get it."

Chapter 24

"I've seen that man," Theresa said without even a trace of surprise. She lowered her head for just a second, then lifted it and looked unapologetically at Derek.

Sam flinched. "Really?"

"Why are you so surprised by that? You guys were the ones who said he was here."

"I know, Derek. It's just...well, it's weird to think I could be close to him right now." Sam massaged his hands to keep them from clenching into fists.

"I've seen him in our woods."

Derek walked away from her. He stopped at an old oak desk, lifted himself onto it and sat staring at her, waiting for the explanation he'd already heard too many times.

"Derek disagrees with me, but I always assume that men like him are homeless, and probably harmless. Most of them are, you know."

Taz spoke slowly. "That...wow, Theresa, it's amazingly tolerant of you to allow homeless to live in your woods." He tried not to look at Derek.

"It's human of me, not tolerant. Those poor souls already have it hard enough living with bugs and heat and cold and rain. They really don't need me calling the police and adding to their problems just because they carve out a few square feet of our dozens of acres. You should try being homeless sometime."

Taz thought about his survivalist hike down the coast of Central America where he almost died because he'd purposely not carried any medicine. He looked at Sam, who shrugged.

"As I said, it's a nice attitude you have. He's a bad man, and definitely dangerous, but that takes nothing away from your concern."

"Our walls can protect them from violence. Do you have any idea how many homeless are beaten each year for fun, usually by teenagers? I can tell you."

"Theresa–," Derek chose his words more carefully than any other time since Taz arrived. "I spent a small fortune building our walls in order to keep people out. I built them so that we would be safe."

"Yes, I know. But I think we are safe."

"He probably comes in from the water side anyway," Taz offered, "by climbing around the end of your wall or over the seawall. That's a big, difficult area to protect. Maybe if you had a couple of watch dogs."

"I don't like dogs." Derek stood and walked over to his wife. He put his hand uncomfortably on her shoulder. "She is obviously compassionate toward the homeless, for reasons I've never quite understood but have tried very hard to accept."

"It would be easy for you to understand, Derek, if you hadn't grown up rich. I lived in a Quonset hut most of my youth and never had new clothes, so–"

"I know, Theresa, your family came close to being homeless many times."

"So I hate that you're so haughty and detached from problems that are all around you."

"But Theresa," Derek said, staying patient, "you had to know that this was the man digging up our yard."

"Of course I did. I'm smart enough to at least suspect it was him, but so what? What he was doing was a little annoying but certainly seemed harmless enough. And just for the record I did tell you about it."

"You didn't tell me that you'd actually seen him. What if he'd attacked you? Hurt you?"

"I told you what you needed to know and nothing more. You of all people should appreciate the subtlety of that."

"You'll probably want to discuss this in private," Taz said, while Pete and Sam sat a few feet away looking very interested in their feet. "Meanwhile, I'd like to remind you that this dangerous man living on your property believes he's about to strike it rich. I understand that you don't want a lot of attention drawn to this matter because it would disrupt the peacefulness out here. I'm starting to appreciate it a lot."

"Don't get too comfortable, Mister Keaton."

"If someone had asked me, I would have bet you'd say something like that."

"You have good instincts."

"Instincts I might as well go against. Is now a good time, Sam?"

"As good as any, I suppose."

"I think so too. Derek, I have a boat tied up at the city docks that would just about fit at that dock of yours. Thanks to your dredging I have enough water, so I'd like to move *Wasafiri* up here where I can help keep an eye on things, with your permission of course. I'll pay the going rate and your electric bill while I'm tied up out there."

"The answer is no. And what would you do here anyway? Join the growing crowd of people digging around for buried treasure?"

"Pretty much."

"Not the answer I expected."

"That wouldn't shock anyone. Yes, I think there might be a treasure here someplace and I'd like to help you find it."

"I'll remind you that whatever bit of gold might be here isn't worth the serenity I'd lose having you three wandering around my property."

"And I'll remind you of the threat Buzz represents to you and Theresa. He hopes desperately to find gold that he feels sure is here. That's already made him determined, which makes him dangerous. We may not look the part, Derek, particularly the skinny kid over there, but I think we can keep you two safe."

"I'm stringy."

"You have to remember what you already know so well from history, Derek, that treasure almost always conveys through bloodshed."

"I do believe you're right, Mister Keaton," he said casually, as though he'd suddenly come to an important conclusion. "If I was this man and living in his conditions, I'd be a dangerous threat to the people who lived here. Any reasonable man would consider him a threat."

"Derek?"

"It's true, Theresa. I'm just putting myself in his place."

"We've met him, Missus Holmes, and I think Pete and Sam would agree that this Tortuga Gold is the one golden opportunity in Buzz's life, no irony intended."

"You met him?"

"And that meeting is what cost my best friend his life."

"How did he even manage to find the gold here?"

"I was hoping you could answer that."

"We don't have a clue. Do we, Theresa?"

Theresa seemed swallowed up by what was being said.

"Theresa?"

"What? No, no idea. I wonder what brought him to our land in the first place."

"Sam can fill in that piece of the puzzle. Sam?"

"You go ahead, Taz."

"Sam's not all that chatty. He loves that cutlass, though."

"Yes, I know. So how did this man Buzz end up here?"

"He worked on a dredger. I saw one working down-river a bit and I imagine it's the same one that dredged your channel so deep right up to your dock."

"Yes...wait, you've been underwater in front of my house?"

"That water is public and belongs to me as much as it does to you."

"We hired the dredging firm to do it as a side job, deepening it to the seawall a couple weeks back," Theresa said. "We're situated on a hard turn in the waterway and it tends to shoal."

"I see that it shoals all the way to the ICW. So the dredger was right at your door, really, and Buzz was most likely working as a crewmember at the time. I'm sure you know, Derek, that every one of the rivers and inlets and sounds and bays that make up the Intracoastal Waterway were right where they are today."

"Of course I know that."

"Engineering and hard work connected them all into one continuous waterway, and some have silted in while other channels have migrated, so to speak. But–"

"You're proposing that the dredger, while deepening the channel in front of my house, brought up some Tortuga Gold from the muddy bottom of a river that's very much the same as it was back when pirates used it instead of crabbers and families. Your opinion is obvious, although completely unsupported by fact."

Taz finished his second beer and said, "That *is* what I'm saying, and my supporting evidence is the gold coin in Buzz's possession. It could only have been one piece that found its way here by chance or accident, or it could have been one piece from the entire missing cargo of gold that's buried in the mud out there."

"In which case there should have been more of it that came up."

"Maybe it did. Buzz only showed Sam one coin, but he might have a ton of it already. I just doubt that he does because Theresa said he's digging holes all over your yard."

"Mister Keaton, what am I to expect from you if I ask you to leave?"

"I'm a gentleman, Derek, so you can expect me to thank you for your hospitality and leave."

"But?"

"But first thing in the morning you're going to see my boat anchored off your point, right about there." He pointed into the darkness toward the river.

"A little closer and a tad farther south."

Taz grinned and moved his finger south. "Thanks, Sam. So maybe a little more over there. I don't like to argue with Sam."

Derek followed Taz's finger out toward the water. "Then you might as well tie up at my dock."

"Thank you,"

"It's late, gentlemen. Good-night."

Chapter 25

November 21, 1718
Aboard the Pirate Ship *Adventure*, anchored on the lee side of Ocracoke Island, North Carolina

"Might they attack tonight, Captain?"

"Aye, they might," Blackbeard said, "and even more likely if aided by some traitorous local what knows these waters. But me thinks no such dog would dare be aboard her, so they'll wait until first light, and use the sun at their backs to see the shoals." He pulled off his hat, covered his eyes, and leaned his strong body toward the two boats anchored nearby. "What be the names of those sloops?"

"HMS *Ranger* and *Jane*, sir."

"I've heard no tales of such named vessels, but perchance some coward has recently commissioned them to avoid looking like pyrates themselves."

"A fast way to gain ships small enough to give us chase into the inlet, captain."

"Aye, Claw. How many men have we?"

"Nineteen, sir. And all guns are manned. Our cutlasses be honed and pistols loaded."

"And the blood to be spilt be of the men upon those yonder decks. To that, my lad, we drink."

"Aye sir, I'll post a watch, and then to your cabin."

"With all hands and a keg, Claw. For to celebrate that if tomorrow brings with her a fight, those ships I now see shall be mine."

"Aye, sir. But if ye die on the morrow, does your wife, Mary, know where ye treasure be buried?"

Blackbeard laughed hard, and then put his hand on Claw's shoulder. "Aside from ye and those poor damned souls, my friend, nobody but me and the Devil now knows where it's hid, and the longest liver will get it all." Then he went to his cabin, where the entire crew gathered and drank through the night, taking turns checking on the sloops to see if they'd moved.

At first light Blackbeard was shaken awake by the watch.

"Captain, their anchors are aweigh and the lightest of breezes moves them toward us. They sent ahead a small boat that's closing."

Blackbeard scratched at his face and winched at the pain in his head. "Fire a volley of shot at the approaching boat, lad, and raise the alarm."

"Aye, sir."

"And the ships?"

"Gun range, sir, but with a bad angle."

"Then hasten to slip free of our anchor and make ready to set sail."

"Aye."

When he got on deck he wore a brace of three pistols, two daggers, and his cutlass. Just then his crew fired a volley at the rowboat, which turned away. Blackbeard breathed in the cannon's smoke like it was perfume, then shouted "To battle, men, if that be our day. Fill my sails," he took the big wheel of the helm, "and carry me through that narrow cut amongst the shoals."

"They're rowing, sir."

Blackbeard looked over to see the two sloops dipping oars. "They plan to board us, lads. Yet they know not the water and will be aground very soon."

"They've run up the King's colours."

"Aye, they have, and proudly at that. Up the rigging now, lads. Catch all of that breeze. And bring me a drink of the night last as well."

As all the ships approached the same spot from different angles, with almost no wind moving any of the vessels against the outgoing tide, the oars of the *Ranger* and *Jane* slowly brought them close enough to prepare for an attack.

Then they ran aground, so close that Blackbeard could see the eyes of the well-dressed captain on *Ranger's* deck.

"Damn you for villains," Blackbeard shouted. "Who are you? And from whence came you?"

"Lieutenant Maynard, sir, and you may see by our colours we are no pyrates."

"Then send a boat over, ye cowardly puppies, that I might see who you be."

Maynard laughed. "I cannot spare my boat, but I will come aboard of you as soon as I can, with my sloop." He pulled his cutlass a few inches out of its scabbard. "Governor Spotswood of Virginia hath commissioned me to bring back your head, sir, and it's that very duty I'm here to perform."

Blackbeard took the mug of liquor that had just been brought to him and held it toward Maynard. "Then damnation seize my soul if I give you quarters, or take any from you." He drank and then turned away.

Maynard shouted, "I expect no quarter from you, sir, nor should I give you any."

Then the breeze all but died. The boats stayed close. As the tide shifted, Blackbeard watched it lift the two sloops off the bottom, aided by the crews' heaving and pulling.

He saw they were digging sharply with their oars, moving both the *Jane* and *Ranger* once again towards his *Adventure*.

"Fill yer cannons, lads, with swan shot, nails, and pieces of old iron. Let fly at those scoundrels on Claw's command."

"Ready, lads," Claw cried. "Now fire!"

The cannons blasted with a deafening single roar and the gun crews immediately began reloading. Through the acrid smoke Blackbeard could see the devastating effect he'd had on the *Jane*, which immediately veered off the chase and fell behind, amidst the groans of the wounded, the silence of the dead, and the lack of a living commander.

"Now get ye an angle on the *Ranger*, lads. They're shooting our fore-halyard to shreds."

"Guns ready, Captain."

"Then give them our shot."

"Ready. Fire!" And again the bright morning filled with the sound of cannons, their effect rocking Maynard's little sloop as cannon balls and shrapnel ripped large pieces of it away, felling many of the crew.

"Captain Teach, our jib and fore-halyards are lost."

"Aye, Claw, I can see. Then make for shore as best you can."

They drifted slowly toward shore as the *Ranger* drifted with the same tide but at a bit faster pace, gaining little distance but eventually getting close enough to see *Ranger's* decks.

"Why, there's no one aboard, sir, save for that young captain and a helmsman."

"Aye, and what a fine tribute that be to our cannons. Gather ye ten men to board with me and take over her command."

"Aye, sir."

Blackbeard looked over at Maynard, who stood almost alone on *Ranger's* decks. He touched his hat, and said, "To your bravery, young lieutenant, which I shall be proud to honor with a quick death."

As they rounded up and turned broadside to *Ranger*, Blackbeard leaped to the rails with his trademark smoking fuses tied into his long black beard, shouting, "Boarding party, follow me!"

With yells and cheers, Blackbeard and his men climbed over the rails onto *HMS Ranger*, but just as they hit her decks two dozen of Maynard's crew poured out of the holds where they'd been hiding, their pistols firing and cutlasses slashing.

Blackbeard ignored the melee of the crews and ran straight to Maynard, who stood waiting, smiling, unafraid. Blackbeard challenged him with his sword and Maynard made a slash that struck Blackbeard's cartridge belt and bent the blade double.

Blackbeard broke off the guard and wounded Maynard's hand, so Maynard threw away his sword and pulled his pistol, then fire a powerful blast directly into Blackbeard's body.

Yet Blackbeard stood as though invincible, and the fight between the two men continued for another forty minutes until a highlander among Maynard's crew stepped up.

"Might I have a go at you, Captain Teach?"

Blackbeard looked up into the big man's eyes. "If you value not your life, and have no time to waste in getting to hell."

The highlander laughed and said "Then 'tis a race to hell between us" as he swung at Blackbeard with his broadsword.

Blackbeard lurched back, but too slowly, and the big sword found a good home low on his face. He stopped and raised his hand to feel the blood gushing from yet another wound.

"Well done, lad," he said, grinning while trying to reload a pistol.

"If it not be well done," the highlander said, "Then I'll do it better." And with those words he swung his broadsword around in a complete circle and gave Blackbeard's head leave from his body that had been shot five times, cut twenty more, and lacked for the blood that had been pouring out in a rush.

What remained of the crew surrendered, and Maynard mounted Blackbeard's head on the bowsprit of *HMS Jane*. His men dumped the headless body into the ocean, where it swam three times around the *Adventure* before disappearing beneath the waves, heading, presumably, for hell.

Chapter 26

"This is quite a nice boat," Derek said as Taz welcomed him aboard. "I expected something ugly with all kinds of pipes and cables hanging off it. I like the style."

"Thank you. Can I get you a cup of coffee?"

"Sure, thanks. It's an unusual boat, and quite large."

"She's called an Expedition trawler."

"It–"

"She," Taz interrupted. "My friend Gordie always joked that boats are *she's* because even the best of them will eventually let you down."

"*She* interests me more than the other big boats we watch going up and down the waterway. I'm not much of a boater, but I think I'd enjoy having something like this. A whole lot smaller, though."

"It was obvious last night when you showed us your collection of artifacts that you value classic things that endure, so I was pretty sure you'd like her traditional lines."

"Particularly how high off the water she is in front."

"At the bow. It must be fun for you and Theresa to live here along the Intracoastal and mark the seasons by the boat traffic."

"It is, as there's a steady line of cruisers heading north in the spring and south in the fall. We don't get much boat traffic in the winter, but during the summer we get plenty of transients that the local kids love because they get to water ski and wakeboard over their wakes. That's interesting to watch."

Taz poured coffee for him, Derek, and Pete. Then he led them up to the high bow of *Wasafiri*. They stared far down at the water, scanning the short distance between them and the shore as though expecting a mermaid to swim up and say hello.

"Fascinating, isn't it?"

"What?"

"Exciting is probably a better word. To think that right now we could be over a treasure site of such historical value."

"Or perhaps we're not. Maybe it's on my property where that man Buzz is digging holes. You know, of course, how unlikely I believe either scenario to be."

"I'm still excited, and where we find it will certainly have significance in court, if it goes to court. If we find Tortuga Gold in the water it's likely that Spain will lay claim to it, maybe the United States Government as well."

"And if it's on my land?" Then he came close to laughing, but didn't quite get there. "Jeez, listen to me. Even I'm starting to sound like it's possible."

"I'm not sure of the impact of finding it on your land other than it will definitely be better for you. North Carolina most likely will want a portion, but if there's a Treasure Trove Law in this state then their cut will be mandated by that. That's the way it is in Florida."

"I see."

"But to be honest with you, Mayday Salvage and Rescue doesn't usually concern itself too much with the sticky legal issues like that." He laughed. "To say the least. But the point, Derek, is that the possibility exists that some day we're going to find at least one coin of Tortuga Gold. I had trouble sleeping last night."

"What does avoiding 'sticky legal issues' mean?"

"Look, here comes Sam."

Sam walked up with an aggravated look on his face, like he'd been waiting for someone who never showed up. "If we're just going to waste all this good daylight I think I'll go work on my suntan. Or maybe shave the hair off my back."

"Last time you mowed that sweater you shivered for a week."

"Then let's get to work."

"Fine," Taz said, smiling. "Go ahead."

"Okay I will." He squared up with Derek, standing only a foot or two away. "Mister Holmes, do you have any idea where the dredger was when Buzz found the gold?" Then he saw Theresa walking down the dock and said, "Good morning, Missus Holmes."

"Good morning, Sam. Morning Taz. Wow, what a nice boat."

Taz went to the gangway and helped her aboard. "Please call me TK," he said. "Like my other friends."

She studied his face before saying, "I heard Sam and Pete call you Taz and just assumed that...well, never mind. TK it is."

"Sam," Derek said as Theresa leaned against the railing alongside of him. "I'm not sure what you're asking me. How could I possibly know where the gold was found?"

"That's not what I'm asking. I'm suggesting that discovering a rare gold coin would shake up the boring routine of a dredger, so I'm wondering if you ever saw anything weird happen out here that might be a clue. Maybe shouting or laughing or some other excitement."

Derek and Theresa looked at each other. "No," she said, and then her eyes brightened. "It stopped once if that means anything."

"What are you talking about, Theresa?"

"Remember that night the dredger stopped? The suddenness of the silence woke both of us up."

"Yes, yes, she's right."

"That was unusual?"

"It was, TK. Derek even got up to see what was going on. I'd never heard it stop before except to move. Other than that it groaned and throbbed constantly."

"Where was it when it stopped?"

"The dredger was right over there," Theresa pointed.

"The barge, you mean."

"Yes, the barge with all the noisy machinery on it."

"Do you have any idea where the pipes led?"

"The pipes that dumped the slime came ashore just over the line from our property, right on the other side of the wall. That's where they're dumping most of the mud from this section on the river."

"I see, and what about the intake, the place where it was chewing up the bottom?"

"I know exactly where that was, too, because I stood there most of the day watching it. I was concerned they would undermine our seawall, worried that the bottom of the concrete slabs might kick out. It was right beside our wall and right over there." She aimed her finger with precision.

"That's very accurate."

"She could say 'around there' and be vaguer if you like," Derek added, "but she's right. It was exactly there."

"Sam, why don't you and Pete get out some gear for you and me. Pete, you stay with the boat and record our readouts. Maybe stand by to haul up the first ton or two of gold." He laughed.

"Just like that, huh? My wife points her finger and you chase off for treasure."

"I don't see a reason to wait to find out if the gold is down there. Sam, do you see a reason to wait?"

"Nope. No reason."

"I thought you already swam around this area and checked it out."

"We did. But not that close to your seawall because we didn't want to risk you seeing us, and the current made it difficult to be sure we covered everywhere else. It's slack tide now, which is why I'm in a hurry to get wet."

"Oh."

"Why don't you and Theresa use these binoculars to watch for Buzz? If he thinks we're on his spot I don't want him shooting me when I come up."

"And if we see him?"

"Don't let him board the boat. Yell shoo or something. Throw rocks or call the cops, but get him out of here. Pete will know what to do."

"Okay."

"I already got the gear ready, Taz."

"Good, Sam. Okay folks, we'll be back soon. Stick around and maybe you'll be among the first people in a couple of centuries to see this gold."

"This is so exciting," Theresa said.

"I'm going to the barn to work. This is foolishness. They'll find nothing."

"Here." Pete gently wrenched the coffee cup out of Derek's hand. "Let me help you and your negative attitude off the boat. You, Theresa, are welcome to join me in the salon."

"Derek, I'll…" She turned away from him and smiled at Pete. "Thank you, Pete. That sounds like fun."

"Derek," Taz said as he and Sam suited up. "I'd prefer you to stick around."

"I have work to do."

"Stick around," Taz repeated, but this time with a practiced authority that kept Derek in his place.

Taz and Sam armed themselves with the same equipment they'd used last night, although Sam had reconfigured it for a narrower search pattern. They slid off the swim platform and moved carefully toward the spot, diving to the bottom as they approached it slowly and side by side, with Sam swinging a big metal detector and Taz stabbing the bottom with a pinpoint probe.

They came back aboard at lunch.

"There's nothing there," Sam said to Theresa as he handed Pete his gear and then climbed up the dive ladder."

"TK?"

"Sam's right. Not even a bottle cap. You folks don't throw litter off your seawall, that's for sure."

"Of course we don't."

"Well," Taz said, "there could be all kinds of possible explanations for what could have happened to the gold that would allow Buzz to find a piece here."

"I'd like to hear a few," Sam said, "because I'm used to finding a ship's cargo on or near the wreck of the ship. We're twenty miles or more from where the *Espiritu del Mar* was found on the bottom."

"Sure. No problem." Taz worked his way out of his wetsuit and then sat down on the bare deck.

"Maybe pirates were chasing the *Espiritu del Mar* and the captain decided to dump the gold overboard at sea so that the pirates couldn't get it, with the hopes of recovering it later."

"I doubt it," Sam said. "It didn't take many crews being slaughtered for revenge after pulling a stunt like that for word to travel fast. Our good captain would have known there'd be no quarter for him if he did something similar."

"Maybe there was some kind of mutiny on board. And in the process the gold went over the side long before the ship went down."

"What kind of mutiny ends up with gold dumped overboard?"

"I'm just brainstorming, but whatever the reason, if the gold went to the bottom somewhere offshore or near the inlet, then it could have been widely scattered by the currents. Maybe just one coin ended up here and Buzz got it."

"Or," Sam said, "someone could have had a piece that just fell in the water here."

"Or a fish could have swallowed it out at sea and eventually died here with the coin still in its stomach."

They all looked at Pete. Sam laughed.

"Hey, it's possible. When the fish rots away the coin falls out."

"Actually," Taz said, "it is possible. After all, most fishing lures are shiny objects because fish do go for them. But I don't like any of those explanations because they take away too much of the fun. I want the gold to be here." He walked away and stared off at Derek's house and property.

Sam kept laughing.

"It's not that stupid an idea."

"A *fish* could have swallowed it? I can't believe you said that out loud. But now I'm thinking that maybe a whale swallowed the whole cargo of gold. Maybe there was a pod of whales that had a thing for gold and they went roaming the ocean scouring through shipwrecks. Maybe their descendants still do, even today. Have you seen any whale pods around here, Derek?"

"I like you better grumpy, Double-M. What's up with Taz?"

Everyone turned to see Taz pacing, slowly, but getting excited and moving faster, taking aim with his fingers as his eyes flashed around Derek's property.

Derek took a step toward him. "Mister Keaton, what–"

"Hold on to that question," Sam said as he grabbed him gently by the shoulder and pulled him back. "Taz is onto something and it's never good to interrupt because his brain could short-circuit. Quick, Pete, go grab a fire extinguisher and watch for sparks around his ears."

"Okay." Pete took two quick steps toward the cabin and then stopped. "Very funny."

"Not as funny as 'a fish ate it.'"

Taz paced faster. Then he stopped, took a deep breath, slowed down everything about himself and said, "Derek."

"Yes?"

"If I'm not mistaken I see concrete pilings holding up your front porch. Am I right?"

"You are."

"So did you add the porch or was it always part of the house? I'm betting the porch is original."

"Yes, it was always a part of the house."

"But you said the house was centuries old."

"That's true, I did."

"But they didn't use concrete pilings that long ago." He walked slowly over and stood right in front of Derek. "You moved your house here from someplace else, didn't you?"

"Yes we did. We moved it from about a mile up the road. It was a plantation home."

Taz smiled. "And you also put in the concrete seawall along the water, I'm sure. It wasn't here before you moved the house."

"We built the seawall. We had it built."

"Then that's the answer. Or at least a clue to the answer."

"What is?"

"Sam, you need to get our equipment moved ashore. Our gold–"

"*Our* gold?"

"Your gold, Derek. It's over there. I've got to get cleaned up now. I'll be back as soon as I can." He ran to the door of the main salon.

"Mister Keaton," Derek shouted. "I'll remind you that I own that property. If you go ashore without my permission you will be trespassing."

Taz stopped, hesitated, then walked very slowly back to Derek. He looked hard into his eyes.

"Derek, from the very first words you said to us I knew you were hiding something? What is it?"

"Serenity, Mister Keaton. And history. I can already see your commitment to doing whatever is necessary and causing who knows how much damage in order to find whatever gold might be here. But as you've seen, I also search for artifacts that are scattered all over this acreage. I will not have you clod-hopping across my land with the singular purpose of finding gold."

"So you want to control where and how we dig."

"That's exactly right."

"Okay, we'll live with that. It's certainly within your rights. Sam?"

"Yeah."

"No clod-hopping around on Derek's property while I'm gone."

"Wouldn't dream of it. I won't let the skinny kid do any hopping either."

"For God's sake, guys, I'm not skinny."

Chapter 27

Taz jumped into Pete's truck and drove Derek's winding driveway that wove its way through a tangle of oaks, slash pines, and holly hedges. Even in daylight it was almost as creepy as it was last night, and if the rotting ghost of some long-dead pirate were to make him stop the truck so as to bum a cigarette, Taz wouldn't have been a bit surprised.

Derek's massive gate opened automatically, and Taz turned onto the narrow, two-lane road back to Beaufort. At the junction he followed most of the cars that stayed on State Road 70 as they headed back over the bridge to Morehead City, but Taz left the pack at Courthouse Square of Carteret County.

He was excited about what he hoped to find, and happy to be at a courthouse, which he loved for the wealth of information they held about almost everything that had ever taken place in a county or city. It always surprised him that so many people chose to speculate about a marriage or birth date or ownership when the truth was so readily available for free.

He'd used courthouses a great deal while completing contracts all over the world, especially since they were such great repository for maps and surveys of an area, often dating back to the first time someone pounded a nail into a tree and said it marked his property. So from that point in time to the lengthy legal descriptions for subdivisions and zonings of more recent years, if something had been recorded, the courthouse could give him the facts.

A very large map of Carteret County hung on the wall and occupied most of it. Taz was still studying it when a young clerk came over and asked if she could help.

"Thanks," Taz said. "It's a nice town you have here. I'm interested in learning everything I can about that large parcel right there along the river." He pointed at Derek's property.

She looked way up, rolling delicately onto her toes as if the extra inch or two might help her see it better. "I'm not sure that's really still in Beaufort proper. It's a little ways up the river, but let's start with the legal

136

description and go from there. Definitely Carteret County, so I know I can give you some information."

"I appreciate your help."

She went back to her neatly organized desk and clicked away at her computer. "Here it is," she said. And then, "Oh!"

"What?"

"That land is owned by Derek and Theresa Holmes. Well, Theresa Holmes now."

"Why the surprise?"

She looked up, and when she saw Taz smiling, she smiled too. "No real reason, I guess. It's just that the sales transaction was quite a contentious issue some years back."

"Why?"

"Because the whole parcel was priced cheaply, based on it's designation as a dump."

"I've been there, and it certainly doesn't look like a dump."

"It was zoned...well, there wasn't really any zoning back then, but basically it was designated as a dump in the early 1800's, and taxed and valued accordingly."

"It's a heck of nice dump."

"Yes, so I've heard. Actually, I don't think it was ever used as a dump, either, at least not in the sense we normally think. But since it was zoned that way Stamford Holmes – he's been the big deal attorney around these parts for years – pretty much forced the county to value it cheaply. His son Derek bought it for nothing. Here's the date of the sale."

"I'm hoping to go back farther than that."

"Sure, how far?"

"The beginning."

"Of time?"

"Cute. What is your name?"

"I'm Cynthia."

"I'll settle for the beginning of your records, Cynthia. I'm really hoping to see the very first maps or charts of that property."

"Are you a history buff? Lawyer? It doesn't matter since they're all public records. I'm just curious. My mom says I'm nosey."

"I'm nosey too. I can't help myself sometimes."

"I know that we have an original survey of the county from 1713. It's really the oldest thing we have." She walked away and Taz followed. "If you want maps or charts older than that you might try the Historical Society on Turner Street. Ask for Miss Lucy." Cynthia giggled. "The joke around town is that she drew most of those ancient maps."

"Thank you."

"Here's the original survey of Carteret County."

It took Taz a minute to orient himself on the plat because parts of it were faded and blurry. It was on a much smaller scale and lacked roads or bridges or significant landmarks. He stared and studied it. Cynthia stood close and waited.

He turned the chart around and stared some more, then finally turned to her and said, "It's not there."

"What's not there?"

"The Holmes property. It's just not there."

She moved closer to him and they stared together. "It has to be there. How could it not be there?"

"I'm sort of anxious to know that myself. The map shows a tiny little island off the shore in that general area, but that's all. At least if that's the right spot. There's nothing else."

"I think that's the right spot."

"What's that little symbol on the island?"

"That means it was inhabited at some time in its past. It could have been Indians, you know, Native Americans. Early settlers, maybe."

They looked at each other and then looked back at the map. They did it again. Finally she said, "I really don't know what else to tell you? It really isn't there. I've never seen anything so strange."

"Can I get a copy of this map? Or at least this section of it?"

"I'm really not supposed to copy these old documents, but I will. I'll have to charge you three dollars."

"Thank you. Where's Turner Street? The Historical Society."

"I'll show you in a sec. Hang on."

She made the copy and then walked outside with him and pointed. He walked down the peaceful street of this wonderful seaport, past marine stores selling anything a long-liner or crabber might need and enough seafood restaurants to keep all those commercial fishermen busy.

The oak floor creaked as he walked into the Historical Society. The old noise was in perfect harmony with the musty smell of ancient records and the dusty shelves that supported them.

"Miss Lucy?" Taz asked a woman who looked to be in her mid-eighties.

"Oh my, heavens no. I'm much too young." The woman laughed beautifully. "But wait right there a minute." She left the room and talked to someone in back, then came to the doorway.

"Do you mind stepping back here, young man? Please watch your head."

"Thank you."

He ducked through a doorway that was only six feet high or less, probably created from an old access door to a coal room that now served as Miss Lucy's domain.

"This is Miss Lucy," she said proudly, while gently waving her hand toward an old thin woman in a wheelchair. "I hope you'll excuse me," she said, and then left.

Miss Lucy smiled and reached out her hand. "What's your name, young man?"

He grinned and shook her hand as gently as possible. "I'm T. Keaton."

"Don't worry, Mister Keaton. My hand won't fall off. I don't think my arm will either, although you never know about these things. And what does your best friend call you?"

"That's a very nice question, Miss Lucy. He calls me Taz. Or at least he did. He died recently."

She kept hold of his hand and rubbed it comfortingly. "I'm so sorry, Taz. Loss is always difficult."

"I'm sure you've suffered your share. Do you mind if I ask your age, Miss Lucy. You must be proud to be so healthy and active."

"You mean so healthy and active for my age, don't you?" She laughed.

"Yes, ma'am, that's exactly what I mean. I find it inspirational."

"Are you trying to charm me, Taz Keaton?"

"I could never pull that off. You're too good at being charming yourself."

"I know. I'm a scamp. Now, Taz, how can I help you, if I can help you?"

He unrolled the survey where Derek's property should have been located and pointed to the spot. "See this island?"

"No. I'm so sorry, but my old eyes...someone should have warned you."

Taz flushed with embarrassment. "I'm sorry, Miss Lucy, I should have–
"

She laughed. "Of course I can see that island, silly. I'm sorry but I do enjoy kidding."

"Actually, I do too."

"It makes things so much more fun. So, yes, I see the island. Now, what about it?"

"It's no longer there."

"I already knew that, dear."

"And there's a big piece of acreage where it used to be."

"I already knew that, too."

"Why?"

"My, you get right to the point, don't you?"

"Too soon?"

"At my age the only thing that comes too soon is tomorrow. Yes, that island disappeared quite some time ago. At one time it was a beautiful oxbow."

"I'm sorry, what's an oxbow?"

"It's a place where the river divides itself around a small island and then flows on either side. They're quite desirable as home sites because they give protected shelter on the backside for boats but allow great views of the river from the other side. Why, my mother told me stories of shrimp and fish so thick in those oxbows that she could scoop 'em up with her hands."

"That must have been a lot of fun."

"Sure must have been. The shores of the river used to have plenty of oxbows, but many of them were filled in. The one you're asking about is now a home, which is nice enough, I suppose, but just a home. Owned by Stamford's son, Derek, who was not nearly as charming as you when he came in here twenty or so years ago asking questions about the land."

"He talked to you about it? Why?"

"He'd played there as a child and found some artifacts, so he wanted to know more about who might have lived there."

"Did he leave here happy?"

"Oh, I should say so. I have a British navigator's chart over there someplace that shows it as a place they once raided. That's probably a clue as to why it's shown as inhabited. That bit of knowledge absolutely thrilled him. He's an amateur archeologist, you know."

"You say the island disappeared, but that's not really what happened, is it? It grew and joined the mainland."

"A poor choice of words on my part, dear, but yes, the island did get connected to the land and became a contiguous part of Carteret County over a hundred years ago, although I'd have to check our records if you want a more exact date."

"Who could or would have connected it to the mainland that long ago? It must have been a big project."

"The United States Government, of course. They asked the county to declare it as a dump so that they could fill in the oxbow with river bottom, making the whole thing land."

"But why?"

"The ICW, of course. They were digging tons of good, rich dirt off the bottom and needed places up and down the river to dump it, exactly the way they're doing today as they re-dredge the parts that have silted in. In fact, if you go to the courthouse you'll find a recent permit issued to the Army Corps of Engineers to discharge and fill the property immediately adjacent to Derek's.

Taz paced. "You don't have any Oreos around here, do you?"

"Fig Newtons?" She opened an old Tupperware and offered it to him.

"Close enough, thank you."

She watched him think while he chewed the cookie. "What's so interesting, Taz? I'm intrigued by whatever it is that has you puzzled."

"You said there was some kind of a settlement there, and that the British raided it. Do you have any idea why?"

"Not really."

"Not really means sort of kind of."

She reached for a cookie but Taz held them out of her reach.

"You're bad," she laughed. "But cute enough that I suppose I could tell you what I think. You must try not laugh at me, though."

"I won't." He sat down on a stool in front of her and let her look hard in his eyes.

"All right, young Taz, I'm going to trust you with my biggest secret. It's just about the last one I have, I guess, so I suppose it's not such a big deal that it's also the biggest."

"I appreciate it."

"Of course, if I'm wrong it's not a secret worth having anyway, so who cares?" She gave an infectious laugh that made Taz laugh too. "I'll be dead soon anyway and no one speaks badly of the dead, do they?"

"I should hope not."

"Thank goodness my ex-husband already died or else he sure would." Then, to the ceiling, "May you have the afterlife you so richly deserve, Ernie." She laughed again and then said, "Pirates, Taz."

"What?"

"Well, at least you didn't laugh."

"Pirates? You mean like Captain Kidd and Henry Morgan?"

"Would you rather talk about Errol Flynn or Johnny Depp? Yes, pirates, and I mean the real pirates of the Caribbean. Buccaneers." She dragged out the word as though to control her growing excitement. "You know how they got that name, dear?"

"Something about a barbecue, I think."

"Yes, yes. On Hispaniola when they smoked their meat for cruises. The French word is Boucaner. Anyway, I think some of those buccaneers, or pirates, lived on that now-missing island. Do you know the countless stories surrounding the many pirates who worked out of this inlet?"

"I do."

"They're all true. Well, maybe not all of them, but there's no question this was a busy port for them. Being a pirate or privateer, which are only slightly different, was a primary occupation here in Beaufort. There were often big and festive parties that drew pirates from all up and down the eastern seaboard. How fun those must have been."

"I know a fair amount of your local history. So you think pirates lived on the island and the British raided it to kill or arrest them."

"I do. Think about the protection that oxbow offered, not only from the storms and current, but from their enemies. What better than an island, inaccessible by land yet with enough tall trees to get behind and hide the nice, fast sloops that most of them preferred for their speed and ability to travel in water too shallow for the king's frigates, schooners or brigantines to get close."

"It certainly makes sense."

"So maybe I'm not crazy? I kind of like being Crazy Lucy."

"I doubt you're crazy about this, and it was nice of you to trust your instincts enough to tell me, Miss Lucy."

"I'm a good judge of character. Lousy at choosing husbands, but that's different. Are you married?"

"No, I'm afraid I'd be one of those lousy husbands."

"A nice man like you should be married. I have a niece."

"Thanks again." Taz stood to leave. "Your theory has given me lots of work to do."

She rolled her wheelchair a foot closer to him. "You're going to leave? Just like that, huh? You don't want to hear the best part?"

He stopped. "May I have another Fig Newton?"

"Help yourself. They keep you regular."

"Terrific." Taz took another cookie and then gave her back the Tupperware. He sat down on the stool.

"The log of the English warship that deployed the troops carries a notation that they raided the island in late November of 1718, only to find it completely abandoned. 'The inhabitants appear to have rapidly dispersed' is the exact wording, 'having left all stores and wares as though fleeing some certainty of death.'"

Taz waited, looking into her eyes and wondering what might come next. "You have it memorized?"

Miss Lucy grinned. "Not ringing any bells yet?"

"Not really, Miss Lucy."

"Ding, ding, ding?"

"Sorry."

She reached over, whacked his head gently, and then said, "I think that island was quickly abandoned by a terrified handful of surviving pirates who'd suddenly found themselves without a captain because he'd been killed in battle. And these pirates had additional reasons to be afraid

142

because they all had a price on their heads from the Governor of Virginia. Think, Taz."

"Because Edward Teach–"

"Ah-hah!" She slapped her boney hand to her thigh so hard that Taz watched for pieces of both bones to go flying off. Then she laughed again. "Now you've got it. Their fearful Captain Teach, old Blackbeard himself, had been beheaded by the British just a few days earlier."

"My God."

"And I've always believed – and this is where I really get to sound like a crazy old bat – that the little island and oxbow that disappeared so long ago was the very last place of residence and refuge for our famous old rogue and his men."

"Blackbeard," Taz said softly.

She giggled. "It's hard not to love the way it sounds, isn't it?"

"Blackbeard," he said again, unable to completely come out from under the spell the name cast.

"Now go, young Taz, and good luck to you. Take my chart and my map and explore as diligently as I would if I wasn't so busy fighting off the liver-spotted men from my retirement home. Come back when you have time and tell me of your adventures. I still love to get my heart racing."

He smiled big as he leaned over and kissed her cheek.

"Just like that," she said, putting a hand over her heart. "I love when it races like that."

Chapter 28

Taz was so excited that he forced himself to drive slowly back to *Wasafiri*, pondering what Miss Lucy had said and wishing he'd gone ahead and told her that a piece of Tortuga Gold had, most likely, been found somewhere around the land that had once been an island.

Over the last several years there'd been a few other times when he'd faced the possibility of salvaging something of real historical significance, but if Miss Lucy was right, this treasure was far more than just historical, it was mythical as well, sought after for generations by those who felt sure Blackbeard had left it buried either on Ocracoke Island or one of the many places on the mainland that he called home.

After Theresa answered the intercom and opened the gate, he drove along Derek's driveway looking for any kind of clue as to what part of his property was once land and what used to be water. All but a few of the trees seemed to be about the same age, so they offered no evidence. The acreage looked like it had never been anything else but solid ground.

He stopped at the house and sat in the truck for a few minutes before getting out. Pete and Sam were on the front porch, watching and waiting for him. Derek and Theresa stepped out of the house and joined them. Taz got out and walked slowly toward the porch, still looking around.

"I really like it here, Derek. This is a nice town. Nice people."

"Except for the guy I've got digging holes. Theresa and I found new ones that must have been dug last night. Did you learn anything worthwhile in town?"

"I'm pretty sure I did."

"And?"

"The treasure of Tortuga Gold, if it's anywhere around here at all, isn't in the river. It was just a fluke that Buzz found a piece there, again assuming that's what happened."

"I thought we'd already established that."

Taz turned around and faced in the direction of the highway, "I think it's out there somewhere."

Everyone followed his gaze. Then Derek said, "That's pretty vague, since 'out there' in that direction goes all the way to California."

Taz smiled and sat down on a step. "You're still fighting me, aren't you Derek?"

"I'm merely pointing out what's obvious as we try to work our way to the truth."

"Really, is that what you call it?"

"What is that supposed to mean?"

"It means that somewhere along the line you should have mentioned your talk with Miss Lucy if you wanted to help us get to the truth."

"Miss Lucy?"

"Quiet, Pete. Taz is on another roll."

"Fun to watch?"

"Usually."

"Miss Lucy is a nice old lady I met in town this morning."

"She's a crackpot. Like so many others."

"Then why did you talk to her about this property before getting your dad to help you buy it so cheaply?"

"The county set the price and I had nothing to do with it other than writing the check. I'm very tired of the allegations of impropriety."

"Pretty lucky for you." He turned to Sam. "Derek bought this great parcel of land at the going rate for a dump site."

"And," Derek continued, "I already told you that I played on this land as a kid. I would come down on my skiff and spend long days digging around looking for arrowheads and the like. I showed some of them to you, if that helps prove a point I shouldn't even find necessary to make."

"And Miss Lucy?"

"I talked to her for no other reason than a strictly historical perspective. She was of little help to me."

"Miss Lucy," Taz said, now performing to the larger audience and pacing his make-believe stage, "believes pretty strongly that this nice piece of ground that Derek bought for its archeological value, which, by the way, is the very same ground Buzz is digging up for the very same reason, was the very last home of – I can't actually believe I'm going to say this – Captain Edward Teach. Or Edward Thatch, if you prefer. No one's quite sure."

"Who?"

"Blackbeard, Pete. Jeez, really, Taz? Blackbeard?"

"Wow."

"It's a foolish, foolish legend," Derek said. "A dreamer's wet dream. And even if Blackbeard did once live on my land, it was probably for a very short time. There's never been any proof or evidence that he even left a treasure of any kind anywhere, by the way. I've never once believed it."

"Maybe he did and maybe he didn't."

"What are you thinking, Taz?"

"Just that Blackbeard never had a chance to buy his way out of his final jam the way he so often did by bribing the Governor of North Carolina. He went to his last battle fully confident that his local knowledge and sailing skills would ensure a defeat of the small British contingent that came after him, probably expecting to come home that evening with another captured ship or two and all of their stores."

"So you're saying he died too unexpectedly to do anything but leave his treasure behind and lost to all time."

"I think it's a good theory, Sam. But even if he knew he was going to die, he kept quiet. Just before they engaged the British, a shipmate who ultimately survived the battle came back and said that he'd asked Blackbeard if his wife, Mary, knew where he'd buried his treasure, to which Blackbeard threw back his smoking head–"

"Smoking head?"

"Yes, Pete. Blackbeard was big and fearsome looking, with a long beard that he braided into pigtails and tied with ribbons. He took on the custom of putting smoking rope under his hat and hanging slow-burning fuses around his face so he would look for all the world like the devil himself."

"That is so cool. An early practice of psyching out your enemy, I guess."

"I suppose. Anyway, Blackbeard laughed at the question and said that no one but him and the devil knew where the treasure was.'"

"So there really is a buried treasure?"

"I believe there could be, and that it could be close to where we're standing, but as I've said before, burying something creates problems. Sam, what do you think?"

"I think he could have thought he was invincible, and that's why he buried it. Maybe he felt the governor would continue to offer passive protection forever. Maybe he liked playing in the dirt, who knows?"

"My question," Pete said, "is why aren't more people than just Buzz and us looking for it?"

"You must mean, why aren't more people looking *here*? Because people have scoured this whole area of North Carolina for centuries looking for it."

"Yes, I mean here."

"Because the information Miss Lucy told me is arcane knowledge and largely intuitive, based on her decades of studying the history of Carteret

County. Plus, this property is private with very restricted access. Derek's made sure of that. This secret is what you've been hiding all along, isn't it Derek?"

"I stand by what I've already told you."

"I really don't think Derek believes there's any gold," Theresa added. "And he's shown you what really does interest him."

"Don't bother to defend me, Theresa. These men have treasure fever and there's no talking them out of it."

"Last night I mentioned gold and your first question, with a little panic I might add, was 'what do you know?'"

"I meant that in a general sense. But it is true that I'm always concerned about protecting the archeology here. It's very difficult because almost everyone wants to rush at a dig and tear it up."

"Okay, Derek, this is your land and it's up to you to make the call. I'm not going to stand here and bullshit with you all afternoon. I think it's reasonable to believe that the Tortuga Gold disappeared because Blackbeard took it off the *Espiritu del Mar* before it sunk. I also think it's reasonable to believe that it's a part, or maybe all, of his treasure, a treasure that might actually be on your property. Sam and Pete and I would very much like to help you find it. Pete?"

"Very much. Mind if I say very, very much?"

"Not at all. But Derek has to start cooperating. And he has to remember that there's a vicious killer here who is racing us to find this same treasure, and I'm willing to bet that the second he finds a gold coin on your property instead of in the river he's going to kill both you and Theresa. Hell, out here in the wilderness, who would ever know, and how long would it take for your bodies to be discovered?"

"Derek, I'm–"

"I'm sorry, Theresa, but I'm afraid that I really did mean to scare you, because Buzz is a bad man and your husband is just about to frustrate me to the point of my disappearance."

"Our disappearance."

"Sorry Sam. Our disappearance."

"You think about it, Derek. We'll be on the boat waiting to find out if you're going to cooperate with us or not."

"And having a beer."

"That's right, Pete. And we'll be having a beer."

"Or two."

"Yup."

Chapter 29

"I'll pass on the beer," Sam said as the three men climbed aboard *Wasafiri* and Pete and Taz flopped down in the main salon.

"I'm not giving good odds that Derek's going to cooperate, Sam. Either he's totally lying to us or just doesn't care. Either way we might as well relax and savor our proximity to the Tortuga Gold. My guess is we're as close as we'll ever get until it's found and put it in a museum."

"I won't want to see it behind a big, thick piece of glass that's reflecting my big stupid head alongside a hundred other gawking faces. That's not my idea of discovery."

"Mine neither."

"I'm going to clean up." Sam went below.

Pete watched him leave. When he was sure Sam was out of earshot he said, "He's sure acting weird."

"He doesn't deal very well with disappointment."

"You mean not finding the gold?"

"I mean not getting to discuss Gordie's death with Buzz."

"Discuss?"

"A very brief discussion in which Sam would say something like, 'You killed Gordie' and then Buzz would say things like 'Ow, ouch, and please stop hitting me."

"Oh."

"The three of us were wonderfully close for a long time. I can't say which of us was closer to whom, but Sam and I both loved Gordie a lot. It was Sam, though, who assumed the role of protector, right from the start. So of course he takes Gordie's death as a personal failing, especially since he was so close by when it happened."

"But he had no idea."

"You think he takes solace in that?"

"I suppose not."

They sat in silence and listened to the shore birds and cicadas starting up their evening rituals.

"So how are you handling it, Taz?"

"By not talking about it. I said too much already."

"Sorry."

After a very long stretch of silence, Pete said, "I'm really frustrated."

"I'm happy to say that I can't help you there," Taz laughed. "I don't think there's any porn onboard either."

"Ha, ha, funny. You know what I mean. It would have been so cool to hunt for treasure. Imagine if we actually found it?"

"It would have been a kick, for sure. I'm sorry that this hasn't really been much of an adventure for you. I'll make you a promise that you will get to see lots of excitement, though. Okay? Trust me on that."

"Yeah, but treasure."

"I know."

"Especially Blackbeard's. He sounds so amazing."

"He really was quite a character. When Lt. Maynard and his men set out from the Chesapeake Bay to find and kill him, assuming such a thing to be possible, Blackbeard had all this local knowledge that should have allowed him to elude them."

"Did he die because he was overconfident in that?"

"I suppose. He miscalculated the tides at Ocracoke Inlet. And if that wasn't enough, he got suckered onto Maynard's ship for his last battle."

"Suckered?"

"Maynard had his men hide below so that Blackbeard would assume his cannons had killed them all. It must have been one heck of a surprise when they rushed out to greet the boarding party."

"Who killed Blackbeard?"

"He was shot five times by pistols and cut more than two dozen times by cutlasses and daggers."

"A painful death."

"It would have been if that had killed him."

"He lived through all that?"

"Yeah, but didn't quite survive having his head chopped off."

"Wow."

Taz lowered his voice. "After they killed old Blackbeard they threw his headless body overboard, which, it was said by many who observed it, swam three complete laps around his ship before swimming toward the bottom."

"I seriously doubt it."

"And Maynard took his head back to Virginia, where he impaled it on a pole where the Hampton River and James River converge – Blackbeard's Point, they still call the place today – which is why, some say, the rather pissed off ghost of Blackbeard still wanders this area looking in vain for his severed head."

Taz lowered his voice to one of eerie spookiness. "His flagship, the Queen Anne's Revenge, was found a couple miles from here at the mouth of the Beaufort inlet in just 20 feet of water. One of his homes – he had several to accommodate his fourteen wives – was, according to Miss Lucy, just a few yards away from where you sit right now, Pete, so I suppose that if the headless ghost of this vicious pirate were to hang around a place, this...matey...would...be...it."

Just then Taz jabbed Pete hard in the ribs and drove him to his feet.

"Shit, what is it with you guys scaring me? How about growing up."

Taz fell over sideways on the sofa laughing.

"I'm taking *my* truck and going to town for a little peace."

Just then Sam came up the steps from below, dressed nicely in khaki pants, a collared shirt, and new boat shoes. He'd shaven his beard and trimmed his scraggly hair.

"My God," Pete said in amazement, "Look at you. Who would have thought you could look so human?"

"That's funny, twerp."

"You do look almost human, Sam. What's the occasion?"

"Nothing really, Taz. It's been a while since I cleaned up, that's all, and the beard was getting tiresome. Besides, I wanted to look good for photos just in case Derek did come around and we got a chance to find the gold."

"Does that might make sense to you, Pete?"

"Yeah, I suppose so."

"You're actually buying that story?"

"I'm...well, I guess I'm not all that sure since I don't know Sam like you do. I think that makes me the luckier of the two of us." He laughed and Sam rolled his eyes.

"Let Pete see you smile, Sam."

"I'm really not in a smiling mood."

"Come on. Just a little smile, like the one you'll use in your mug shot."

"What do mean, Taz?"

"Sam's cleaned up so he'll look good when he gets arrested. People tend to be influenced by the mug shot that shows up in the news, and some of those same people end up on juries. If they remember you looking friendly and nice the first time they saw your photo they tend to remember that at your trial. Come on, just a little smile?"

"I said no."

"But why would Sam get arrested?"

"For killing Buzz."

Pete jumped again. "What? When did he do that?"

"He hasn't. Not yet. Is that your plan for tonight, Sam?"

Sam mumbled something as he sat down.

"I didn't quite catch that."

"Yes, Taz, for God's sake, tonight. Derek could throw us out of here any minute now and I'm not leaving without Buzz's scalp."

Taz walked over and as gently as possible sat down beside Sam, smiling.

"Come on, Sam, you know we were never meant to be killers. We're just not the type."

"It's a small step."

"But we agreed a long time ago, you and me, that we'd try to never get anyone killed, and that if it did happen it should only be by accident or when absolutely and unquestionably necessary, and even then within the law as much as possible."

"Yeah, but Buzz murdered Gordie."

"You think I don't know that? You think my insides aren't as kinked as a cheap hose knowing my best friend's murderer is hiding out a couple hundred yards from me?"

"Then you should understand."

"I do, and you should understand that I've got a plan to get justice for Gordie."

"Justice isn't possible."

"But there's nothing noble in your goal, Sam. It's nothing short of cold-blooded murder."

"Those are just words."

"Words that carry a high price, and I don't just mean jail."

"Gordie would do it for me. Or you."

"No, Sam, Gordie would not." Taz kept smiling as if determined to do it. "Vengeance is poison. Gordie knew that and so do you."

"It's hard for me to think of anything else."

"Of course it is, but you have to let it go. If not, you know I won't be a part of it."

"Since I left Key West I've been thinking about what to do, knowing full well that you'd draw the line."

"But you still decided to go through with it? Even though it will end us?"

Sam stared at the floor in front of his feet, and then quietly said, "I guess this is where we part ways."

Taz got up and walked away, his back to Sam while he thought it through. Then he turned and just as quietly said, "I don't have a choice."

"I know, Taz. Look, I'm sorry to put you in a tough spot. You'll ship my gear to me?"

Taz had managed to keep a smile on his face, but it was looking more and more difficult. "Damn it, Sam, I....yes. Of course I will."

"Know where to find me?"

"Where you've always been, I suppose. Somewhere on the other side of safety. Hopefully not in jail."

Sam walked over and hugged him. "I love you, Brother." Then he turned to Pete and said, "I've watched over Taz since the day he was born. It's your job now. Do it well, and good luck. Try to keep up with him."

Pete just stared at the two of them as Sam moved sadly toward the door. When he opened it Taz said, "To adventure, Sam."

Sam stopped and turned. "And to those of us with big enough balls to seek it."

They all waited for Sam to leave, with none of them wanting it to happen.

He finally moved, and when he did Taz jumped up. "How about one last dinner out together? Buzz won't go anywhere before we get back, Sam. And besides, you're not that keen on jailhouse food."

Sam smiled slightly. "That does sound nice. I'd like that. One last meal together. You can come too, twerp."

"Are you two really brothers?"

"Don't you see the family resemblance?"

"Not in the least."

"We have different fathers, but we're brothers all the same. Come on, let's go spend a big chunk of Sam's money. He's not going to need his fortune while serving twenty to life."

Chapter 30

It was well after midnight when Taz and Pete came back from town. They'd woken Theresa by repeatedly buzzing the intercom to get the gate opened, but Derek was waiting on the dock as they walked up singing a two-part variation of an old Elvis song. He was too alert to have been sleeping.

"I've made my decision," Derek said.

"I'm in love," Taz sang as the duo danced along toward him. "I'm all shook up."

"A bottle in front of me–"

"A frontal lobotomy–"

"Hey, hey, yeah."

"Oh, man, we should start a band, Pete." Then Taz walked straight up to Derek and flopped his head against Derek's chest. "You decided to stop being a dick?"

Pete laughed and Taz did too.

"You're drunk, Mister Keaton."

"Yup. But Pete drove us home. He's a better singer anyway."

 "Where's Sam?"

"I meant driver."

"Pete, where is Sam?"

"Arrested."

"In jail?"

"If not," Taz laughed, "then check the Empire State Building for a giant furry man batting down airplanes."

"Really?"

"Don't be ridiculous. Sam couldn't have gotten to New York this fast."

"Sam had a little run-in with the law."

"What happened?"

Taz turned and wandered to the edge of the pier.

"Hold on, Holmes," Pete said as he went after Taz and then guided him back, where he once again leaned against Derek. "A guy at the bar aggravated Sam until he hit him."

153

"Hard!" Taz added.

"Yes, Sam hit him hard."

"It's difficult to imagine anyone stupid enough to pick a fight with Sam. Any idea who it was?"

Taz looked up and smiled, his swollen face now catching the moonlight. "Meet Mister Stupid." He rubbed his jaw. "Ow."

"I'm kind of surprised you're not Mister Coma." Pete turned back to Derek. "Taz ground on Sam's nerves so much that even I wanted him to hit him."

"That was the point, Petey. But did you notice how my big ol' brother tried to pull that punch of his tire-sized fist?"

"I saw you intentionally step into it."

"Yup. I had to be convincing enough to get him arrested."

"So Sam's in jail?"

"Safely so, Derek. And Taz is lucky he's not in a hospital."

"I *hate* fighting with Sam. So, Derek, are you still a dick? And stop moving."

"You're a ridiculous drunk."

"Yeah, but in the immortal words of Winston Churchill, tomorrow I'll be drunk and you'll...wait, that's not right. Anyway, your answer please, sir."

Derek pushed Taz off his chest, but Taz fell right back against him. "I was going to let you stay," he said, mostly to Pete, "because Theresa felt safer having Sam around. I'm not sure what to do now."

"Pete, he doesn't think you and I can project him. Protect him."

"You're right I don't."

Taz laughed, which made him grimace in pain. He grabbed his face. "Ouch! Well that's honest."

"Let me think about it until the morning."

"Fine. I don't feel much like talking now anyway. Pete, has the swelling gone down any?"

"You haven't kept the ice on it."

"Nighty-night," Taz said as Derek walked away. Then to Pete, "I think I'm going to lose a tooth."

"If you just lose one then I'd say you're lucky. I couldn't believe that Sam's fists just about covered your whole face." Pete laughed.

"Yuck it up, laughing boy."

"I am."

"Next time is your turn."

"Wait, what? How often does this happen?"

Taz spit out a mouthful of blood. "Once a year or so."

"Really?"

"Maybe twice. Sammy's a good brother."

"I can tell."

"But he doesn't always play nice with others."

"With people like Buzz. I get it."

"So I occasionally have to get him penned up somewhere." He started laughing and blood shot forcefully out of his mouth.

"What's funny?"

"I just had an image of terrified jailors worrying about Sam bending the bars and coming after them."

"He's not that strong."

"Are you *sure*?"

"No."

"He's probably not. Dump me into bed, Pete. Or the river. It's been a tough night. I'll do the same for you when it's your turn."

"Such a wonderful thing to look forward to."

IT WAS almost two in the morning when Derek shook Theresa and woke her up. He'd paced and pondered and finally came to a decision that he couldn't allow her to challenge or stop.

"You should take these pills, Honey."

"You called me honey. Why?"

"They'll help you sleep."

She looked confused. "I *was* asleep."

"I know. But you've been so worried about this Buzz fellow and sleeping so badly since this started that you were bound to wake up before long. So I figured these will let you sleep through the rest of the night."

She rubbed her eyes and took the pills from his hand. "Buzz scares me, Derek. When I saw him I thought he was homeless, and that's all I noticed at the time, a man who needed help."

"You're nice like that."

"But thinking back on how he looked, well, he's pretty scary."

Derek sat on the bed and rubbed her arm. "Nothing's going to happen."

"He could crash right into this house tonight and attack us. TK made a good point when he asked how long it would be before anyone noticed we were hurt, or dead."

"He's not going to attack us."

"He killed TK's friend Gordie."

"I know. Here, wash down the pills with this water and get some sleep."

She took the pills and slid down into the sheets. "Where are you going?"

"I'll read downstairs for awhile. And think about whether or not I should allow those misfits to stay here and look for gold."

"Do you think it's possible the gold is really here?"

"Absolutely not. I am willing to believe that Buzz found a piece of gold on or near our property, but as we've all said there are lots of ways it could have gotten here. I've never found a single gold *anything*, not even in the big excavation, so it's hard to have any faith that a treasure exists, especially since I've been digging around here for most of my life. Good-night, Theresa. I'll be right downstairs."

"Good-night."

Derek waited an hour before tip-toeing back into the bedroom to make sure Theresa was asleep. He dug out some old clothes, dressed, and then went out of the house through the garage.

He walked cautiously into the ominous darkness surrounding his home, knowing pretty much where Buzz had to be living in order to search where he did and watch the house without being spotted. He found Buzz's little campsite, even though it was masterfully disguised and carefully hidden.

Buzz wasn't there, which meant he was probably out spending the long night digging somewhere on the vast acreage of their property. Derek thought about looking for him, but in truth, Buzz scared him too.

At dawn Buzz would most likely come back and sleep, and then it would be easier, with much less risk.

Derek crouched behind a small jungle of untamed vegetation. In his lap he cradled the double-bladed battle-axe he'd discovered years ago and carefully restored. The heavy head of twin blades gleamed like diamonds and the oak handle he'd made fit well in his hand.

In his mind he pictured a pirate of long ago, boarding a magnificent sailing vessel and swinging this very same axe in battle. He could see him rushing along the wooden decks, terrifying the crew as he waded through them, crushing skulls and splintering bone and gashing flesh.

Derek waited in the darkness, playing the scene over and over in his mind and determined to wield the battle-axe just as viciously.

Chapter 31

Taz and Pete slowly walked the two hundred yards from *Wasafiri* to the Holmes' house. When they rounded the corner they found Theresa sitting in a rocker on the front porch.

"Good morning, Theresa."

"Good morning, Pete. Nice face, TK. Tough date last night?"

He smiled. "That's the problem with liking feisty women."

"It looks a lot better this morning, by the way."

"Thanks, Pete, but I feel as though the Hunchback is banging my skull like a bell. Can you get him off me?"

"No Hunchback around, buddy. You're good."

"I'll get you an aspirin and make you boys a new pot of fresh ground coffee."

"Thank God for coffee. And aspirin. And nice, pretty women who have both."

"Are you ever serious, TK?"

"About what?"

"About, gosh, I don't know. Anything."

"I'll give it some serious thought and get back to you."

"That's what I mean."

"Sorry. In all seriousness – and I mean it – I try hard not to be serious. I have the choice, like most of us, to be happy. It makes no sense to me to frown instead of laugh."

"It must be nice to live like that and have fun all the time."

"It takes practice and dedication." He made a painful grin. "It's a lot of work, and especially without coffee."

"Have a seat. I'll be back soon."

"Is Derek up yet?"

She stopped and hesitated before saying "I think he got up early and went to town, but I'm not sure. He didn't leave a note like he usually does."

"Is his car still here? Maybe in that building over there?"

"Good lord, there's no way he'd ever put a car in there. Be back in a minute."

Taz and Pete sat down.

"Does my face really look better?"

"Yeah, it does. And by the way, you take a hit really well. I was going to say that last night but decided to wait so that you'd remember."

"You'll probably never see me that drunk again. I usually have a few stiff pops before taunting Sam into teeing off on me, but it got away from me last night because of his talk of vengeance. That and the fact that Buzz is close enough to make it a possibility."

"I understand. A lot of emotions going on in you. You're a funny drunk, though."

"Yeah? Being a funny drunk ranks right up there with being the smartest kid in woodshop."

"Still want to start a band?"

"Did I say that?"

"In between choruses of "I'm all shook up.""

"Off-key?"

"Terribly."

"In that case let's get to something I know how to do." He pointed out towards the driveway. "Now, assuming Derek doesn't toss us out on our ears, we'll use that old barn as a solid reference to start a search grid. We'll measure it out precisely so we don't miss a spot or over-search another."

"What will be looking for, besides the gold, of course?"

"We have seismic equipment that should help us determine what was filled a hundred years ago when they dug the Intracoastal Waterway. Then we'll know where the island was."

"We can do that?"

"Oh, sure. It'll be easy, actually, and certainly easier than diving out of a helicopter hovering over the very hard deck of a very big ship."

"That was kind of fun. It wasn't really an audition, either, but is that what convinced you to let me join the team?"

"That was always Sam's decision."

"Really? Right from the start? I thought you were the boss."

"I suppose I am, but I delegate a lot, especially about the people we work with. If I like someone I sometimes let that blind my judgment. Sam doesn't have that problem."

"I bet."

"A safe bet. He always had his finger on your eject button."

"I probably didn't help things by giving him static when we first met."

"I'm actually surprised you made it through that without some sort of permanent injury, but I'm positive it impressed Sam that you stood up to him. I've never seen anyone do it before."

"Stupid of me."

"Yup. But when he finally said you would belong on the team it was like swearing an oath to you."

"Nice."

"You'll be in on the fun from now on, and you'll see how far Sam will go to protect you while we're doing it."

"I'm looking forward to it."

Taz laughed. "You're killing me, Pete. Here you are in the middle of a quest for one of the most mythical treasures of all times, like looking for the Titanic or King Tut's Tomb or Noah's Ark, and all you can say is that you're looking forward to what's next."

"You know what I mean. After last night I don't think Derek's going to let us stay. You did call him a dick."

"That I do remember. But I said it in a nice way, right?"

"No."

"We'll get to do this. I'll find a way. I'm a man of contingency plans, Pete, so even when you think we've lost – *especially* when you think we've lost – expect me to pull a groundhog out of my hat. And before you bother to ask, a rabbit is too easy."

"I'm going to hold you to that."

"So let's go back to work and assume we're able to determine what was filled and, with luck, how much. Then we'll probably just have to search the areas that were only filled a few feet."

"Your logic?"

"I've always doubted the idea of pirates burying their treasure. Blackbeard was more likely than most to do it because he lived in relative safety."

"He had the locals on the take?"

"Even the governor protected him because he got a share of the booty."

"That's such a fun word."

"Even so, I suspect it's more likely Blackbeard would have put the treasure in water that was shallow enough to have been a good accessible hiding place."

"A man of the sea puts it under water at a very low tide?"

"So that it'd be completely hidden yet still accessible."

"I'm getting excited again. You really do think the gold is here, don't you, Taz?"

"I'm sure the gold is still somewhere, and this theory seems like the most logical explanation for what happened to the enormous amount of treasure on that ship. Everything else I can imagine has someone spending it at some point."

"Another ship could have sailed off with it."

Theresa stepped out and said, "Just a few more minutes, guys."

159

"Black for both of us, thanks. But Pete, if another ship took it away, again, they would have spent it or melted it down. But there's no record of the Tortuga Gold being melted down, and no one's ever spent a single coin of it, so yes, when added to the location of the ship's sinking, the pirate activity in the area, the coincidence of Blackbeard's treasure and the Tortuga Gold both missing, and the private ownership of this large property that means it's one of the only places no one else has been able to search, logic almost dictates that it's here."

"You apply logic to everything, don't you?"

"It was my favorite subject in college, although my under-graduate degree is in mathematics. There was a time I could use exponential generating functions to find a closed formula for recurrence relations in my head. Not with today's painful head, but a normal day's head."

"I used to be able to do that too."

Taz smiled. "But it's been years since I've even bothered to balance my checkbook. Logic, though? Yeah, I use it everyday."

"I'm learning that. I'll be glad to get Sam back. I'm not sure I can protect you like he can."

"No one could, or would. He's amazing. And as I said, he'll also protect you, now more than ever after not being there to save Gordie."

"That's, wow, that's nice to know."

"Pretty comforting." Taz looked up and then off in the distance. "Pete, take a look over there."

"Holy Jesus."

Taz stood up. "Doesn't look holy or like Jesus. This certainly gives me a bad feeling."

"Jesus."

They went down the steps as Derek walked slowly up to the house. He was shaking just slightly and a little disoriented, like he was kind of lost mentally. He did not seem afraid, though, or ashamed.

He was covered in blood.

"Where have you been, Derek? Painting a barn or a fire truck, I hope."

"Keaton."

"You have blood all over you."

Derek looked down and almost seemed surprised. "Apparently I do."

"So you decided to just take the law into your hands and kill Buzz. Or is he out there in the woods wounded and suffering?"

"You said it the other night, Keaton. Treasure conveys through bloodshed. Yes, I killed him to preserve mine, just another step in the preservation I've done all of my life."

"What treasure? You don't even believe in the gold."

160

"The treasure of the peace I had here before he showed up. The security. Excuse me. I want to clean up." He walked up two steps and then stopped. "You won't tell the sheriff, Keaton, because it would be the last thing you'd ever do on my land. You would prevent yourself from finding the gold."

He went inside. Theresa screamed. Then she cried. Then she ran out the door and down the driveway.

"Should I go after her, Taz?"

"I don't think so. She's got stuff to figure out and just needs a quiet place. Let her be."

"Sure."

Taz shrugged. "This is a hell of a mess."

"I couldn't believe all that blood."

"Let's go get Sam out of jail. There's no reason for him to be there now."

They wandered slowly to the truck and drove off, passing Theresa as she loped around in circles on a patch of lawn.

Chapter 32

Derek stood on the porch next to Theresa as Taz, Sam and Pete returned from town and parked the truck. He'd changed clothes and cleaned up, but even from a distance Taz could see that he hadn't been able to scrub the stain of murder from his eyes.

"I've seen that look too many times," Taz muttered as they got out and walked slowly toward them.

"It sure makes a man ugly. Thanks again for saving me from it, Taz. I'm sorry about your face."

"It was my turn to protect you. Let's go see what he has to say."

They stopped at the bottom step.

"How do you feel, Derek?"

"I'm fine, Keaton, and here's what I propose. I'll let you search my land, within reason. For your part you'll need to appreciate that I was merely protecting myself and my wife. He was, after all, a threat. You said so yourself."

"It's not my place to judge anyone, Derek. How about you, Pete?"

"Mine neither."

"Sam actually has the most experience with the judicial system. What do you think, Big Man?"

Sam shrugged.

Derek waited in the silence. Then, "Fine, so I'm going to assume we're in accord. Be gentle on my property and remember that this isn't some jungle or desert or war zone. It's my home."

He walked inside. Theresa stood a half minute longer before joining him, leaving the three men staring after them.

Sam was the first to break the silence. "That guy really killed Buzz?"

"Thank goodness I can't testify to that, but he said he did."

"He sure looked the part when he came walking up," Pete said.

"It's just so hard to imagine him pulling it off. Buzz is–"

"*Was*, apparently."

"Buzz was almost as big as me."

They walked slowly to the dock and boarded *Wasafiri*.

"Derek's right, you know, in that it was justified to some extent as self-defense. Buzz was clearly an intruder, and although he hadn't yet been convicted of Gordie's death, odds are good that he would have been, which means he was already guilty of killing the little girl and Gordie. I guess I'm guilty too."

"Of what?" Sam cracked open a beer.

"A little early, isn't it?"

"A just-released-from-jail beer. So what role did you play, Taz?"

"I was the one who scared him enough to do something so awful."

"All you did was tell him the truth. He didn't have to take it on himself to kill him. He owns a phone and could have used it to call the police."

"Come on, Sam, Derek knew as well as we do that the police could have only arrested Buzz for trespassing, and maybe vagrancy. That wouldn't have kept him in jail long."

"You did this, didn't you, Taz?"

"What's that Pete?"

"This was the plan you talked about. This is how you managed to avenge Gordie's death without our getting our hands dirty."

Taz turned away from Pete. "My mouth hurts, Sam, Next time try hitting me in the stomach, just for a change. And grow your beard back, you too-handsome devil."

"You manipulated him."

"Leave it alone, Pete."

"It's okay, Sam." Taz turned to Pete. "A man, Pete, any man, has to have it in him to be a cold-blooded killer like that. I showed him the cliff and gave him a push, but he would have jumped on his own."

"A guy who could do that," Sam said, "has other dark secrets in his past, too, I bet."

"Then how about me? How bad should I feel? I mean, I don't feel bad, but maybe I should."

"You did nothing wrong, Pete. And I imagine that one day the courts will decide whether or not Derek was justified. Things like this don't stay secret for long."

Taz stepped to *Wasafiri*'s port windows and pointed toward the far side of Derek's property. "He walked back from that direction. Let's go take care of the body."

Sam took a quick glance and then finished his beer. "I can do it alone. There's no point all of us getting into this mess."

"The way we discussed on the drive back?"

"Yeah. I need a gold coin."

Taz went below and came back with a gold doubloon. He rubbed it adoringly and then handed it to Pete. "This one holds lots of good memories for Gordie."

Pete's eyes popped open. "Wow, so this is what we're looking for."

Taz handed it to him. "Careful, Pete. They're addictive. This is a doubloon. That's what the English call them. We're looking for Spanish escudos, but yeah, gold like this."

Pete passed it on to Sam with a quick sort of reluctance.

"Thank you for doing this, Sam. Don't forget the stuff in the truck, okay? And don't let Derek see you."

Sam walked off without saying another word.

"An oasis of calm in a very noisy world, Pete."

"Sam?"

"Yeah."

"Am I right, Taz?"

"About what?"

"About you manipulating Derek?"

"What do you think? Because that's what it comes down to. What I say doesn't matter."

Pete leaned against the wall with his back to Taz, staring out at the ICW and the boats she carried along with her current. After awhile he said, "I think we should really consider starting that band you mentioned."

"Apparently we need a singer."

Pete walked over and held out his hand. "Not sure why, but I want a grip-to-grip from you."

Taz slowly reached out and the two men shook hands. They squeezed tightly. Then Pete smiled and said, "So what do we do now, boss?"

Taz looked out the windows at the sky. "It's a beautiful day to look for what might be the greatest treasure of all time. Are you ready?"

"Yes."

"I said," Taz repeated, raising his arms like a revivalist preacher. "Are you ready, boy? Are you ready to find some gold?"

Pete couldn't help but laugh as he said "Yes, sir, I am. I don't want to sound too excited, man, but I'm naked-with-Mary-Ellen ready."

"Then what do you say we get started."

"Wa-hoo!"

They grinned like young fools as they climbed up to the bridge deck of *Wasafiri*, which had four crates on it that Sam had loaded aboard while Taz and Pete made their way up from Venezuela. They'd opened one the other night to get the dive gear, underwater metal detectors, and probes, but Taz and Pete used the forward boom to lower the other three crates to the dock.

"What is all this stuff?"

"These, Pete, are a few of the tools of your new trade. It's the best equipment that exists, all of it military spec or better. If we're looking for needles in haystacks, water in the desert, or nuclear warheads buried underground, almost anything at all, this stuff should do it."

"Cool."

"Help me with this seismic pounder."

"That's not a very technical name."

"Sam has trouble saying the word, the way others mispronounce cavalry as calvary and nuclear as nucular, so we just call it the pounder. Feel free to correct his usage if you like."

"I'll pass."

"Good call. And it's heavy because it has to send a big, variable shock wave through the ground."

"Of course it does."

"Then by measuring the speed, resonance, variations, and dead spots we'll learn a lot about what's underneath."

"How do we move this stuff around the property?"

"That's why you have a truck. And don't let Derek give you any crap about driving across his grass, either."

"Okay."

"In fact, go get it right now and drive it down to the dock. I'll study the maps and pinpoint a good place to set up and start."

"Look, Mom, I'm a treasure hunter."

"To adventure, Pete. Let's get moving."

Pete ran for his truck while Taz unrolled Miss Lucy's chart and map. They were so old, brittle, and valuable that he felt honored to be entrusted him with them. Both of them showed the island that no longer existed, along with the large slough of water that at one time kept it separated from the mainland behind it.

The map also showed the abandoned settlement noted on the county's first survey, but only in rough detail with an approximated location of two buildings. The navigational chart, on the other hand, hardly showed anything at all on the land other than a tree to be used as a range marker by captains making the dangerous turn into an adjacent waterway.

He looked back at the map and found that it, too, had a notation about the tree, saying that a large stone was at the bottom of the tree to be used as a reference for measuring distance, much like a modern concrete monument or surveyor's pin.

Taz figured it was as good a place to start as any, especially since it would help locate the past and current buildings and contribute to a better sense of bearings.

Sam came back aboard looking disgusted. "I took care of Buzz. Jesus what a mess. Derek used an ax on him. He used it a lot."

"Where's the ax now?"

"It's still out there. I hid it close by."

"That's good. Did you find any gold?"

"He only had the one piece that I saw in Key West. No more. Here it is, along with the gold coin you gave me to use."

Taz stared at the two bloody coins in Sam's hand, particularly the one he'd just taken off Buzz.

"Tortuga Gold," Taz said with quiet reverence. "I...did you ever think you'd see a piece of it, Sam?"

"I told you I almost crapped my pants when I saw it. I don't think I've ever been so excited."

"Funny, I'm almost afraid to touch it."

"Few hands have held it since it was struck at the mint, I'd bet on that. Probably just whoever lost it, Buzz, me, and now you. Here." He dropped the coin into Taz's hand.

"Tortuga Gold. I still don't believe it."

"I see the equipment's down. Want to go look for more? I know I do."

"Yes. Let me have the other coin I gave you earlier."

Sam delicately put that coin in his hand too.

"You can have this piece of Tortuga Gold, Sam. In case we don't find any more. You earned it." He went to drop it into Sam's hand, but Sam closed it into a fist and said, "I don't want it. Gordie got killed over that piece of gold."

"Then put it away for some other purpose down the road. Are you hungry?"

"You're kidding, right? We're finally ready to go after that gold and you think I want to take time to eat?"

"Sorry. But go get cleaned up a little and throw all those clothes away."

"I like this shirt."

Just then Pete came back aboard and said, "Holy shit, Sam!"

"Okay, I'll throw away the shirt."

"Thank you."

An hour later they and a few cases of equipment were in Derek's front yard looking for some indication of the original location of the big tree shown so well on the chart, but they didn't see anything that gave a clue.

"I don't appreciate Pete driving over my yard," Derek said as he walked up.

"Yeah, we're really sorry about that. Look, Derek, once upon a time in a magical land of pirates there was a tree somewhere around here that was used as a reference by ships and surveyors alike. If we knew where that tree was we could measure out to where the water used to be and save a lot of time."

"I bet it would. Probably preserve my property better, too."

"We could certainly be more careful if we knew. I bet Miss Lucy might be able to help locate it if you don't know where it was."

"I know exactly where it was. The tree was long gone when I bought the property, but I did receive a survey that showed its location exactly. Since I thought it might be useful in my archeological explorations I marked it by driving a metal rod into the ground."

"Great. Let me take a look at the old survey."

"I lost it. Actually the wind caught it and blew it away while I was driving the rod into the ground. I was regrettably careless that day."

"I'll say. Where's the rod?"

"Over here." He walked about fifty feet away and then stopped. "I marked the rod with this birdbath, which I centered precisely over it so that I wouldn't ever have to move it or dig up the ground covering the rod."

"Smart."

"I thought so."

"Sam, how about you and Pete setting up radius rings using this birdbath as the center. Since we now have a solid reference point you can measure out to where the water once was. Make your sweeps in five foot increments."

"Will do."

"While you're doing that I'll measure over to where the old buildings were noted on the map and see what I can find. How are you feeling, Derek?"

"I'm tired, but relieved."

"What you did was wrong."

"So you say. But it wasn't you and your wife who were being threatened."

"Still wrong.

"Doesn't really matter anymore, now does it?"

"Your guilt to live with."

"Just so you know, Keaton, I've searched for years for the old buildings on the map you have, but there's nothing here. I think someone must have carried away the remains and used them for something else. Either that or they were washed away by a storm, or removed when the government filled the land. I have no idea why they would have spent the money to do that, though, so I'm guessing it's one of the first options."

"What's in that old barn over there?"

"Stuff. My personal stuff."

"It looks old, but certainly not old enough to have been part of the original settlement. Did you move it here along with the house?"

"No, I just built it to look old. It adds an air of history, or at least I hope it does."

"It does. You didn't happen to build it on top of a treasure, did you?"

"I'm an archeologist, Keaton, even if just an amateur one. Don't you think my first consideration in any construction project would have been the historical ramifications?"

"I'm just making small talk to calm me down. Getting excited about finding something that no other living person has ever seen."

"I'm pretty sure you'll find nothing, so don't get too excited."

"Sam said he almost crapped his pants when he first saw Tortuga Gold, so if I pee in mine it will be a clue."

"Wonderful imagery, that. Be damned careful with my landscaping."

Chapter 33

By early evening the three of them had managed to make a rough sketch of a big chunk of Derek's property. The seismic soundings had enabled them to draw accurate topographic lines that showed what had always been solid ground and what had once been the slough that ran behind the island.

"We're lucky that the majority of Derek's acreage was always a part of the mainland," Sam said. "That really cuts down on the search area since we've already searched the island, assuming Blackbeard actually hid it in the water. You're confident of that, Taz?"

"Nope."

"Wonderful."

"If we have to search the entire property it's going to take months, maybe years, and I don't think Holmes will tolerate us that long. So we need to concentrate our efforts, and doesn't it seem likely to you that the bank of the old slough would be a great hiding place?"

"I guess. I'm a little exhausted."

"We're all tired, so let's start working in shifts. I'll take the first one. Pete, you and Sam get something to eat and some sleep. One of you take over from me at midnight."

"I want to stay."

"You need to rest, Pete. If I find something I'll call you. Keep your radio on."

"I'll make sure there's hot food ready when you get back to the boat."

"Don't use all the hot water. I'm going to be even more of a mess than I am now."

Sam and Pete left as Taz hoisted the metal detector and probe, took another quick study of their topographic lines, and headed off through the woods toward the long-gone riverbank.

Pete came to relieve him at midnight, and Taz worked with him until Sam showed up at four.

"It's not looking too good, Sam. We're pretty much finished and have nothing to show for it. Only six grids left, so you'll be done in an hour or two."

"Okay. See you around sunrise."

Taz and Pete went back to *Wasafiri*. Taz took a quick shower and crashed. His boat was as dark inside as the late night water in which she rested. The only sound was the air-conditioner blowing cold over Taz's exhausted body as he lay facedown on top of his sheets, immediately falling into a sleep as deep as a clubbed seal's.

A hand pushed his face into the pillow as the point of something sharp cut slightly between the ribs of his back.

"Shh."

The control in Taz's muffled voice earned him a gasp of air and a chance to say, "You've got my face in a pillow. How loud do you think I can I be like that?"

"Just stay quiet, Mister Keaton. I know you can do that."

"Are you going to keep that blade in between my ribs?"

"It's only made a scratch."

"Try to not sneeze so we can keep it that way."

"I'll try."

Suddenly the door burst opened and Pete jumped into the room. He snapped on the lights and leveled a massive pistol at the Arab standing over Taz. "Drop the...drop whatever the hell that is."

"Damn, Pete, what took you so long?"

"You know how hard it is to find a gun on this boat?"

"That's because Mister Keaton does not like guns," the Arab said, speaking as calmly as if he was ordering coffee. "But I'll bet there are T-ball bats all over the boat."

"I said to drop the gun."

The Arab twisted the blade slightly in Taz's back. "If you shoot me, Pete, I'm afraid I'll make quite a mess on this beautiful carpet."

"Yeah," Taz said, "But if you do shoot him, go for the hip or his skull. Something that might be thick enough to stop the bullet so it doesn't put a hole in my boat."

"Drop it."

Just then Sam stepped through the door, filthy and muddy from searching. He grabbed the gun from Pete, walked over to Taz's bed, put the barrel against the stranger's head, and said "Mind if I look at that lance? What is it, Etruscan?"

"Very good, Sam. From quite early in their era, actually. About 750 years before Christ was born and 250 years before that part of Italy slipped from their power." He carefully slid the tip of the short lance out of Taz's skin and handed it to Sam.

"Thank you."

"You're most welcome. Consider it a gift."

Taz climbed out of bed and stood up with them. Then he hit the Arab in the face, hard enough to knock him back against the wall and then to the floor.

"I was quite sure that was coming," the Arab said.

"You know each other?"

"Yeah, Pete. Meet Hassan. We call him Joey because it pisses him off." Then, turning to help Joey to his feet, Taz said, "What the hell were you thinking, boarding my boat like that? Never mind. Nice lance."

"Thank you."

"What time is it?"

"Almost dawn."

"You couldn't have come by during office hours?"

"This was Sam's idea, actually. He wanted to show once again that you aren't invincible."

Sam looked a little ashamed. "You really do need that lesson once in awhile, Taz."

"Thanks for the concern, Sam. Next time you get the skewer treatment."

"No need, because I already know that I am *vincible*." He suddenly let out an enormous laugh, and everyone stared as if Bigfoot had just tap-danced across the floor in front of them.

Taz poured four cups of coffee when they got to Wasafiri's main salon. "There are only four of us, right Joey? Your entourage isn't in a rubber boat hanging onto the side and about to storm aboard?"

"Want me to check?"

"Don't bother, Pete. This is Joey's idea of a social call."

"Yes, Pete," Joey said. "If it were a professional visit there would have been more blood."

"Probably," Taz agreed. "It's always hard to know for sure."

"Who are you? And how did you know about me."

"Knowing things, Pete, plays but a small part in my profession. My name is Hassan Abdul-Qadir, which means beautiful servant of the powerful."

"We think he changed his name to that. What's the Arabic word for thieving back-stabber? That's probably what we'll find his name really is if we ever get around to checking."

"I assure you, Pete – and I hope it's alright to call you Pete – that it is the name my parents gave me. I am in the recovery business, you might say, not unlike your colleagues here, except that I collect treasure for The Louvre."

"In Paris? Nice."

Taz sipped his coffee. "Don't let him bullshit you, Pete. The UAE is building a branch of The Louvre in Abu Dhabi, funded by oil money and a bunch of sheiks determined to make it the best in the world someday. Right now it's Joey's job to make that happen. Tomorrow he might be stealing cadavers for some mad scientist."

Joey rubbed his jaw where Taz hit him. "My job is not an easy one."

"I've owed you that from Tripoli."

"You are correct. You know, of course, why I'm here."

"Because you missed hanging out with me?"

"Pete, your boss and I have such good times."

"When we're not out to kill each other. And I'm not Pete's boss. He's a partner."

Joey looked surprised. "Then congratulations are in order. I envy you. They've never offered that chance to me, perhaps because it's quite competitive between us. But we still manage to have fun, particularly because Keaton, you see, is an intriguing enigma in my world, and those things hold unlimited fascination for me. He has no formal education in archeology, but is blessed with a natural instinct that puts him near the top of the field. It's really quite impressive."

Taz sipped again. "I'm lucky."

"He is that too. For instance, how did you happen to end up here?"

"Gordie's dead."

"I know. I am very sorry. He was an excellent adventurer."

"The man who killed him came back here."

"I know that too. But it does not explain your interest in the local records you've been studying. What *I* believe is that it is once again your incredible luck, connecting your desire for revenge with a quest for treasure."

"I don't condone revenge."

"But you just hit me in the face."

"That was an accident."

"So tell me about the treasure you seek here. I assume it to be Blackbeard's, as I, too, have heard the legend for years, even back in my country. Or is it the fabled Tortuga Gold you seek?" He turned to Pete. "Legend alone can often lead us to treasure, but a legend like Blackbeard's, combined with a fact such as the Tortuga Gold's disappearance, is an irresistible combination of very high odds."

"We're here to make sure there's justice for Gordie. Nothing more."

"You know I don't believe you."

"And you know I don't care. Was Isabelle working for you when we saw her in Panama?"

"Ah, yes, Isabelle. She helps me on those occasions that require her special talents, but Panama was a private matter of hers that involved her own clients. She does send her love to you, of course."

"She blew up a hell of a nice boat in order to get away. And Belgians send chocolate as a token of love."

"Sorry, I have arrived empty-handed, at least from her."

"Finish your coffee, Joey. It's time for you to go."

Joey set down his full cup and bowed graciously. "You still know how to get hold of me, I assume?"

"By the neck if I get the chance."

"You Americans are always so clever. It's been a pleasure, gentlemen, as always." He stepped out of the cabin and disappeared as the first rays of dawn splintered the darkness.

Pete followed with his eyes long after the man had gone. Then, "Taz, do you know many guys like that?"

"A few."

"That was Weirdsville."

"It's even weirder when he brings his men along. They're very well trained and hard to anticipate. Sam, now that Joey's involved we're going to need some support up here from contractors. Use helicopters or chartered jets, whatever you need. Err on the side of overwhelming firepower."

"I'm on it."

"If there is a treasure, Taz, do you think they'll beat us to it?"

Taz set down his cup and smiled that great grin of his. "Nope. Not if I can help it, Pete. Any luck on the last few grids, Sam?"

"No. There's absolutely nothing under the ground where the water once ran. Not even an old sewer or water line. I covered it twice and even cut down a couple of trees that were making it difficult to search around them."

Taz looked at Pete. "You look a little discouraged."

"A little, sure."

"Me, too," Sam said. "In my mind I could already see us finding it. What's funny is that I feel better now that Joey's here."

"He's not one to waste time, that's for sure, so his presence probably means we're onto something. I wonder what he knows that we don't."

"He obviously followed up on your visit to the courthouse."

"Yeah." Taz got up and grabbed an Oreo. He walked out onto *Wasafiri's* main deck. He looked over at Derek's property, and kept staring as the sun rose and brightly illuminated it in morning light. "Do either of you think it's possible that Blackbeard might have hid his treasure on this side of the island?"

Pete stepped up beside Taz. "He would have had to deal with an awful lot of current on this side. You've seen it roar through here during the tide changes."

"But he might have seen that as a natural form of security."

"There would have also been a lot of erosion," Sam said. "Or silting. Erosion would have caused his gold to sink farther into the mud, or wash away completely. Silting would have covered it up more heavily. Besides, we searched on this side of his property already."

"You're right, we did."

"So what's your point?"

"I'm going to see Miss Lucy tomorrow."

"Got a thing going with her?"

"Maybe. Are you jealous?"

"Only a little."

"I want to see if she has a chart that shows exactly where the river flowed along this bank way back then."

"What makes you think it was different then than now?"

"Because, Pete, rivers like to change. Often it's on their own through erosion or accretion, which might take a long time or happen from one season to the next. People change them, too. The Army Corps of Engineers sure changed this one."

"Maybe they're the ones who found the treasure."

"There's no chance the Tortuga Gold was found that recently, relatively speaking, and then kept a secret this long. If it had been found during the Civil War, the South might have melted it down and never mentioned it to anyone, but not during the domestically peaceful times when this river was dredged."

"You're driving at something, Taz."

"What do you see over there, Sam?"

"You know what I see. You also know I hate games."

"Pete?"

"Sure I'll play. Trees and a house. A long dock. Mud. Cattails. A skiff in the yard."

"You see a seawall, you knucklehead."

"I thought you didn't want to play, Sam?"

"Jeez, Taz, numb nuts was never going to get it."

"A seawall is the right answer, though. What do you think the odds are that Derek already knew where the treasure is, or was, either before or shortly after he bought the property?"

"He says he dug around here all his youth. I'd say the odds are fair."

"Now let's also suppose that Blackbeard did hide it in the river on this side of the island, and close to shore. What would have been Derek's best way to protect it. For all time, forever, really."

"By building a seawall that created a concrete fortress around his treasure."

"Exactly, Pete."

"But wouldn't that have risked the marine contractor who installed the seawall finding the treasure?"

"That depends on where he put it. With his powerful father and obvious wealth, Derek could have claimed an extra fifty or hundred feet of land, especially this far from town where no one really seems to care."

"You mean he could have built the seawall a hundred feet farther into the river than where the shoreline really was. So that's why you want to see Miss Lucy."

"Maybe she can tell me exactly where the river once met the shore, as measured from that stupid birdbath where the tree once stood."

"I'm getting excited again."

"Stay that way, Pete. And while we're digging at non-sequiturs—"

"Digging at what?"

"Things that don't make logical sense. Literally, facts that do not follow logic."

"Oh. Like a billionaire digging around in the Carolina mud."

"Hear that, Sam, I just lost half of my wealth."

"I did hear that. Which means that I'm suddenly only half as excited about being in your will."

"Does it strike anyone other than me as peculiar that a devoted archeologist and lover of all things old would be careless enough to let a map blow away?"

"I was surprised when he said that."

"Me, too," Pete said. "And have you noticed how much Sam and I are starting to think alike."

Sam groaned. "Really? Are you thinking you're wearing out my nerves? Because that's what's I'm thinking."

"I'm starting to wonder," Taz said, "if Derek might have suspected we'd come to this idea eventually. To be honest, I'm not even sure there is a rod under the birdbath, and if there is, heck, it could mark where he buried a dog or found a dime. Who knows with a guy like that?"

"What do we do while you see Miss Lucy?

"What's the schedule with Gordie's family? Anything we need to do?"

"I think Fran and I have covered everything. They'll be here Friday. They're bringing his ashes."

"How about checking out the hotel that my office booked for them and making sure it's the best around. I want to make sure they're comfortable. It's a sad time for them."

"It's a sad time for all of us. Drop us off there on your way to see Miss Lucy and we'll double-check the arrangements."

"I'll drop you off, Sam, but this is a good time for Pete to come with me and learn a little about the local history."

"That's exactly what I was thinking. Sam, is that what you were thinking?"

"Shut up."

Pete laughed. "See, I'm also thinking that I should shut up. Another weird example of how we think alike."

Pete leaped back into the salon just as Sam lunged for him.

Chapter 34

Taz stopped the truck and Sam jumped out like an agile beast.

"We'll meet you for lunch, Sam. Find us in one of the restaurants along the waterfront."

"I'll check out the hotel and then wander around a bit. Maybe buy some new shoes."

"You really think you'll find your size in this small town?"

"It's possible."

"Two words," Taz said. "Mail order." Then he drove off toward the historical society. It was only a few blocks but he took his time, pointing out some of Beaufort's interesting architecture to Pete.

"I once thought I could live here," he said. "I actually looked at property in Oriental, which is nearby."

"Why didn't you buy something?"

Taz laughed. "It gets cold in the winter. Not cold like up in the Great Lakes, but too cold for my thin blood."

"It's hard to imagine you being a wimp about anything."

"Then don't imagine me cold because I'm Super-Wimp."

"Is that when you learned about Blackbeard and the Tortuga Gold, while you were house hunting around here?"

"Like all kids, I heard about Blackbeard long ago when growing up. I did learn more while visiting here, though. It's impossible not to be intrigued by the local legend."

"And the gold?"

"Sam and I funded and worked on the team that eventually found the *Conquistador del las Americas*, the galleon that carried half the Tortuga Gold before transferring it to the *Espiritu del Mar*."

"Did you ever think you'd be chasing Blackbeard's lost treasure?"

"I've never had sufficient reason to believe it even existed until Buzz showed up with that escudo he'd found in a place that's legendary for holding the secret of Blackbeard's lost treasure. Then it was just logical. Here we are."

"Neat old building."

"Yeah."

They parked, walked in, and found Miss Lucy near the front door. "Hello, Taz Keaton. I expected to see you again."

"How could I resist your charm, Miss Lucy?"

"Not many men can. Or could." She looked at Pete and winked, "Back in the day I was quite the number."

"You still are. Let me introduce you to Pete. Pete, say hello to Miss Lucy."

"Hello, Miss Lucy."

"Hello, Pete. My, I'm such a lucky old gal to have so many handsome young men visiting me these days."

"I'm a little jealous," Taz said, with his hand gently touching her shoulder, "that other men are coming to visit. Let me guess, was he a handsome Arab man?"

"Why, yes. How did you know?"

"He's like a shadow to me."

"Seems like more of a cloud."

"Right, Pete. He's more like a cloud."

"That's just about what he said, too. Don't worry, though, I didn't tell him my theory about, well, you know what."

Taz looked around to make sure no one else was there. "It's okay, Miss Lucy, Pete knows. We both have faith in your theory, by the way."

She grabbed both of Pete's hands. "It's exciting, isn't it? Will at least one of you come back and tell me what you find, even if it's nothing?"

"Yes, ma'am, we promise."

"Would you mind letting us in on what you told Joey? I mean Hassan?"

"The Arab? I only answered his questions. It's my job here and I can't play favorites too badly."

"What was he asking?"

"Pretty much the same as you, about Derek Holmes's property, the island, the dredging project. And you, of course."

"Of course. Did he make the connection to Blackbeard on his own?"

"No. In fact I don't think he's even made that connection except in the most abstract way. At least he never mentioned Blackbeard. But he did refer to the gold that was missing off that shipwreck."

"The Tortuga Gold."

"Bingo, Pete," Miss Lucy said. "Give that player a kewpie doll."

"What's a kewpie doll?"

"Before your time, Pete. Before mine, too."

"Oh, far before my time, too, dear. I heard my mother mention them once."

"We're going to have to work fast, Miss Lucy. Joey probably seemed nice, and he is, actually, but he's dangerous and very fast in executing his decisions."

"I'm *raring* to go."

"Derek–" Taz stopped. Then he laughed. "You are really something, Miss Lucy."

"Oh, I know."

"Derek told me that he got a survey when he bought the property. He says it showed the exact location of the tree you pointed out to me on the chart, the one that captains used for navigation. The one with a stone at its base that was used like a surveyor's pin."

"I believe I saw that survey. In fact, I think I'm the one who gave it to him."

"He says he lost it."

"He doesn't seem like the type to lose old things of value."

"That's what I thought, too. Any chance you have a copy of that survey?"

"What are you trying to determine?"

"A survey could have a scale. If it did, and I knew exactly where that tree had been, I could scale out to the river. I suspect it was wider at the time of the survey than it was after Derek installed the seawall. Would the survey show the distance to the river?"

"So you think he claimed some land. Well, that used to be pretty common. Yes, a survey should show the distance to mean low water."

"Great."

"Not really. I don't have a copy. Derek took the original."

"Damn. Sorry, I meant darn."

"Damn," she said, and then smiled. "But I do have the original documents filed by the Corps of Engineers, though. In all likelihood they used the same information when they did their site restoration report as the surveyors did when doing the survey. Let's check."

She turned her wheelchair and took off for a back room. "Do you want us to follow you?"

"It's too crowded with stuff back there. I'll return in a jiffy."

She left them alone. "Cute old lady."

"I think so too."

They sat down and waited. It took more than an hour before Miss Lucy returned.

"Got it!"

"You're amazing."

"Of course I am, although I'd be more amazing it I'd filed it with the other information about Holmes's property years ago. Addled by old age, I

179

guess, or at least I will be when I get old. Let's see what we have." She unrolled the faded Army Corps of Engineers site restoration drawings.

"The primary building that originally stood on that site is shown clearly enough. And here's the scale. Here's the distance to the river. There's the tree, about 275 feet from the original building."

"I need a reference that's still there in order to pinpoint its location. I think Derek is lying to me about the tree's location because he wants us off his land, and finding nothing is the fastest way to get rid of us."

"There aren't any remains of the building?"

"None that I've seen."

"The well?"

"No. All of it was probably filled in or covered up along with the land. Can we take this, Miss Lucy?"

"Will you bring it back?"

"I'll do my best."

"I can't resist blue eyes. Take it."

"Thank you."

"But just a second, let me make a call and try something else." She picked up the phone and dialed.

"Hello, Cynthia, it's Miss Lucy. How are you?"

"I met Cynthia at the courthouse," Taz whispered to Pete. "Nice girl."

"Well, I'm happy for you, Cynthia. Now could you do something for me right away, dear? Good. Please pull the permit from when Derek Holmes moved the old Grady place to his land. Yes, that's right. Of course I'll hold, but I'm with two handsome men so don't leave me alone with them for too long." She laughed and winked at Taz. "Yes, as a matter of fact one of them is a very cute blond guy."

"I hope I'm like her at her age," Taz said.

"Heck, I'd like to be like her at my age."

"Great, Cynthia, now check and see if there's any reference to an old tree that's shown on a very old survey. There is? Why that's fantastic. Can you determine a distance and direction from a known point?" She covered the phone and spoke to Taz. "We're just about to make this very easy for you."

"Terrific."

"Yes, I'm ready." She handed Taz a pen and tablet. "The tree is roughly 245 degrees and 180 feet from the southwest corner of where Holmes was permitted to put his house. Got it. Thanks so much, Cynthia." She hung up and turned to Taz and Pete. "Ta-da."

"I'm taking you out to dinner soon, Miss Lucy."

"Keep in mind that I'm an early bird."

"I will."

"I can't wait to hear what you find. Don't forget that."

Taz and Pete rushed out. "Let's get Sam. We'll grab something we can eat on the ride back."

Sam was staring in the window of a candle shop when they pulled up to the curb. "Jump in, Sam. Let's go."

Sam hopped into the back of the truck and slid open the rear window. "Have you seen what amazing stuff they can do with candles? I'm coming back here when I have some time. What are you looking at, twerp?"

Pete looked at Taz and laughed. "Really, Sam? Candles?"

"Yes, candles. Do you have a problem with the fact that I like candles?"

"How about incense?"

"Yes, I like incense, too. But not as much as I like pounding the snot out of jackasses."

"That's rich."

"We know where the tree was and the distance to the river before the seawall was installed."

"I made that assumption when we passed up all the restaurants, Taz. Time to go to work?"

"Precisely that time."

"Candles," Pete muttered.

"What did you say? I'm not sure with all the wind back here, but I think you're still giving me crap about candles. Are you really that stupid?"

"Candles," Pete repeated, laughing. Then he slammed and locked the sliding window.

Chapter 35

"Go to the boat," Taz said to Pete as all of them dove out of the truck, "and grab the longest measuring tape you can find. And some shovels. Sam, you get the metal detectors. I'll take the survey and get started with some rough bearings."

"Ten minutes."

"I'll race you to the boat, Sam."

"No."

"You're not still mad at me, are you?"

"You certainly can be irritating."

"I'm sorry. I'll buy you a candle to make up." Pete took off running for the boat with Sam right behind him.

Taz went to Derek's front yard and stood there with the report from the Corps of Engineers, estimating some distances, and getting his first real sense of the way the island looked before the Corps totally made it disappear. Even without measuring off the distances exactly it was obvious that Derek had lied about the tree's location. The birdbath was northwest of the house, not southwest where Cynthia said it had been.

"Hold the zero end on Derek's foundation," he said to Pete as he and Sam came running up."

"I got it. Go."

Taz held the compass in one hand and let the tape pay out of the other. When he'd measured off 180 feet he stopped and kicked a mark in the ground with his heel. "This is where the tree used to be."

"And the river? How far and in what direction?" Pete's voice carried his enthusiasm.

"Do you know why we can't just measure to the water?"

"We need a compass heading, Sam, in order to be accurate. We could be off by yards otherwise."

"Okay, Pete. I just wanted to know that you're catching on."

"I am. Taz?"

He didn't answer.

"Taz," Sam said. "How about a compass heading?"

Taz stood studying the Corps drawing. He looked around the yard and then toward the river, then back around the yard. "Something's not right."

"Don't tell me that Derek managed to dummy up an old report."

"I'm not sure. Give me a minute."

Taz got down on the ground and oriented the drawing. He checked his compass several times. Then he stood up and said, "How about measuring from right here" he pointed to the heel mark he'd dug into the ground where the tree had been, "to that barn over there. If it's about 272 feet I'm going to need an ax or a sledgehammer."

"Looks like it's going to be just about that far, so Pete, go back to the boat and get a maul. Taz, stand over your spot and hold the end of the tape."

Pete ran off as Sam walked toward the barn, stopping when he ran out of tape at two hundred feet and waiting for Taz to move forward to his spot before proceeding.

"Right on it, Taz. 275 feet, more or less. That's got to be within an acceptable margin of error."

"That son of a bitch."

"Yeah, Pete bugs my ass too."

"I meant Derek."

"I know. Just kidding. Let me guess, okay?"

"Damn if Derek didn't build this barn precisely over the remains of whatever building once stood here."

"And I wanted so badly to guess. Do you think it might have been Blackbeard's home, or at least one of them?"

"We'll know soon enough. Here comes Pete."

"I brought both an ax and a sledgehammer."

"Give me the ax."

Taz stepped up to the big lock on the heavy barn door and took a giant swing that hit the lock squarely. It bounced off and the lock didn't break or even look like it might.

"Maybe we'll just chop through the wood siding."

"I don't think so," Sam said. "Look at this." He removed a small air grate, about four inches by nine inches. It was one of several installed around the barn. "The building is solid concrete block behind this wood paneling. Jeez, he built a block building and then covered it with old wood siding to make it look as old as his house."

"Take a swing with the maul, Sam."

"Gladly." Sam stepped up to the door and swung the heavy sledgehammer like it was light plastic. It hit the lock and something splintered.

"Again."

Sam took a small step farther back. "I'm going to make it groan this time."

"No you're not. Put down those tools or I'll shoot all of you."

They all turned to see Derek standing there with a handgun. Theresa was on the porch.

"That's right," Taz said, "I'd forgotten that you had that gun, I guess because I would have expected you to use it on Buzz."

"Then don't make another mistake and doubt that I know how to use it. With Buzz I didn't want to wake you or Theresa. Now we're all here so it really doesn't matter."

"You lied about the tree's location."

"That really doesn't matter either."

"We all know you're not going to shoot us, Derek."

"I'm no so sure," Pete said, "but then I don't have your experience with people waving guns around."

"I'm not sure either, Taz. I think he might shoot us. He killed Buzz without a problem."

Taz looked at both Pete and Sam. "Well thanks for your support guys. Don't think it's not appreciated while I'm trying to defuse this situation gracefully."

"No problem."

"Glad to help."

Taz looked back at Derek. "Listen, I'm just trying to solve a mystery, a riddle of sorts. It's what I do."

"What we do, right Pete?"

"Right. Thanks for including me. I would have felt a little bit slighted otherwise."

"Let's you and I try to ignore Pete and Sam for the time being, Derek. I believe there's treasure behind these doors, and I also believe you're entitled to all of it, depending on the law. I just want to know. I have to know. You understand that, don't you? And it's not like I need the money."

"I'm still amazed that you don't think I'll shoot you. Lots of people die over gold."

"A-ha! I told you, Sam. You heard him say gold, right?"

"I did."

"Pete?"

"Yup, I heard him too."

"I meant that people get hurt in their hunt for gold, the way they go crazy over the pursuit of it and end up dying."

"Why don't you put that gun away and give me the key. Swinging a sledge hammer is going to get heavy eventually, even for Sam."

"I'm not at all afraid of you."

"You know what, Derek, I'm convinced of that. I'm surprised by it, but convinced that you're really not afraid of us. But you need to know that somewhere hot on my tail is a merry band of men who'll roll over you like you're asphalt. Trust me that you will be afraid of them."

"He's talking about Joey, right Sam?"

"Hassan, that's right."

"Hassan or Joey, it really doesn't matter. You're still not getting into my site."

"There he goes again, Taz. He called this place a site. You built this whole massive barn over an archeological dig, didn't you, Derek?

"Yes, Sam, I did, but I assure you there's no gold in there. Just artifacts from a long ago settlement here, maybe a storage barn or armory or warehouse. They are things I discovered years ago and continue to explore, some of which were the things I showed you the other night."

"If that's the case then Hassan will have little interest, and I'm pretty sure that he'll take my word for it and leave you alone. Weird, isn't it?"

"So weird as to almost be unbelievable."

"I think it's weird, too. But on the other hand, Derek, if the Tortuga Gold *is* in here, Hassan and his boys won't give a damn about you or Theresa or whether or not you live or die. And even if you do manage to live you can forget about getting to keep any part of it."

"Honey?"

"Stay out of this Theresa."

"Derek," Taz said, "I can make sure you keep your treasure, whether it's artifacts or gold. I've got men close by to protect it, and protect all of us."

"Now you're the one who's telling lies. I don't see any other men."

"You know, that's a very good point. Hang on just a minute, okay?"

"I've got nothing else to do today but protect what's mine."

"Sam?"

"Yeah, Taz."

"I'm just a little bit curious about something."

"Let me guess."

"Where is the support I asked you to get?"

"You never, ever let me guess. Okay, most of them are standing by in a hotel out by the highway. I didn't think we wanted them on-site yet. I do have a couple of guys out there."

Taz turned back to Derek. "Sam and I have, apparently, had a little communication breakdown. Most of the men are not as close as I thought, but they can be here in minutes if we need them to keep us safe."

"Keep you safe, you mean."

"No, I mean us. Sam and Pete and I, even with your helping out with that little popgun you have in your hand, won't be able to hold off Hassan's men for more than a few minutes if it turns out there's Tortuga Gold behind this door. So will you please, pretty please with a cherry on top, unlock the door so we can see and then take appropriate actions?"

Derek looked back at Theresa and then lowered the gun.

"I'm sorry I ever laid eyes on you," He said as he handed Taz a big key.

"I wish I could say you were the first to tell me that. Sam, no wait, Pete?"

"Yeah, Taz."

"Open the door. Let's take a look."

Pete took the key from Derek. He was almost trembling when he put it in the lock and turned it.

Chapter 36

Pete pushed the door as though it might be a fragile, creaking old relic, but it swung open easily on smoothly operating hinges. Although there were several windows on the outside of the barn, the inside was completely windowless.

"Those fake windows were pretty convincing with the dust and cobwebs. It's mighty dark in there, Derek. Any booby-traps or trip wires?"

"Don't be ridiculous, Keaton."

"Great. I still think I'll let you go first."

"That would probably be best. Please stay where you are until I turn on the lights so that you don't fall into one of the holes or the main excavation."

"You don't have another gun inside, do you?"

"As a matter of fact I have several, but if I were going to shoot any or all of you I would have done it outside."

"Makes sense to me," Sam said. "Pete, go with him to be sure."

"Another initiation?"

"I'd go but I'm afraid of the dark."

"Yeah, I'm sure you are." Pete put his hand on Derek's back so as not to get lost in the dark. "Lead on."

"You men are a bit dramatic, don't you think?" Derek took four steps inside and then clicked on the lights.

"I had no idea how far you were going."

"I was going to bet four steps," Sam said. "Jeez-Louise, would you take a look at this place?"

They all stepped inside. The building seemed cavernous, much bigger than it did from outside. Huge bright lights hung from the rafters twenty feet in the air. Ladders went down into the dig at several locations, and an old stone foundation was centered in the immaculate building, about ten feet lower than where they stood.

"This is perhaps the best preserved digs I've ever seen," Taz said.

"It took me decades to do this secretly, only to have the secret get out because of that fool Buzz finding one gold coin."

"Don't be so glum. Or so sure your secret will get out. I don't see any gold, nor do I see anyplace that looks like it could hold tons of gold. If Tortuga Gold was here, I'm sure you would have found it by now."

"Is that supposed to make us happy, Taz?"

"No, Sam. Sorry. It's supposed to make Derek feel better, because if there's no gold here then the rest of this find is probably safe, even though this stuff is certainly museum quality. I think this must have been an armory."

Sam walked over to a wall where close to a hundred gleaming swords hung on a rack. "These are incredible. It's almost like they're new, stored carefully by whoever made them and never unsheathed. It's obvious they've never been underwater."

"I'm sure you realize that I already know they're incredible, but thanks all the same for appreciating them."

"There's probably a half-million dollars worth of swords right here on this wall."

"I would say more like eight hundred thousand, if I ever chose to sell them. Which I wouldn't. You'll understand when you take a look at the markings."

Sam reached for one of the swords, then hesitated. "Do you mind, Derek?"

"I'll request that you use a pair of the soft gloves over there so as not to leave oil from your fingers."

"Sure." Sam put on the gloves and then picked up the sword. "Spanish," he said, "carrying the mark of King Phillip the Fifth. That puts it in the time frame of when the *Espiritu del Mar* sank off the coast."

"Is it like the one found on board?" Taz turned to Pete. "Ballard only recovered one sword off the wreck," he explained. "One lousy sword, and it was broken. The ship had been completely looted of anything worthwhile."

Sam examined the sword closely. "It's exactly like the one he found."

"So this," Taz turned around slowly, fascinated, "solves the mystery of where everything from the ship ended up."

"I've always known it," Derek said smugly. "My first real find in this excavation was a collection of pewter mugs with the ship's name on them."

"So whoever boarded, looted, and sunk the *Espiritu del Mar* brought most if not all of it back here. But you never found any gold. That almost seems impossible, you know."

"I agree, Keaton. I certainly know the legend as well as anyone and better than most, so of course I've always expected to find some gold here someday. But it was never what I sought, even though it would have been nice."

188

"Nice?" Pete looked at Derek with disbelief. "A fortune in gold would have been nice. What would you call a good meal, Derek?"

"That would be nice, too."

"Your lack of emotion amazes me."

"Anyway, as you can see, there is no gold here. Look around if that's what it will take to assure you, but after that I must ask you to leave my property. You've learned what you came to learn, and if you came here to see justice given to that man in my woods, well, you've seen that done too."

"Fair enough, Derek, but I think it would be good for you to let Joey take a look in here too, just to make him go away."

"The man you warned me about? You said he would take your word for it."

"He would if this was anything close to a normal excavation. But if all these crates you've stacked on the floor and the stuff hanging on the walls is from the *Espiritu del Mar,* you can imagine his skepticism when I tell him that everything from that galleon is here, it seems, except for the gold."

"This won't ever end, will it?"

"Actually, Derek, I think it's about over. We just need to get Joey out of your hair and that's that. Tomorrow we're going to bury Gordie at his favorite wreck, and after that there's really no reason for us to stick around here either."

"And you expect me to believe you're going to give up so easily on Blackbeard's long lost treasure?"

"It really doesn't matter anymore since we've looked everywhere we know to look. It's not here. I can't explain Buzz's coin but life's too short to waste. Look how many decades you've already invested."

"I've enjoyed every minute I've spent here."

"It's a big world out there, Derek. Pete and I were on our way to the West Indies when this came up, and we're anxious to get back underway before it turns cold up here. I hate the cold."

"He really does," Sam laughed. "I remember once when we were kids–"

"I think he believes me, Sam."

"Oh, right."

"Besides, Derek, men and ships both rot in port. It's not good to spend too much time in one place."

"Then call this man Joey and tell him what you've found. If he needs to come out and see for himself, let's do this quickly so Theresa and I can get back to our lives."

Taz grinned, stepped outside, and shouted. "Joey!"

Half a minute later his cell phone rang. "Hey, Joey," he said. "I figured you were watching us. Did you happen to see any of my men in the woods yet? You did? That's good. Surprising, but good. Sam assures me there are more on their way too. Look, why don't you come on over to the barn. We've got something to show you."

Pete and Sam and Derek dragged themselves from the lure of the excavation and scanned the woods.

"He saw some of our men?" Sam asked.

"He almost stepped on one who was proned out in full camo under a bush. Joey's very confident he has us outnumbered, though. Let's hope that changes."

"There really are armed men in my woods?" Derek asked nervously.

"Yeah, but Sam already told them there's a body out there, and to ignore it. They've seen bodies before, trust me."

"You have men and Joey has men? And they're ready to fight each other?"

"They are, although right now they're probably playing cards together or catching up on each other's news, waiting for word to kill each other over gold."

"Any idea on his manpower?"

"Plenty, I'm sure, as always."

"There he is," Pete said.

"Joey is the consummate professional, Derek, so just let him look around and then he'll take off. As nice as your stuff is, none of it is part of this particular scavenger hunt of his."

"I'll be as tolerant as I can."

"One important safety tip. If you show that silly little gun you have in your pocket you'll catch about twenty bullets in an instant."

"I've deduced that on my own."

"Taz?"

"Yeah, Sam?"

"It might help for you to tell Joey that we're leaving too. After he sees *Wasafiri* pull away to bury Gordie, he'll lose any remaining interest he might have."

"Especially if you and Theresa come with us, Derek. You will have shown Joey your excavation and proven there's nothing to hide. There will be no reason for him to be here, and you and Theresa coming out with us will drive home the point that he's just wasting time. As far as I know there's nothing Joey hates more than wasting time."

"You, maybe."

"True, Sam, he might hate me more." Then Taz shouted, "Keep on coming, Joey. Our men won't shoot you."

"I'm quite sure they won't."

"You need to take a look inside. This is an incredible excavation, although I'm afraid we've all wasted our time and money looking for Tortuga Gold."

Joey was much less comfortable than he was as a nighttime intruder on *Wasafiri*. "You do know about my men, right, Keaton?"

"Yes, yes, I know they're ready to cut us in half if anything happens to you."

"It's good that we understand each other." He stepped up to Derek. "Hello, Mister Holmes. I am Hassan Abdul-Qadir."

"That's nice. Please just take a look around and then leave."

Chapter 37

Sam and Pete spent the next morning doing jobs on *Wasafiri* while Taz went in a limousine to pick up Gordie's family.

Pete stopped to watch a squadron of pelicans circle around and then dive at a school of baitfish in the river. "Do you think Joey left without searching the grounds, Sam?"

"Not one chance in a million."

"And probably less likely than that with so many millions involved."

"Good point."

"I thought so, too. It makes me nervous that he'll probably go over every inch of Derek's property while no one is there."

"I worry a little bit, too, but we couldn't find any treasure and Derek never found it. However I do accept the possibility that Joey has a clue we don't. I will never make the mistake of underestimating him, just like Joey never underestimates Taz. "

"I'm bummed we didn't find the gold. I'm also kind of surprised Taz gave up so easily."

"Taz has his reasons, I'm sure. This adventure will cycle back to us someday. They almost always do."

"Here come Derek and Theresa."

"Nice of them to dress up for a man they never met."

"They're probably decent enough people when they're not dealing with all this swirl." Then, "Good morning and welcome aboard. Taz should be back any minute with Gordie's ashes and his wife and son. Then we'll get underway."

Derek looked back at his precious property. "I'm still not sure about this, Sam."

"You can take Joey at his word that he won't plunder your site. And letting him poke around on his own is the smartest thing you can do because he's going to do it anyway. He'll convince himself the Tortuga Gold isn't there, and that's really the only way to get rid of a guy like that. Not to mention that it also proves to us that you really don't think there's any gold there."

"I've always said that."

"Yes, you have."

"I just want this to end."

"Me, too," Pete said. "Did you feel the cooler weather this morning? I'm as ready to get down-island as you are to get rid of us."

"Look," Derek said as he looked up toward *Wasafiri*'s high bow. "Here comes a southbound sailboat, with another one behind it. It's the twice-a-year parade I always enjoy watching, so I can appreciate your desire to get underway."

"I'm ready to go right now. Here comes Taz."

Taz jumped out of the limousine and ran around to open the other door. A plainly dressed but pretty woman stepped out, followed by a young man about eighteen.

"That's Gordie's wife and son," Sam said. "Great people from our hometown. I'll fire up the engines."

He left as Taz led them down the dock.

"I pictured your boat as something just like this, Taz, because I just couldn't imagine you with one of those fancy showy yachts. This is...well, it's you."

"It fits me pretty well, Angela. Are you ready to go to sea on her?"

She looked down at the urn she carried tightly in her arms. "Not really."

Taz hugged her gently. "I'm not ready to let him go either. I never will be. Do you want to sit here at the dock for a while?"

"No. No, I guess not. He's already gone, I know that. I just like having his ashes."

"We don't have to bury him at sea, Angela, and certainly not today. You can keep them at home until you're ready."

"I'd like that a lot, but Gordie loved the water as much as you do, and maybe even more. He would never be happy stuck on a mantle or table."

Taz laughed lightly. "I'm not sure he ever owned a mantle or a table. He sure didn't care about that stuff so I think you're right that he wouldn't want to spend eternity there."

"He hasn't owned real furniture since we split up. He loved us a lot, and his only other love was chasing adventures with you and Sam. He lived for each time some new crazy challenge came up."

"He was a good team mate." Taz turned to Gordie's son. "Roger, just so you have no doubt, Gordie has been my very best friend since we met in high school. I never expect to have a better one."

"He loved you, I know."

"He was a fearlessly brave man who loved his family and friends. I can't think of a much better eulogy than that."

"He was a good husband and father. Probably better at both once we divorced."

"I'm getting sad," Taz said, "so let's get underway." He looked at Pete, who threw off the lines so that Sam could idle *Wasafiri* away from the dock. At the inlet he turned southeast and headed out to sea while everyone else sat in the salon listening to Taz tell stories about Gordie that managed to make Angela and Roger laugh, and gave Derek and Theresa some idea of the man they'd come out to honor.

After three hours of cruising, Sam approached the spot Gordie had years ago chosen to be buried. He slowed down and Taz announced their arrival.

"This was Gordie's first dive using nitrox. He's always called it his favorite wreck. He once said to 'put my ashes upon the waves right here and let them sink to where I'll have this amazing ship to enjoy for eternity.'"

"His will requested his ashes end up here, without any long speeches or praise."

"I didn't see the will, Angela, but that's what he told me. Are we ready?"

Angela didn't move. They all waited for her. It was as though she never intended to get up from her seat again. "Roger?" She finally said. "Will you do this for me?"

She lifted the urn and pushed it slowly in her son's direction. He looked around, hesitated, and then took it from her.

"Let's go to the stern," Taz said as he put his arm around Roger's shoulders. "And let's try to be half as strong as Gordie."

Roger carried the urn to the rail and then opened the lid. He looked at his mother, who nodded, and then he turned it over, crying as the ashes drifted down to the ocean in the still air.

"Check the urn, dear," Angela said. "There may still be some ashes inside and I want your father together and at peace in one place."

"Empty," he said sadly.

They stood silently watching as the ashes settled to the calm surface. As they began to sink Taz took out the gold coin Sam had taken along when he took care of Buzz's body, and then brought back to Taz with it covered by Buzz's dried blood.

"Treasure," Taz said, "so often and sadly transfers through blood, my true and wonderful friend. The blood on this golden eight that you recovered from these waters is the blood of your killer. So rest now, Gordon Windsor, in peace."

Derek leaned closer to see the blood on the coin as Taz tossed it into the water. He looked concerned.

After a few minutes of staring as the ashes sank, Taz asked if anyone wanted to say anything. No one did, or if they did, they couldn't. So he nodded at Sam, who went to the lower helm and slowly headed back to home. Derek and Theresa moved to the bow and sat there alone. No one spoke until they were back to port.

"I've always had the impression," Taz said to Angela as they idled toward the dock, "that Gordie sent home a fair amount of his share of the fees generated by Mayday. He always wanted to take good care of you two, and he loved doing it. But if you ever need anything from me, you know you only have to ask."

"Then you don't know, do you, Taz?"

"I'm not sure. What do you mean?"

"Gordie has always sent home everything he ever earned on your adventures, every penny of every share. He endorsed your company's checks and then mailed them directly to me."

"Gosh, that would have been many millions of dollars."

"He would never take any of it back. He worked the Conch Train, the marina, and all those other jobs just to pay the few bills he had."

Taz was, perhaps for the first time in his life, shocked. "I did not know that. I wished...wow, I've got to tell you that I'm kind of blind-sided by that."

"I told him it was far too much money for me, but still he wanted us to have it. I put aside enough for Roger's education and a modest retirement, but gave most of it to charities. Roger and I really don't need much to live."

"I've always admired how you've kept your lives so simple. It's a great way to live, and a skill I'm only recently starting to learn."

Angela studied the dock as they approached, as if touching solid ground might heal some pain. "You'll stay in touch with us?"

"Of course I will. I hope to get back for Christmas if I can shake free of Sam and this knucklehead." He nodded at Pete.

Angela laughed a little. "Please do, Tanner. We'd love to see you back home."

"Pete," Sam said. "Go stand by with the lines."

"In a minute."

"What? Don't 'in a minute' me, kid."

"I'm busy."

Angela and Roger stepped out onto the main deck, but Pete stopped Taz as he tried to join them. "Tanner?"

"Sure, that's my name. Tanner Zachary Keaton."

"Tanner Zachary. Taz. I've always wondered where that came from."

"Well, while we're confessing our wonderings, you once asked me if this trip I offered was worth taking. Now I'm wondering what you think."

Just then Sam turned to see what was going on with the lines.

"You know, I think I'm going to need to get a little further down the road to know for sure."

Taz gave Sam a look and Sam laughed. "This is your lucky day, kid, because Taz and I just happen to know the way a little further down the road. So stick around."

"I have to, Sam. I still owe you a nice candle."

"Go handled the lines, twerp."

As Pete left, Derek stepped cautiously inside the salon. "I'm sure you gentlemen have noticed that the sheriff is waiting on my dock. Keaton, this was your doing, I suppose?"

"No, Derek, it was yours. You murdered a man. Did you really think I would just let that go?"

"I suppose it was foolish of me to think so. Honey?"

"Don't you dare say you did it for me, Derek. I was the one who let Buzz live on our property in the first place."

He looked at her and then back at Taz. Then he stepped outside and shouted to the sheriff. "I want my father's office to send an attorney to be present before I speak again."

"I already called them, Holmes. He's waiting at my office. And by the way, you're under arrest for the murder of a John Doe we found on your property. Get a little closer and I've got some Miranda rights to tell you about."

Derek turned to Taz. "As I said once before, I am truly sorry to have ever met you."

Taz moved close to Derek. "I really hope you are. The man you killed is the same man who killed my best friend, the amazing man we just honored, yet I was never going to take my vengeance on him. For all of your money and education, you're nothing but a murderer."

As soon as Pete had secured the lines, the sheriff stepped aboard. "Nice day, don't you think, Holmes. Turn around."

He handcuffed him. As he turned to take him away the sheriff said, "Thanks, Mister Keaton. I appreciate the information."

"You're welcome, sheriff. You found the body okay?"

"Right where you said it was."

"See anything else around there?"

"I'm not sure what you mean. Like what?"

"Oh, I don't know, but I heard a rumor that there's close to two-hundred armed combat veterans in those woods ready to go to war. You didn't see them?"

The sheriff laughed. "No, Keaton, I didn't see them. Or Merlin's castle or the boogie-man. Next time, maybe."

Taz laughed too. "Yeah, maybe next time."

Taz didn't say anything else until Angela walked up and hugged him good-bye. "You and your crazy adventures, Taz."

"I'm sorry?"

"That's what Gordie will miss most about this world. You and your crazy adventures."

Chapter 38

Taz walked Angela and Roger to the limousine and hugged them goodbye. Then he went up to the porch and sat in a chair beside Theresa. "I'm sorry," he said to her.

She was calm and quiet, as if in a daze and unable to believe what had just happened. "Are you sorry? I have trouble believing that."

"Theresa," he said, slowly choosing words he could say without being a hypocrite. "What allows us to live together is a system of laws. I'll be the first to admit that I stretch those laws almost to their breaking point, and sometimes, regrettably, beyond. But I try, I mean I really try, not to cross to the dark side. It's just too easy to get lost over there."

"How would you know about the dark side?"

He took the question seriously and wanted to answer with the truth. He thought about the evidence he'd seen in some of the black-hearted men he'd fought, and the ruthless men who'd sought fights with him, but they weren't really that much unlike Derek, so Theresa already knew all of that. And besides, whatever he could say was just an opinion.

The only truth he knew for sure was what he'd learned during a long, hard time in a jungle a couple thousand miles away, but that lesson was all about the light side, the good side of the coin where doing the right thing and being as fair as possible always paid off better than anything he could steal or withhold. It didn't really apply now.

"I guess you're right. I wouldn't know about the dark."

"Will he get convicted?"

"I could only make a guess. Will you testify against him?"

"I hate that he killed a man, even if Buzz might have been a threat. Derek should have just called the sheriff, but he was too protective of his big secret. God how I hated that excavation of his."

"If you do decide to testify, I imagine he'll get convicted. Probably without you, too, because I went to see the sheriff before picking up Angela and Roger and gave him a sworn statement about everything I saw and heard. Sam will testify, too."

"Then that pretty much seals his fate, I guess." She turned to look back at the home that Derek had filled with his treasure, and for the first time Taz realized that he hadn't seen any family photos or personal items inside. Their home was a museum, a tribute to Derek's discoveries and nothing more.

"What will you do?"

"Me? That's funny."

"What's funny?"

"I can't remember the last time a man asked me what I wanted to do. But I suppose I'll go back home to Waynesville. I've wanted to go back there for a while, but Derek was dug in here." She laughed. "Dug in. That's funny too."

"You have a very pretty smile when you laugh. Do you have family back there?"

"Just my parents and a sister. But I like small. I like private, too, although seeing some old friends would be nice after so many years secluded away on this land."

"When I was checking the courthouse records I noticed that, for whatever reason, all of this property is in your name."

"That was Derek's idea. He hit a bicyclist three years ago with his car and killed him. No charges were filed but Derek has always feared what a civil suit might cost him."

"Cost him?"

"Cost us."

"I have no idea what you have in savings, Theresa, but I'm sure you can guess that his defense is going to be expensive. And it sounds like you want to get out of here and start over."

"You're offering to buy this place. I was already sure you'd ask."

"I am, because I think you're going to sell it anyway, either because you have to or because you want to."

"I want to. I hate this place. Hmm, that's funny too. I've only just now allowed myself to think that way."

"You know that most buyers won't place much value on Derek's dig, and I don't get the impression that you know how to market those valuable relics since Derek never sold anything."

"What are you suggesting, then?"

"What seems most fair is that I buy this place for its fair market value. If you want I'll also sell off his collection for the best price possible. You'll get one hundred percent of the profit for the items Derek has already discovered. I'll also include you in a full share of anything new we find, subject, of course, to any reductions due to successful legal challenges by foreign nations or North Carolina. That could turn out to be a fortune, even if Derek didn't believe it's here. Sound fair?"

"I can do all that without Derek's permission?"

"You can, although I think you should talk to him first."

"It would kill him."

"That might be a better way to go than what faces him. North Carolina has the death penalty, and he did commit murder, probably premeditated. I'm sure a defense lawyer will make his best case, but I can't imagine it being compelling enough to avoid life in prison or death. Does Derek have any kids to consider?"

"No."

"Well, then it's your decision. Let me know. My lawyers can have the papers ready in a few days and you can be gone."

"Let me think about it until the morning."

"Please take all the time you need."

"Thanks, TK. And thanks for, gosh, it feels weird to thank you for taking us along to Gordie's service when it turned out so strangely, but, well, thanks."

"You're welcome."

Theresa walked to the door. Taz looked as he walked away and saw her staring into her house as if taking it all in for one last time.

Sam was at the bar pouring shots when Taz came aboard *Wasafiri*. He handed one to each of them and then raised his glass. "To your new adventure, Gordie," he said.

"To your new adventure," the others repeated, and then raised their glasses to the sea and drank.

"I guess there's no point in hanging around here, huh, Taz? You sure didn't show much interest in his dig."

"You're right, Pete, I didn't, because there's obviously no gold in there."

"It's still pretty cool. I've never seen so much old stuff, and it's in such good shape. To be honest, I hate to leave now."

"Oh, we're not leaving."

Sam knocked back another shot. "What am I missing? If you're sure there's no gold, why hang around? Fran's called twice with a new job she thinks we should take in Egypt."

"I think I'm about to buy this place from Theresa."

"Great," Sam muttered. "Another land distraction."

"You told me you looked for a house here once before. I remember. So you still think you might want to live here, then."

"It's too cold in the winter."

"Then why?"

"The gold's here. It has to be."

200

"You just said that it wasn't."

"I said it's not in the excavation."

"Jeez, are we playing another game now?"

"When we went into Derek's dig we all saw how far below current grade the foundation of the old building was. The Army Corps of Engineers must have added ten feet to this whole site in order for Derek to have to dig that deep."

"So?"

"Ten feet! Let's go with our original assumption that this really was Blackbeard's last hiding place."

"I'm good with that," Sam said. "But if that assumption is wrong then we're really wasting time."

"Let's further assume that Derek's find proves that Blackbeard plundered the *Espiritu del Mar,* that he was the one who brought back the swords and relics."

"I can go with that, too."

"I'm getting excited."

"Good, Pete. So why would Blackbeard hide all that stuff instead of using whatever he needed of it? Heck, he could have outfitted several more ships with crews and expanded his fleet. But he didn't. Why?"

Taz stared while Sam and Pete looked around as though the answer was about to fly by on a banner. "Fear," Sam said, finally.

"That's it, I think so too." Taz turned to Pete. "The Spanish were already bled white by all the years of war with their European neighbors, so the loss of that shipment was pretty much a death sentence to them. Without it there was no way to fund a defense or even take minimal care of their people. So they sent an armada over to find it and spent two years looking everywhere they had any clue it might be."

"And so Blackbeard," Pete said, taking over the line of thinking, "figured they would come looking, and also figured he'd be better off hiding everything until the heat died down."

"We've always assumed that he would want his treasure to be accessible, yet hidden well enough so that it couldn't be found. So what better place than down a well?"

"The one on the chart Miss Lucy gave you? Pete and I already probed all around the area where it must have been."

"Sams's right. We had the same thought at the time and spent a long time probing every inch of that area. If there was gold within a hundred yards of there we would have picked it up with the metal detectors."

"I would have thought so too," Taz said.

"See that, Pete? Taz is pacing but not looking for an Oreo. Which means he's already thought this through and is just waiting for us to catch up."

Taz laughed. "But what I didn't take into account was that the well, and the gold in it, would be buried under an additional ten feet of dirt."

"Wouldn't matter," Sam said as a matter of fact. "I'm an expert on that equipment. I handpicked the best gear available and I'm telling you it should have been able to penetrate ten extra feet of dirt without a problem."

"Of course it could, Sam."

"I know. I just said that."

"Did you notice the stones in the foundation Derek was exploring?"

"Yeah. "So?"

"I did," Pete said excitedly. "They were nice, flat, and easy to stack. I saw them all over the property when we did the seismic survey."

"So," Taz continued, "if whoever built the well used those same kinds of rocks to line it, as they most likely did–"

"And," Pete added, "let's assume the well was already ten or twenty feet deep in order to reach the water table. So if the Corps filled in the well and then added ten more feet of fill dirt, could the detectors have penetrated all of that?"

Taz looked at Sam, who stared back. Then Sam grinned and said, "Absolutely not."

Chapter 39

November 7th, 1718
15 days before Blackbeard's death in battle
On a small island near Russell Slough, just north of Beaufort, North Carolina

Blackbeard watched five of his men hoist mud-filled buckets from the bottom of the small island's well. Trees overgrew the spot and the men worked in shadows. An oxbow of slow-moving water with a heavy tangle of vines separated the island from the mainland.

The wide river on the other side of the small island flowed swiftly, and the oxbow provided the shelter and safety that Indians and conquerors had used for centuries as they settled, abandoned, and resettled the small island so many times in its past.

"How many days more, Claw?"

"'Tis a great deal to hide, Captain. And treacherous digging out the sidewalls without reinforcing timber."

"Then with reluctance shall I put my carpenters to the task. Yet go ye deeper still."

"We've but one good man left, sir, what can hold his breath and deny the water its right to drown him. The other found his peace at about three fathoms."

Blackbeard laughed. "A mere three fathoms of well water is a bit ignoble for a man of the ocean, says I."

"And I as well. He be resting now, though."

"And taking no quarters in my hiding place, lest there be ample room."

"Aye. No quarters for him, sir. Nor the man what stole a coin from the five chests what got broken."

"His body I did see lodged among tree roots in the river."

"Shot him through, I did. And the time I'll soon find to wade out and retrieve that coin from his purse."

"A single coin is of little matter, Claw, as yer service be more needed here."

"As you say, sir. 'Tis a privilege to undertake this task for you."

Blackbeard turned to leave, his dark and scary features dappled with sunlight and shade.

"Captain?"

Blackbeard stopped and turned around. "What troubles your mind, Claw?"

"Spain, sir."

"Aye, and mine, if I'm to be honest. With their fortunes gone bad this treasure they must have, and soon."

"They be readying a fleet as soon as they hear of the loss. The season of hurricanes 'tis about to end, so a dozen warships or more would be my guess, with more soldiers than any band of pirates could ever prevail against. All of us to the grave would go."

"'Tis good, says I, that the *Espiritu del Mar* is now resting well in her watery fate."

"Not a man beyond our own crew shall know it be us what took her, sir. The amaranth never bore close enough to catch sight of our colours, so to search this place for her bounty would lack all merit and reason, especially if no coinage bearing that stamp be traded here."

"The carpenters and timbers tomorrow, then two weeks more, Claw. That gold what was Spain's is now mine, and to be buried within a fortnight and no later, as word has it that an enemy of lesser concern approaches from the Chesapeake."

Claw laughed. "Truly, sir, have I heard rumor that the right honorable governor of Virginia has dispatched ships with soldiers for us to slaughter at our pleasure."

"A waste of their blood and our time, says I, with no prize for us to claim but some armament. Make haste upon this spot and be done with it. Bury me goods and then rebuild the well as though never accosted."

"Aye, sir."

Blackbeard stood next to Claw as they both looked over at his men working to exhaustion. "Damned ye be, my lads, for I can do nothing but dispatch ye for your loyal service."

"To that unpleasant task I'll commit, sir."

"With my gratitude, then Claw, for it does my black heart pain. See ye well to any families and favored whores after the deed be done."

"Aye, sir."

"A fortnight, Claw. And not a sunrise beyond."

Claw looked at the enormous stack of crates still waiting for space in which to be lowered into the well. "Aye, sir. A fortnight and no more."

Chapter 40

"I can feel rifles aimed at about a dozen spots on me," Sam said as he single-handedly carried the heavy seismic pounder. "You ever see a guy driving the golf cart and picking up balls at a busy driving range? I feel like him."

"You only feel a dozen rifles? You must feel unloved." Taz couldn't help but look up and scan the surrounding woods. "I think I feel a hundred."

"I feel nothing," Pete said. "What...I mean, how do you feel something like that?"

"They're probably not aiming at you, Twerp, because you're insignificant."

Taz laughed. "I guess there isn't yet any glory to shooting you, Pete. But Sam and I have worked with or against most of the men out there at one time or another and they've come to respect us, I suppose."

"Even the guys on Joey's side? You actually know the men who might kill you?"

"They're just contract workers doing a job. Ours and Joey's alike. Next time they might be on different sides, with Joey's men working for us and the other way around."

"This is weird."

"No," Sam said, "what's weird is that I'm carrying all this heavy stuff while you two ladies chat it up. Here." He handed Pete the pounder's amplifier.

"Do you think you hired enough men to establish a balance of power, Sam?"

"Yeah, Taz, I did, almost a hundred men."

"There are a hundred men out there on our side alone?"

"I know it sounds like a lot, Pete. Might be a few too many, but you have to remember that they're working shifts, too, keeping this place protected twenty-four-seven. They're all out there now because none of them wants to miss the fight that's coming, but the woods won't typically be that full."

"And Joey's got a similar force?"

"The reports I get say he has fewer men."

"That's good," Pete said hopefully.

"Not really. Force equality often encourages some finesse and perhaps even dialogue inspired by the fear of mutual annihilation. But if one side is undermanned it's often a sign that things will get messy."

Taz dropped his gear and started measuring out distances, looking absolutely unconcerned about the number of mercenaries aiming at him "You promised them their expenses plus a share?"

"Yeah. At first there was some grumbling about just splitting one share among all of them. Especially since they're going to be on-site for a long time if this gold is as hard to recover as I suspect."

"But they're cool?"

"They got cool when I gave them a clue of how much money was involved. That also got them more determined to go Chernobyl if required."

"I didn't think they could possibly get more ready to fight. Any sign of Joey?"

"No, Taz. And Pete, just so you know, if you don't see Joey it's a good indicator that he's around."

"He's sure a hard one to guess," Taz said. "I don't like it at all when I know he's around, but I absolutely hate it when I'm not sure where he is."

"Even if he is gone, that big nose of his can smell treasure from a continent away. If we actually do find Tortuga Gold, he'll be back. Man, I wish I had that good of instincts."

"You've got the nose for it."

"Are you insulting the size of my nose, Pete? Every time you open your mouth you create another reason for me to crush you."

"I can outrun you."

"Yeah, but you sleep, don't you? Some dark night out at sea and..." Sam grabbed his own throat and stuck out his tongue like he was choking.

"That's cute. Taz?"

"Don't choke Pete to death, Sam."

"You heard him. Don't choke me to death."

"At least don't do it until we find the well and send Pete to the bottom of it."

"Oh, swell."

"I'll be the one to lower you," Sam said, grinning like some kind of fiend. "I'll really try my best not to let you fall. I bet that doesn't sound like as much fun to you as it does to me, though."

Taz finished measuring over from where the old tree had stood. "Set the pounder up here, Sam. What would you guess the typical diameter of a well would be?"

"Three feet. Maybe four?"

"That's what I think too. Let's move."

"Why the sudden hurry?"

"I'm getting the feeling."

"The feeling?"

"Yes, Pete, the feeling. Taz gets this feeling when he locks onto the scent of something. It's an uncanny trait, kind of a sixth sense sort of thing similar to Joey's. Neither of them is wrong very often."

"It must be hard for you to relate."

"He's wrong sometimes, like when he invited you along. Here, secure the base and let's start sending some shock waves into the ground."

Pete leveled the equipment and tightened down the screws. "Done. Ready?"

Sam hit the button that fired a blast. Pete recorded the results and said, "It's solid here, all the way down." He drove a stake into the ground to mark that spot. "Let's move two feet."

Sam and Pete moved, fired, and then moved again, repeating the process and ignoring Theresa as she walked over to Taz. "Find anything, TK?"

"Not yet. We're searching for an old well somewhere around here."

"I've never heard Derek mention a well."

"It was only noted on one map I was shown at the historical society. Maybe he didn't know."

"That would surprise me."

"No one's perfect."

"And certainly not Derek. I've decided to accept your offer."

"Are you sure, Theresa? I don't want you to feel pressured or taken advantage of, and there are probably dozens of other ways to structure this if you want to stay or retain ownership."

"You're not pressuring me, but I talked to Derek's family last night and, as you can probably imagine, they're extremely private and not very close with each other. They're angry about the attention Derek's attracted to all of them by what he's done."

"They're distancing themselves from him?"

"Yes, which means he'll be completely on his own. He'll need the money. So I'll take half of the money for the house and use it to start over. He's going to need the rest."

"I doubt he'll need all of it. A share of such a great fortune is a lot."

Taz was distracted by Sam, who hurriedly moved the pounder so that Pete could drill deep into the ground.

"Okay, Theresa, I'll have the closing set up if you're sure. We should be able to do it as soon as we get an appraisal, unless you have a number in mind."

Sam hurriedly screwed long sections of a probe together and inserted them into the hole.

"I thought a half a million would be fair."

Taz looked back at the house and then around the property. "Not to you it wouldn't. Or Derek. Even in this market it's probably worth somewhere between nine hundred thousand and a million three."

Pete began to jump up and down. Taz tried to ignore him, but it was hard to do, especially when Sam hugged Pete and lifted him off the ground.

"My, they're certainly happy."

"Must have found a lucky clover."

"Then call it a million, Taz, if that's fair to you. I'll be happy with half of that. Give Derek the other half and all the treasure money. I doubt that he and I will speak again." She turned and left.

Taz watched her walk away. She seemed taller than before, but perhaps lighter. She was, it seemed, happy.

"Taz, get over here."

"You two giggling like that is embarrassing."

"We found it, Taz."

"Are you sure it's the well?"

"That's not what I mean," Sam said. "It. We found *it*."

Taz stared at them for a second and then said, "Let me have the headphones."

"The gold is covered by something so thick that Pete had to drill through it, and he even had trouble doing that. A big chunk of cap rock, I think. The Corp must have covered the hole rather than fill it in."

Taz smiled, and his smile grew even bigger as Sam handed him the probe's monitor and headphones, "No way would we have found it the first time around," Sam continued. "The well is only two and a half feet across, way under ground, and covered by a stone lid. Take a look at this." Sam held the meter so Taz could see it.

Taz started to put on the headphones, but Pete said, "Don't bother. You won't need them."

The needle was pegged. Taz put on the headphones anyway and heard more noise than he'd ever heard it make before.

"That's one enormous amount of metal down there."

"An enormous amount," Sam repeated. "And how much Tortuga Gold was on the ship?"

"Around a hundred thousand pounds."

Pete was wiggling, "Well I'm going out on a limb to guess there's a hundred thousand pounds of metal down there."

"My God," Taz said in a hushed sort of reference. "Tortuga Gold."

"Blackbeard's treasure," Pete whispered.

Sam looked back and forth between them. "Blackbeard's treasure of Tortuga Gold. This, my friends, is the most significant find of that period ever to be discovered."

Pete stared at the ground and couldn't say anything else but "Wow."

Chapter 41

"It's getting dark. We're going to need lights to continue digging."

"I'll go to the boat, Taz."

Sam climbed out of the hole they'd dug beside the well and stretched. "I'll go, Pete. Taz might need your help in the hole. We must be close but it's too small now for me to go further."

"Measurements show us beside the cap rock," Taz said. "Another couple of feet and we should be able to dislodge some of the well stones and make a hole in its side big enough for me to wiggle into it."

"Are you sure you want to go in first, Taz?"

"No one has seen this gold in almost three hundred years, and who knows what other treasure might be down there? I hate to be selfish about it, but yes, I want to be the first."

"I don't blame you. If I could fit I'd be arm-wrestling you for the chance."

"And so, once again, I find myself rejoicing in the size of your shoulders, Sam."

"There might be creepy things down there too." Sam smiled. "It really might be best if you go first.

"Just hurry back with a bunch of lights."

Taz climbed down the ladder and dumped several more shovelfuls into the bucket that Pete hoisted out and dumped in a pile.

He dug into the side of the hall and hit rock with his shovel. "We're there, Pete. I'm hitting stones similar to what we saw in the foundation, stacked in the same way. Lower the pry bar," he said, while continuing to scrape away at the outside wall of the well.

"Here's the bar, and here comes Sam with some more light. Man, he can really run. Not sure I really could outrun him." Then, "Hey Sam! We're there."

"Great. Rig up these lights, Pete. Taz, headlight coming down."

"Light the hole from up there too, so that if I lose my light in the well I'll be able to see which way is out."

"Up is out."

"Funny, and if the well is just one hole, you're right. But I'm prepared to find a labyrinth down there."

"Good point."

"I'm having trouble getting the first rock out. The stones were already stacked tight and the weight of the cap rock and dirt just makes them tighter."

"Can I help?"

"Do you see any room down here for anyone to help?"

"No."

"Then that answers...wait." Taz grunted. "I got one to move."

"Try not to let it fall down into the well."

"I've got it." He wriggled the stone free and set it carefully into the bucket. "Let's get a heavier rope on that before we haul up any more."

"Just stay out of the way if this rope snaps."

"Oh, sure, I'll just stand over here." Taz moved an inch to the left. "Or over here." He leaned two inches to the right. "Or maybe I'll walk over here–"

"Yeah, yeah, it's a small hole, I got it. But the rope is new and I'm willing to trust it."

"Me, too," said Pete.

"Help me pull, Pete. Again. Here it comes." They lifted out the stone and then lowered the bucket. "See, the rope held."

"I'm so happy. I've got another stone ready to come up."

"How many more before you can get your head in?"

"This stone and one more, then I should be able to wiggle through. I already have them both loose."

Sam and Pete hauled up those stones. They sent the rope back down and Taz tied it off around his waist. "To adventure," he grinned, his white teeth reflecting back the intense lights above him.

"Good luck."

He squeezed his head between the stones and shimmied far enough into the well to see, a waterproof LED headlight helping him pick out objects in the darkness. He looked around for more than a minute, half in and half out of the well, and then struggled to get his shoulders and head back out.

"The well seems to have shifted. It turns a couple feet sideways a few feet down. It still might be passable, though."

"Might be?"

"I guess I'll find out."

"Are you sure you want to do this, Taz? If you're going to own this property we could just get some heavy equipment and excavate. You don't have to go down there."

"I know, but it takes away too much excitement. And heavy equipment could collapse the well. Who knows what might be down there besides gold? Might be a lot more lost history, and some of it could be fragile. Maybe–"

"Blackbeard's headless corpse," Pete interrupted, "hanging around and ready to devour some poor soul that enters his lair."

"Oh that's helpful. Thank you."

"Don't worry," Sam added. "If he's headless he can't devour you. So you're good."

Taz took several deep breathes. "Okay, here I go."

"Are you really sure?" Pete asked nervously.

"Sam, please make him stop asking me that."

"Sure."

Taz took another deep breath. Then he worked his way back into the hole, twisting his body completely around as he managed to squeeze between the stones and into the well.

"There he goes," Pete said.

Sam sat down, wrapped the rope around him, and braced his feet so he could stop Taz if he fell. The line paid slowly through his hands. "Stay behind me, Pete, and make sure this line doesn't knot up. And back me up if I need help."

"Got it. Did you hear something splash into the water down there?"

"Taz," Sam shouted. "Are you okay?"

There wasn't an answer, but the rope kept paying out slowly.

"He must be okay because he's still taking line. Probably dislodged a stone. I need more line."

"More coming."

It was almost an hour later that the line went slack.

"He's coming up, Pete."

"Or devoured."

After another twenty minutes Taz's hands poked through the sidewall and groped around at the bottom of the hole.

"Can we help you, Taz?"

"I just have to get the angle right in order to fit through here. Hang on."

"Hanging on."

One of his arms stretched out, followed by that shoulder, then his head and the other shoulder. Then nothing. "Great, I'm stuck."

"Want me to pull hard?"

"Definitely not, Sam. You'd just end up with half my body dangling at the end of your rope."

"Ew."

"There!" Taz slipped his hips free and pulled his legs out. He stood up in the hole and climbed up the ladder, then sat on the ground at the edge of the hole, soaking wet, covered with dirt and mud, and breathing deeply.

"Well?"

Taz didn't say anything. He just kept sucking in air.

"Man, this is so un-cool of you to keep us hanging," Pete said.

Taz looked at them both. "I really can't believe it. I mean–"

"What did you see?"

"First I went all the way to the water. At the bottom of the well. Let me catch my breath."

"So the well hadn't been filled in with dirt?"

"No. The water reflected my light back at me and made it hard to see anything along the way down, but when I got there I took a lot of line, held my breath, and dove."

"Now that had to be seriously creepy."

"I've got to admit that it was, but only for about ten feet. Maybe fifteen. The bottom had...oh, it's hard to guess, but maybe five chests worth of gold coins on it."

"Five chests?"

"Really difficult to guess because they were all loose. I couldn't dig to the bottom with my hands, but did manage to get to mud at one place where they weren't piled so deep."

"Wow. Five chests of gold."

"Easy, Pete. Taz finding five chests is a big deal, but there's many times that amount missing from the *Espiritu del Mar* and the *Conquistador de las Americas* shipment. Is it another find, Taz? Did you see the mint mark?"

"It's Tortuga Gold, Sam."

Sam looked around the property. "Then where's the rest? If not here, where else could Blackbeard–"

"As I was coming back up I found an opening in the side. I hadn't seen it going down because it was on my backside and I was light-blinded. I assumed it was a washout, that the sidewall of the well had collapsed there and created a cavern of sorts. I was working around it when my light hit something white."

"Gold?"

"He said it was white, Pete."

"White gold?"

"Don't be an idiot."

"Bones," Taz said. "An enormous pile of human bones were stuffed unceremoniously at the entrance."

"A grave?"

"A mass grave. Or maybe they were sentries of sorts. Who knows?"

"Anything else in the cavern?"

"I climbed through the bones–"

"Ew."

Sam hit Pete on the shoulder. "Damn it, stop saying that."

"It was kind of gross. But once I got through the bones the whole place opened up into a huge room. It's a marvel of engineering."

"And? Come on, man, give it up."

"I'm not sure I'm ready. I kind of like being the only person in the world who knows something."

"You're being an asshole."

"Good." Taz stood up. Then he smiled. "It's there."

"It's there?"

"It looks like it's all there."

"All of it?"

"Yes, Pete, there are crates and crates of gold bars and coins down there. They're all neatly stacked and numbered, almost like they'd just been shipped and inventoried."

"And you checked the stamp? You're sure it's from the lost mint?"

"I did, Sam. I can't believe I get to say these words, but gentlemen, we've found the Tortuga Gold."

Sam whistled low between his teeth. They were all surprised to hear an echo. They turned as Joey walked up.

"Good evening, gentlemen."

"Shit," Pete said.

"From the self-congratulatory looks on your faces, can I assume you found what we've all been looking for since, well, perhaps forever?"

"Sam," Taz asked nervously, "you did get our men out here, right? We are protected?"

Joey held up his hand in a simple protest. "Mind if I answer that question for you, Sam?"

"Be my guest, Joey."

"Yes, Keaton, Sam has quite literally filled the surrounding woods with your men. There's actually a bit of détente at play, as my men and yours have squared off quite nicely. Teams are about even, I'd guess, although you, of course, have Sam."

"So if we're so well protected, where did a guy like you get the guts to walk out here like you just did? It should have been suicide."

"Ah, well, you see, the leader of your sniper teams, who seems quite competent by the way, allowed me the privilege after a pleasant conversation that he and I had."

"Sam?"

"Don't worry, Taz. He's talking about Jean-Louis. We're good."

"Sam's quite right, because I've been promised by – Jean-Louis, was it? He's made it quite clear that I am, even now, carefully in their sights."

"Especially now, I imagine."

"Quite right, Sam. Especially now. And they seem rather intent on killing me merely for unspecified reasons, but they're particularly keen to kill me if I do anything that might be considered foolish. Keaton, do you have any idea of what their standards are for foolish behavior?"

"Apparently not. I would have figured you being here was foolish enough."

"Hmm, as would I." Joey peered down into the hold. "The treasure is there? The fabled lost shipment of Tortuga Gold?"

"Yup."

Joey smiled. He rubbed his chin and smiled like a child on the Easter Bunny's lap. "Really, that's quite remarkable."

"Yup," Taz said again before turning to Pete and saying, "This might be a great time to consider a new career, my young friend. There's no telling how this is going to go down but the odds call for bloodshed. Joey, will you let Pete walk away if that's what he chooses to do?"

"Of course I will."

"I'm staying." Pete took a threatening step toward Joey.

"So cute," Joey laughed. "He's very brave for such a skinny man."

"One more skinny comment and I swear I'm going to pound someone."

"At least he called you a man, twerp."

"But it would be foolish of Pete to leave," Joey said. "Especially at this point. Am I to understand that this sweet young man is really a partner?"

"He is," Sam said powerfully. "Pete's a full partner. He's taking Gordie's place, or at least trying his best to do so." He looked at Pete. "That might sound like I'm trying to get you killed, but I'm really not."

"I took it as a compliment."

"I didn't mean it as a compliment, either."

"Then by all means he should stay, because, you see, a fight of the magnitude necessary to better your impressive forces and then somehow get away with all these tons of gold would be, well, let's just say it would be a tad too dramatic for this bucolic setting."

"It would be pretty exciting though."

Joey smiled, "Ooo, I think so too, Keaton. Another day, perhaps."

"Another day."

"But on this particular day I've been authorized – and sadly, now, restricted – to a mere expenditure of money, not blood. Have you any interest in such a proposal?"

Taz turned to Pete. "What do you say?"

"Me? Why me?"

"Because it's a tough decision. You need more practice with them than Sam or me."

"Come on, don't make me decide what we do."

"You'll do fine. Just remember that the adventure – actually finding the treasure – is the real prize. Possession of this gold will gradually pass to hundreds or thousands of people sitting in easy chairs wondering what it would be like to do this. But we *know*. So we already got what we came for."

"You don't care about the money? What about this property? The stuff Derek recovered?"

"It's important, of course, and you'll need to be honorable to Derek and get a good price for all of it."

"I'm still–"

"It's simple, Pete," Sam said. "We came for adventure and found it. Now it's time to move on to the next one. Taz and I aren't willing to bog ourselves down for the next two years handling this find." He turned to Taz. "I do want to stick around long enough to see it, though."

"Of course. Now go with Joey, Pete, and see what he has to offer."

"I really think you should do this. I mean, come on, Taz. Sam?"

"You'll do okay, twerp."

"Besides," Taz said, "I've got to shower and then go wake up a cool old lady so I can tell her an amazing story."

"I hope that story ends with her earning a full share, because we wouldn't have found it without her."

Taz grinned. "It most certainly does, Sam. Now deal fairly with Pete, Joey."

"I shall, of course. After all, it is not my money."

As Pete walked uneasily away with Joey, Taz shouted out to him. "Hey, tell me something, my suddenly wealthy young friend. Now do you think it was worth the ride?"

"And more importantly," Sam added, "do you want to stick around for more?"

Pete looked at Joey, and then Sam. Then finally he looked at Taz and said, "To adventure, Taz. To adventure."

"To adventure," Sam laughed.

Taz didn't say anything as Pete and Joey walked away. Then he turned toward the Atlantic where they'd left Gordie behind and softly said, "And to those rare and beautiful souls with the courage to seek it."

The End

About the Author

Wes is a real-life adventurer, one of those people who turns life on its head and shakes the change from its pockets. A global traveler, yacht rat, intellectual, surf bum, bow-hunter, actor, romantic, former F.B.I./S.W.A.T. Agent and Security Consultant, raconteur and all-around fun guy, Wes can debate Voltaire and Rousseau while wrenching on a greasy diesel far out at sea, or drop into a point break wave as skillfully as he's crept within grasp of wild game.

Over the past dozen years Wes (wesdemott.com) has garnered international acclaim for his novels about prisoners of war, the FBI, military assassins, and spies. In his beautiful but heartbreaking novel, *Loving Zelda*, he wrote about hope and loss and the chance to change our lives if we're fearless enough to try.

Tortuga Gold reflects a fun new chapter in Wes's own life as he's joined in his adventures by his beautiful Belgian wife, Sabine, a human rights/refugee lawyer who spent seven of her fifteen years with the United Nations living in Africa, including full-time residency in the war zones of Rwanda, Burundi, and the Congo during their bloody genocides.

Wes's love of the ocean often plays into his short stories and novels. He's boated thousands of miles on dozens of his own boats, surfed world famous breaks, and caught or speared game fish since he was thirteen. In 2010, after sailing from the Chesapeake Bay to Florida's West Coast and selling their home, Wes and Sabine made a permanent move aboard their new boat, a trawler they named *Wasafiri* ("The Wanderers" in Swahili). After a shakedown cruise of 1200 miles, Wes took off for Bocas del Toro, Panama, planning to pick up Sabine in Isla Mujeres , Mexico. But the voyage was cut short when Wes shipwrecked in violent seas off the western tip of Cuba and was rescued by the Carnival Cruise ship, VALOR.

When Wes abandoned ship he left behind all their possessions except their cat and his American flag. Immediately after the Coast Guard told Sabine of the rescue, she texted a friend a message that well defines the way these two live: "Boat lost at sea. Wes and crew alive. All possessions gone. New adventures ahead."

The couple rented a flat in a Mexican beach town for a few months, and then, on June 1st, 2011, they moved to Portland, Oregon to begin exploring America's Pacific Northwest. Their shopping list of replacement items included backpacks, a good knife, Merrill hiking boots, and of course, another adventure hat for Wes.

There is really no way to guess where the couple will be by the time you read this.

NOVELS BY WES DEMOTT

THE TYPHOON SANCTION

CIA Field Officer Cruiser is a master at manipulating people and circumstances. Be careful or he'll manipulate you in this story of vengeance, murder, and global terrorism.

Mixing spies and counterespionage with old vendettas and small town murders, The Typhoon Sanction pits the protagonist, CIA Agent Jay Stewart, against a Chinese enemy who hunts him halfway around the world to the Outer Banks of North Carolina. Stewart's mastery of misdirection provides a whodunit element to this international thriller as the reader tries to make sense of four mysterious small-town murders. The more obvious the truth appears, the further the reader gets from it, ultimately being captured by the same skills that made Stewart such a successful operative.

THE FUND

How deep does the conspiracy go? Who's in charge and how many more will die? Aerospace engineer Peter Jamison is determined to find out.

While trying to save his contract for a tactical weapons system, Jamison uncovers a crime of corruption, power and violence that draws him into a deadly game he cannot win but still chooses to fight, any way he can.

This thriller has been translated into several languages and is an international best-seller and IPPY Gold Medal Award Recipient for Best Fiction. Robert Ludlum, the wonderfully gracious man that he was, hosted the launch party for this novel.

HEAT SYNC

Heat Sync takes you through the U.S. Assassination School exposed by NEWSWEEK Magazine just prior to this novel's publication.

Experience the pain and process of sanctioned murder from Lt. Henry Thompson, who was recruited for JASPERS from the U.S. Navy SEALS. Thompson believes he's training to assassinate foreign threats to this country, and it's only after he graduates and gets his orders that he realizes his true mission is to kill the President of the United States by using the White House access his girlfriend provides, and that he's already too boxed in by his handlers to refuse. Heat Sync provides an exciting but non-traditional thriller that deeply probes the emotions and psychology of a patriotic killer.

WALKING K

America's leaders haven't faced a Prisoner-of-War crisis since the debacle over POWs left behind in Vietnam. Walking K is an exciting thriller that exposes the reasons it can't be allowed to happen again.

DeMott, a former FBI Agent, analyzed intelligence documents, Nixon's White House tapes, Congressional Records, and interviewed POWs and their commanding officers while researching this tragic story of a reluctant conspiracy lumbered upon the shoulders of each U.S. President since 1975. Crosscutting between dramatic battlefield scenes, heartbreaking torture, American businesses protecting their investments, and a continuing refusal by the White House to reveal the shameful truth, the emotional ending of this thriller sadly shows why the United States Government stopped wanting the prisoners of that war to come home, and perhaps sheds light on the government's attitude toward the POW classification in wars since Vietnam.

LOVING ZELDA

The humanity and hope of this beautiful novel makes it the work for which Wes would most like to be remembered. Loving Zelda's emotional range includes pieces of everyone's past, and provides hope that we can all find love if we're brave enough to take a chance. Loving Zelda is an extremely rare glimpse of the soft-as-cotton heart of internationally known tough guy Wes DeMott.

Loving Zelda explores the emotional pain and damage inflicted on a writer's relationship with the woman he loves as she struggles with manic-depression. Through ten years of joy and hardship he loves and cares for her with unwavering devotion, but when she marries another man he becomes a recluse on his sailboat, waiting for a chance to be together again in this or any world.

TORTUGA GOLD

Throw your sea bag aboard WASAFIRI to join Taz Keaton and the Mayday Salvage and Rescue gang in fun adventures and a chance at Blackbeard's treasure.

Tortuga Gold is a fun action story that follows Taz's fast adventures after he rejects his wealthy lifestyle and starts Mayday Salvage and Rescue in search of excitement. After Taz and his two partners race the Panamanian National Police to recover a metal case from the wreckage of a private jet in a muddy river, they meet a man with a coin from an historic but never recovered Spanish shipment that vanished in 1715. From there the adventure rolls from modern day pirates to blood-sucking leeches, exploding yachts to beautiful international competitors and a sea battle with the legendary Blackbeard himself. This is the first novel in a series involving Taz and the Mayday crew.

CNN, Fox News Network, the Huffington Post and many other news outlets referred to this novel after Wes' rescue off the coast of Cuba by Carnival Cruise lines. Now you can read the scene that inspired so much discussion.

COMING SOON

TEQUILA BOOM BOOM

Tag along with the gang of Mayday Salvage and Rescue in their next adventure. Due late Summer, 2012.

www.ingramcontent.com/pod-product-compliance
Lightning Source LLC
Chambersburg PA
CBHW060805120626
46557CB00001B/93